SONATA OF THE DEAD

Also available from Conrad Williams and Titan Books

DUST AND DESIRE
HELL IS EMPTY (NOVEMBER 2016)

DEAD LETTERS: AN ANTHOLOGY

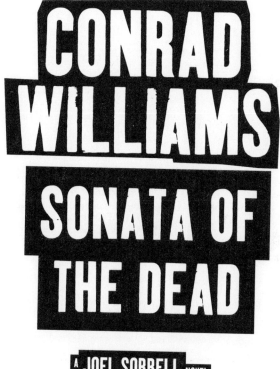

CONRAD WILLIAMS

SONATA OF THE DEAD

A JOEL SORRELL NOVEL

TITAN BOOKS

Sonata of the Dead
Print edition ISBN: 9781783295654
E-book edition ISBN: 9781783295661

Published by Titan Books
A division of Titan Publishing Group Ltd
144 Southwark Street, London SE1 0UP

First edition: July 2016

1 2 3 4 5 6 7 8 9 10

A CIP catalogue record for this title is available from the British Library.

Printed and bound in the United States of America

To the memory of Graham Joyce (1954–2014).
Brilliant writer, cherished friend.

"All i know is what the words know, and dead things, and that makes a handsome little sum, with a beginning and a middle and an end, as in the well-built phrase and the long sonata of the dead."

SAMUEL BECKETT

Red sky. White thighs. OPen ~~mouhts~~ mouth. You and me both. This night youll be too terrified to scream. But Ill make some noise for you, dont you worry. Wheres all your fury now? Wheres your cocky little grin and your smartarse backchat? No friends to back you up. No daddy dearest to shoo you into the car after youve effed and jeffed and blinded and kicked and spat. Just you and me and some tools. A soundproofed cellar. Dead space.

Clean page. White. Crisp. At this point, there is nothing separating me from the gods of literature. In this moment, I am on an equal footing. Me and Hemingway and Greene and Orwell. Me and King and Brown and Rowling. Empty page. The vacuum. The tease. Endless possibilities. I know the same words that the bestsellers use. The same words as the critically acclaimed. All I need to do is write about eighty thousand of those. Put them in that magic configuration that will tick all the boxes and open the doors to the room filled with milk and honey. It is in me. I can feel it. I almost know its odour, its flavour. The taste of failure is keen, but it hasnt yet dulled my appetite. I am fictions apostate. I guard that edge of hunger jealously. You need the hunger or the words wont come. I was born to this. It is my destiny. I wont be dissuaded. I wont be denied my birthright.

Years of practise have led me to this place. This is the coalface. Writing is mining. It is hard graft. It is in this place that I opened the seam. I work that black gold. I pick at it until the sweat is lashing off me. No windows here. A view is a distraction. A tree will take your mind away from where it needs to travel. The strict pattern in a brick wall will infect the plans youve made. Neutral colours. One wall is plastered with rejection slips. That's my skin up there. Thickened. Toughened. No noise. I soundproofed this room. Only the clack of the Olympia as I plough through the ream. That's right. A typewriter. I need that physical connection with the words. I need to feel that Im doing some work. The thought coalesces, the words form; I nail them to the paper. No winking cursor. No cut and paste. No Control-Z. It seems you are trying to write a novel. Would you like some help?

I am beyond help. Maybe not once. There were classes and courses and conventions. Feedback and encouragement. Endless platters of shit sandwiches. This is good, this is great… but this bit here… The arm around the shoulder. You must keep going. Dont ever stop. Dont let the bastards grind you down. Its a subjective industry.

Its not a rejection of you. Its not a rejection of you. Its not a rejection of you.

There are only so many writing exercises you can do. There is only so much shit youre prepared to eat.

Bare room. A single, nude, 100-watt bulb. No chair. A table elevated by breezeblocks. I stand to write. Like Ernest. This is work. This is craft. This is sculpture. It is the hew and hack of an axe. It is the whisper of a scalpel. I am pugilist and pacifist. I am a lover, a clown, a shadow at the door. I am a mummer, a mother, a murderer. Bare-chested. Hot in here. A furnace. A foundry. Ideas white in my mind. Soft, malleable, searing, desperate to find their shape. I am on fire.

The byline. The review. The signing. The guest appearance.

The awards. The acclaim. The lucrative contract. I can feel it. I can feel it. And you realise, after a while, that you have to play the game. You realise it isnt just a solid plot or a jazzy name or a pretty face. You need backstory. You need history. You need heat. Get in bed with the market men. Whats the angle? Wheres the hook?

Yeah, well Im working on something that will have the bean-counters drooling. I've got something going down that will have every agent in London slapping their cocks on the table. Publish and be damned. Thisll be some page-turner.

Sometimes I hit these keys so hard I leave bloody prints behind.

I come down the wooden steps from the attic slow and heavy. Maximum creep. Hes still face down on a filthy mattress where I dropped him hours before, and there are cockroaches mating in his hair. I sing to him while I drag the blade this way and that across the tiles. I let him hear the heavy gritting steel: the clearing of some monstrous throat. I let him hear my words, my promise, turning wet in the saliva building up around my teeth.

PART ONE

AUTHORIAL INTRUSION

1

Pulling out of Leighton Buzzard, the Gyuto Monks hitting the vinegar strokes: Om Tare Tu Tare Ture Mama Ah Yuh Pune Jana Putim Kuru Soha, I received a text from Lorraine Tokuzo.

make it crisp, white and expensive. Lxxx

I toyed with the idea of buying her a shirt from Turnbull & Asser, but beating the crap out of my wallet for the sake of a not-very-good gag was hardly worth it. And Tokuzo, when she's got a jones for a decent glass of white wine, is not a woman to be dicked about with. I messaged her that I was on my way and settled back in my seat. It's just a forty-five-minute clip down to Euston from this arse of the woods, but I needed a nap. I'd been up to Northampton to visit my younger brother, Adam. He plays bass guitar for a beat combo called Motel. There had been some kind of weekend 'battle of the bands' competition and he asked if I wanted to go. I think he felt a little guilty about not coming down to visit when I was in hospital. So I spent seventy-two hours with him and his mates, drinking in various bars while a cacophony of power chords reamed out my earholes, sleeping on badly sprung sofas and eating pizza, curry, burgers and chips for breakfast, lunch and dinner; beer at all times. It was a great laugh. He gave me a lift to the station in their touring van, an old Toyota Space Cruiser with a sound system that was probably worth three times the value of the vehicle. The interior smelled of spilled beer and stale smoke. Adam was wearing shorts and flip-flops and an oversized cream jumper peppered with dope burns.

'I talked to Mum last week,' he said. 'Told her you were coming up.'

'Oh right,' I said. 'What'd she say?'

'She said "Joel who?"'

'Really?'

'She said she never hears from you. No visits. No phone calls. No postcards. No homing pigeon. No smoke signals.'

'I'm busy.'

'She doesn't know that. She misses Sarah too, you know. She was devastated after what happened.'

'I didn't want to burden her.'

'She felt… I don't know… underused.'

We parted on good terms and promised to spend more time with each other in future. He didn't ask me about my scar and I didn't tell him. Quite possibly I didn't need to; the story had been all over the news.

I always thought a scar – you know, one of the visible ones – would work for me in my job, give me a head start, an edge over the monsters I would invariably come across. They might think twice, or at least for long enough that I might launch their nads into the troposphere before they worked out that I was about as substantial as a piece of granny piss. In the books, James Bond had one (a scar, not a piece of piss) and he divided his time between saving the world and reclining on mattresses that teemed with women. My Eagle Eyes Action Man had one (a scar, not a mattress teeming with women) and he was the epitome of cool when I was eight years old. What you have to remember though, is that for every scar there is a story. Which means there must also be an author too.

Four months previously I was slashed in the face by a seventeen-year-old meathead called Steven Blythe. He had a problem with me (you don't say!) that went back to a time when his mother and I had been an item. It ended and he didn't like that. He came after me, not because I treated her badly (I didn't; many did) but because I broke it off (I wasn't up to a proper, grown-up relationship... I was actually doing her a favour), but she thought I was The One. She committed suicide and he blamed me for it. Anyway, he tried to kill me and instead ended up ploughing through the roof of an intercity train at St Pancras. He got to stay young and beautiful. I ended up looking like Frankenstein's practice corpse.

And now people tend to steer clear of me in public. And when I say 'people', we both know I really mean 'women'. I was married, once, but she's gone, thanks to another monster. My daughter left home on the heels of that and I haven't seen her in the flesh for five years. She's eighteen now. I bounce around from bar to bed to breakfasts in rancid cafés that smell of diesel and blood, trying to find her. But I don't try too hard because I'm scared that when I do find her it won't be the tearful, happy reunion I've rehearsed time and again. I worry she might not recognise me. I worry she might hate me. I'm always kind of looking for her, though. Just like I'm always kind of cruising for work. Work isn't too bad at the moment. There are a lot of monsters in London.

So I sat on my own on the train, snoozing, and not one person bothered me. At Euston I picked up a bottle of William Fevre 2011 Chablis, a pack of smoked salmon, a bag of salad, a pot of double cream and some tagliatelle. I jumped in a cab to King's Cross. Within five minutes I had the bottle in Tokuzo's fridge. She was on the balcony in a pair of bikini bottoms, reading one of her fat novels, snapping gum and listening to old Bowie on the iPod dock.

I gritted my teeth at the sight of her curves – we'd had something going a while ago, until I ruined it – and concentrated on getting some food going. Her flat, her rules. Not that I was living here, but I was a little more sociable than I had been, and I wanted to make it up to some of the people I hadn't treated so well over the years. It's quite a list; maybe it's a subconscious rehearsal for the most important person on it.

'Where's the wine?' Lorraine asked, coming back from her sunbathing session. She'd pulled a light jumper around her shoulders at least, sparing my blushes and bulges.

'I couldn't find any,' I said, 'so I got you some Tennant's Extra, which we all know is your day-to-day tipple of choice.' I caught a glimpse of my face as I reached for the polished glass of the cupboard where Tokuzo kept her wine goblets. The scar has calmed down a lot since I received it (why do news items always talk about victims 'receiving' stab wounds, as if it's some sort of gift?) but it's still angry, still red. The surgeon who treated me ('treated' – that's more like it) reassured me that the colour would fade in time, and that plastic surgery might be something to think about 'going forward', once everything had calmed down.

'If you're not joking I'll give you a matching one of those on the other side,' she said, tactfully. 'Make you look like a pair of brackets.'

We've always had what you might call a spicy, spiky relationship. She was a rebound job after my wife's death and she's never let me off for that. But I count her as one among maybe three people I can trust implicitly. She helped me when I needed her, when I was at a low ebb, and I would do the same for her.

We ate, and I stole glances at the tanned slivers of flesh in the scoops and scallops of the thing she was almost not wearing. We were on to our second glass of wine – she was impressed by my selection – when my phone rang. I almost left it. A beautiful summer evening in London with some decent plonk and a gorgeous, engaging woman. Why would you allow anything to get in the way of that? But, well, I couldn't not answer. I can never switch it off. What if, this time, it was *her*?

It wasn't. Of course it wasn't. It never is. It's unlikely ever to be. It was Mawker. 'Bête noire' is too elegant a phrase to describe this guy. 'Cunt' works better. He sounded far away. Lost. He sounded kind of broken. Maybe it was the job. He'd been a copper too long. I couldn't hack it – I was out within six months – but Ian Mawker was a career plod. You could see it in his grey, crumpled report-paper face. He was in it till the bourbon or a bullet put him in a box.

'I'm up Enfield way,' he said. 'I'm in a cul-de-sac—'

'Just for a change?'

'How soon can you get over?' he asked. 'Corner of Cheyne Walk and Uplands Way.'

My watch-it gland went into full spaz. Mawker was using his friendly voice, reserved only for higher rank and women.

He wasn't biting at my lures. Not a good sign.

'What is it, Ian?'

'It's a body,' he said. And then he was saying something else but the world had gone grey and uncertain and I could feel my heart congealing in its cage. *Sarah*, I thought. *Here it comes. Sarah.*

But instead he said: 'It's easier if you just come over. Give us twenty minutes and we can have a squad car pick you up.'

Lorraine didn't utter a word, and that's another reason why I like her. Sometimes you need your best friends to zip it, not proffer any advice. Sometimes they just know when you need some space to breathe. She sipped her wine and fiddled with the spacers between her toes as her plum-painted nails dried.

'You can use my car,' she said.

I parked the car where I could on Uplands Way – there were squad cars and forensic vans blocking any further progress – and walked to the top of the street where it is taken over by waste land. People were standing in doorways with their arms folded, wearing sucked-lemon expressions. Mawker was waiting for me at a barrier with a duty officer so keen you could have served up dollops of him on rare roast beef sandwiches.

'Mawker.'

'Sorrell.'

Mawker was wearing his trademark shit clothes ensemble. More shit, even, than mine and believe me, that's saying something. At least I put my best bit of gear – my nubuck leather jacket – away for the summer. Mawker is one of those freaks who wears his cement-grey raincoat on days when even a mankini seems too much. His frayed shirt was infecting his skin. He and a duty officer traded looks and then Ian gazed back at me. I knew that look. I had worn it a few times when I was on the beat. It was the face you put on when you visited a house to convey bad news.

You might want to sit down...

I'm terribly sorry to inform you...

'Sarah?' I said, and my voice was Sahara-dry.

Ian held his hand up. He was shaking his head. 'It's a body. Male. As yet unidentified.'

'Why all the deep and meaningfuls, you and your glove puppet there? Why am I here?'

'Shall we?' Mawker said.

I followed him and his excitable uniformed puppy under the barrier into an ecstasy of white tents and SOCOs wearing protective suits. Every so often I heard the crunch of a camera shutter and the whine of a recharging flashgun.

'I'm a big crack and you're Polyfilla,' I said. 'Fill me in.'

'Got a call this morning, about ten a.m. Kid on a bike rode over what he thought was a big pork chop. Only a big pork chop doesn't have fingers. Thankfully he didn't go mooching about by himself otherwise he would have found what looks like an explosion in an abattoir.'

We were nearing the first of the tents. I rubbed my nose and smelled smoked salmon on my fingers. I felt my stomach arch and flop like a dying fish. To our left I watched as three guys in daft clothes stalked Enfield golf course. To the right was a series of allotments. Further east was another golf course: Bush Hill Park. And there was the railway too, bisecting these expanses of green. Plenty of escape potential in all directions. I thought of the PCs going door to door. I bet nobody saw a thing.

Mawker pulled open the tent's entrance and we stepped into a theatre of red. 'We have reason to believe this person knew Sarah. Probably knew her quite well too.'

I stood there making guppy faces, waiting for the next moment to arrive.

There were body parts strewn around the ground, only partially hidden by clumps of nettles and dock. Whoever sliced this poor guy like an Iberico ham half-arsed it when it came to concealing his crime. I was getting tired of Mawker and his slowly, slowly approach. I didn't know what I was going to do, but it seemed to involve a variant of grabbing him by the lapels and screaming at him until the skin of his face boiled off.

'Do you know him?' Mawker asked.

'Difficult to say,' I said, marshalling all my self-control. 'He seems to have gone to pieces. Why not just tell me why you think he knew Sarah and remove the possibility of me punching you until your head is less offensively potato-shaped?'

'*His* head's over there.' Uttered with all the tenderness of a man referencing a bowl of cold porridge.

I went over and had a look, if only to stop myself adding to the confusion with some of Mawker's own limbs. A SOCO very kindly tipped the head to one side so I could get a better view. It was gritty and blood-spattered, and slashes made it look as though he'd evolved gills, but I knew the guy. I just couldn't put a name to what remained of the face. He'd been at school with Sarah, I knew that much. He was a couple of years older than her. He used to walk her to the Tube stop. Protective. Very sweet. His parents lived around here; I remembered taking Sarah to his birthday party once.

'Never seen him before in my life,' I said to Mawker.

Now his face hardened as he scrutinised me. He was

hoping for an in. He'd get it, but not yet.

'Your turn,' I said.

Mawker put his hand in his deep raincoat pocket. 'We found these in a rucksack he was carrying,' he said, and pulled out a glassine bag.

Photographs. I received them with a hand that did not seem like mine, as if I'd picked up one of the strays from the ground. I teased open the lips of the bag and peeked inside. It took a moment to recognise her, but there was Sarah, doing some teasing of her own. All I could think of was how much she'd grown up, how much like her mother she was.

'Anything else? Anything with an address for her? A phone number?'

I needed to keep talking. Rage was filling up the gaps inside me. I was thinking of Sarah on her back on a threadbare carpet, smiling for some wet-nosed chancer, falling for the spiel and the promises. I stared at the guy's severed head and tried to understand how the boy who held an umbrella over Sarah while he got wet could turn into someone who took advantage of women. A little voice kept piping up, telling me that might not have been how it played out, but I stared it down.

Mawker shook his head. 'We're still doing a forensic sweep,' he said. 'I shouldn't really have taken these, but, well… There was a book too. Collection of short stories. Anthology jobby. You get me. What's the title? *Something Something Dying Planet*. We don't know if it's relevant. The victim could have been carrying it.'

I nodded and thanked him through gritted teeth. My desire to visit terrible violence upon his tuber had retreated, but only a tad.

'You sure you don't know him?' Mawker asked, and a

name rose up out of the murk. Martin Gower.

'Nope. Maybe if you can find out why he had these photographs we can ask Sarah.'

'We'll work on it,' he said. 'While we try to find the killer, if that's all right with you?'

'Mind if I have a look around?' I asked, knowing full well the answer.

'It's a crime scene, Sorrell,' he said. 'Suspicious death, believe it or not. If there's anything else here that can help lead us to Sarah, I'll let you know.'

I nodded, feeling impotent. I couldn't help but think Mawker was making some kind of point; lording the privilege he had worked for and I had voluntarily given up.

'I'll need those photographs back,' he said.

'Come on, Ian,' I said. 'It's my daughter. I don't want every plod in north London drooling over them.'

'They're evidence.'

'Let me keep the more… salacious ones then. Please.'

Mawker sighed and stared out over the fairways and rough. 'Pick 'em out,' he said. 'But get a move on. If anybody asks, I didn't see a thing, right?'

Clutching half a dozen photographs I turned my back on them and trudged to Tokuzo's Honda. I felt protected once I'd got my shoulders against the soft, scuffed leather of the driver's seat, heard the reassuring chunk of the door as it shut out the shit of the suburbs. The glassine bag felt slippery under my hot fingers. I wanted to open it again and see my daughter, see more evidence that she was alive. But I didn't want to acknowledge, in the arch of her body and the cat-sleaze eyes and the just-fucked hair, how alive she had become. She was a woman now, without my knowledge or understanding. She had become an adult, as bizarrely as it sounds, without my having any say in the matter.

I felt myself wishing this Gower character had survived just so I could kill him.

Love the camera, baby. Oh yes, show me all you've got. Your figure and my lens? We'll make a fortune.

But I knew that was wide of the mark. I hadn't seen Sarah for five years, and I couldn't remember what her voice was like, but I know that even at the age of thirteen she was a feisty fucker and wouldn't put up with even a speck of shit from anybody. She'd have seen some shyster with a camera and a come-on from a mile away and she'd have sent him packing with the business end of it hanging out of his arse. So no, it was nothing to do with model work – for which she only ever had withering contempt. Which meant that she had disrobed and positioned herself like that because they were involved. She got her tits out because she wanted to. And if she'd done *that*; if she could do *that*, then…

I threw the photographs to the floor and put my hands on the wheel before my nails started gouging holes in the palms of my hands. I wanted to go back and punch Mawker so hard that his inbred cretin ancestors, lying in their pauper graves, felt it. I wanted to glue together all the pieces of Martin Gower they'd found so far, shake him alive and then strangle him. Instead I gunned the engine, wound down the window, turned on the CD player and whacked up the volume until my ribs were shaking. I was so wound up I couldn't tell you what was playing, but by the end of the first track the red had vanished from the edges of my eyes and I could no longer hear my breath snagging against my teeth.

I'd driven less than a mile. Somewhere very nearby was the house where Gower had lived with his parents. I tried to remember the name of the street, but it had been ten years or so since I'd last been here. An unusual name, I remembered that much. The something... And then I turned left and I was there. The Chine.

2

This bit of north London is particularly leafy, and the residents seemed to be competing for the title of most verdant foliage. Hostas in ostentatious plant pots, rude bursts of flower on a magnolia tree, the barely controlled froth of wisteria. I fully expected to see Treebeard or a couple of Ewoks come bumbling out of the undergrowth. I parked in front of Gower's parents' house – I vaguely remembered the panelled front door with the bullion pane – and waited. There was a metallic blue Jaguar XE in the drive. I saw a shadow pass across the window. *Christ.* It hit me what I was about to do, but if I hung around any longer Mawker would turn up and that would be that.

It was with him in mind that I drove up the road a bit, and parked near the junction with Old Park Ridings. I got out, walked back to the Gowers'. I leaned on the doorbell. I heard a woman's voice inside – *I'll get it!* – and then a smiling face, a cream-coloured blouse and red fingernails.

'Mrs Gower?' I said.

'Yes.' Her face creased with faint recognition. I felt the same way. I might have traded pleasantries with her from the car as Sarah jumped in or Martin jumped out. I might have waved once or twice.

'My name's Joel. You won't remember but—'

'Joel Sorrell! Sarah's dad. Of course.'

'You do remember.'

'I'm good with faces,' she said, and Martin's own flashed horribly across my mind. 'Come in. What can I do for you? How's Sarah?'

I followed her into an expansive, brightly lit tiled hallway. A staircase led off to the right, carpeted in something that looked as soft as sable. A glass-topped table was covered in framed photographs. *Hello again, Martin.* There was a vase of white lilies. I had to just throw it out there. Nip the chit-chat in the bud and get her life ruined right now so she could begin to recover.

'Martin is dead, Mrs Gower. He was found this morning, just a short distance from here, near the golf course.'

She was looking at me as if she'd discovered that I wasn't Joel Sorrell after all, but an imposter who had somehow inveigled his way into her house on false pretences. She kept looking back over her shoulder at the kitchen.

'Do you mind?' she said, and her voice was thinning by the syllable. 'Only the rhubarb will catch.'

I followed her to the kitchen. I could see through the patio windows into the garden where a man in a pastel-pink Ralph Lauren polo shirt and steel-coloured hair – Mr Gower… Tom, as I recalled – was emptying a wheelbarrow of grass cuttings on to a compost heap. Mrs Gower – June? Joan? Joan – took a simmering pan off the hob. The hot, sweet, acidic smell of it filled the room.

She looked at me levelly, a hard look. She reminded me of someone agonising over a tough question on *Mastermind*.

Very carefully, she said: 'Martin is due back any minute. He was at a friend's house last night.'

'The police will be here shortly, Joan,' I said.

'In fact, he might even have slipped in while I was outside with his dad.'

She wasn't listening. She wasn't accepting it. This wasn't going the way I'd planned, but then why would it? What did I really expect? A tear in the eye, a thank you and an invitation to have a poke through his things? At least she wasn't screaming. At least I was still here.

We went up the stairs to an empty bedroom. Posters on a wall: Jimi, Kurt, Eric. A stack of PlayStation games. A stack of music magazines. How old was Martin? Twenty? Twenty-one? His room was pretty sparse. Perhaps he was in the process of moving out. I spotted the kind of things that stand out: a karate kit with a purple belt, a Teeline shorthand course book, a guitar, boxes of photographs. I wondered if any more shots of Sarah resided within them. I itched to search.

What I'd said seemed to catch up with Joan. She sagged on to the bed. A deep, agonised wail sounded from deep inside her, animalistic, ineluctable. I should not have been there. As soon as Tom came in I would be through the door, possibly before it had a chance to open. I did not have much time but I didn't know what I meant to do. The karate gear and guitar meant contacts I could interview: presumably he trained at a local dojo; maybe he was in a band. The Teeline shorthand book suggested he was maybe training to be a journalist, presumably at a college or university nearby. There would be something I could dig into regarding his photography. There was action to be taken.

Joan was sobbing into his pillow now. Maybe she could smell his scalp on it.

'Joan,' I said. 'Has Sarah been in touch? Has Sarah been here?'

But I was locked out. She was cocooned within her son. I heard the patio doors skid shut downstairs. I heard the roar of a tap.

On top of a cupboard lay a stack of notebooks. I skimmed through them. Photography stuff in the main: film speeds, apertures, timings. A purist then. No digital exposures for Martin Gower. Maybe that extended to his appointments. And yes, here was a diary.

Feet on the stairs. Tom calling Joan's name.

I riffled the pages. Nothing in the previous day's space. No mention of Sarah. He hadn't entered any information in the names and addresses section. There wasn't much of anything, actually. Except, once a month, a single word: ACCELERANTS.

'Who are you?' Tom came into the bedroom, the glass of water in his fist. No recognition here. He looked from me to Joan and then back again.

'Joel Sorrell,' I said. The name seemed to make no impact on him. But he was no longer listening. His wife was crying. A stranger was standing nearby.

'I'm calling the police,' he said.

'He *is* the police,' Joan cried at him, lifting her head from the pillow.

'Actually—' I began, but Joan was clawing her way towards her husband, her face slicked with tears and snot.

'Martin,' she said. 'MARTIN!'

Tom was shaking his head. Water from the glass sloshed over the rim. He didn't notice. 'What about Martin?'

'He's dead,' Joan managed, the words struggling out of her as if they were barbed wire snagging in her throat.

Tom dropped the glass. He went to Joan and held her. He didn't take his eyes off me.

'Sarah Sorrell,' I said. 'Have you seen her? Did Martin—'

'Get out,' Tom said. His lips were drawn back from his teeth. He was shaking. He was shaking so hard I thought he was having convulsions.

'I'm sorry,' I said.

The doorbell rang when I was halfway down the stairs. I didn't answer it, and went out through the patio doors at the back. I hurried down the garden and skipped over the fence. I jogged along the train tracks until I hit a road and followed it round to where I'd left the car.

I was on Spaniards Road, gunning through Hampstead Heath, when Mawker called to give me holy hell.

3

I picked up a litre of Grey Goose on the way home. I had maybe three inches left in the bottle in my freezer, but today was a four-inch kind of day. Mengele was laying in wait for me when I got in, pouncing on my leg like a furrier, more tuna-scented version of Cato. I let him bully me for a while until there was a real danger of him reopening some of his previously administered wounds, and poured him some Fishbitz. I carried the bottle and a shot glass and went out on to the balcony where I got on with the serious business of destroying my internal organs. The heat of the day had been captured by the floor tiles and I kicked off my shoes and enjoyed the warmth in my feet. I could hear the buzz of early evening traffic. In the windows of flats opposite I could see people sitting down for meals or TV or, like me, a restorative gill or two. I poured. I tossed it back. The vodka shot was a syrup slug of iced purity; I held it still on my tongue for a few moments and then let it roll down my throat. Cold became heat. I closed my eyes.

We used to have a bush in the back garden at Lime Grove. Dianthus. It produced red flowers with attractive grey-blue grassy leaves. You'd smell it on summer evenings when we sat outside with a glass of something, watching the Tube trains clatter over the tracks above the roofs of Shepherd's Bush market. It had a spicy smell about it.

Whenever she'd been naughty Sarah would pick one of the flowers and leave it by the bedside. She never confessed to this, but I'd seen her doing it once or twice. I smelled that flower now, across the years, as if some old, dying pocket of my mind had cruelly opened up to let me in.

I wondered how close I'd come to finding a path to Sarah. Somewhere in Gower's house, in a notebook or on a computer file, was a phone number or an address that might lead me to her. Martin Gower. Childhood sweethearts. I'd never thought to consider childhood friends as possible sources of information. How many of us retain the relationships we built at school? I tried to think of the other kids Sarah had been friends with but couldn't for the life of me dredge up any names. I guessed Sarah wasn't the kind of person to use social networking sites because I'd tried any number of them without success, both with my surname and Peart, her mother's. But that didn't mean her old friends didn't populate them. I made a note to ransack my brain for names, or contact the schools she'd attended.

I tried to push her from my mind, just for a while, but it was easier said than done. She was like Long John Silver infecting the dreams of Jim Hawkins, albeit in a much less frightening way. And then I thought about Martin Gower and how his parents would be plagued with thoughts of their son, and which version of events I'd rather have. I poured another shot to help blot out the vision of Gower's face, like so many rough leaves of bacon on a slicer. Whoever had done for him was committed. He wanted to make a statement. And this was not his first. Or if it was, it would not be his last.

Mawker's voice drifted through my thoughts. It had been punched around and exhausted by this murder. You could hear it in the empty threats. I'd accepted the caution without argument and told him I was sorry. I wasn't thinking straight. Sarah, and all that. He came round, a little, but only because he thought he might be able to benefit from my knowledge.

'You know what I know,' I told him.

'What about this Accelerants thing?' he asked. 'Any ideas?'

'What did Joan and Tom say?'

'Not a lot. They didn't have much to do with their son. He was out a lot. Busy, busy, busy. Click-click. Kick-kick, karate chop. Press passes and arpeggios. He was about to move. Shared flat in Crowthorne Road. Him and two other guys.'

'Names?'

'What have you done for me lately?'

'Well I was thinking the Accelerants might be a band. Maybe he's moving in with the bass player and drummer.'

'Owning a guitar does not turn you into Bob Dylan.'

'Well, he was musical when I knew him,' I said. 'At school, I mean. I dropped him off once after guitar practice.'

'He might not have kept it up. I ditched the cornet after six weeks.'

'Says the man who is so fond of blowing his own trumpet.'

'Funny, Joel. You're such a funny fellow. My ribs are on fire whenever you're around.'

'Anyway, you might want to follow that up. Local music venues. Pubs, clubs. See if they've done any gigs. Any more photographs I might be interested in? In those boxes of his?'

'Not as yet,' Mawker said. 'I'll let you know. Mainly

wanky black-and-white stuff. Wet landscapes. Black crows on rotting fence posts. Woe-is-me junk.'

'So are you going to let me in on these Crowthorne Road posers or what?'

'No, I'm not. You've been formally cautioned. Stick your wanger through the letterbox one more time and I'll chop it off. If anything relating to Sarah crops up, I'll let you know.'

'I'd rather there was some *looking for* instead of *cropping up*.'

'Yeah, well, this is a murder inquiry, not a search for a woman who is apparently alive and well, an adult holding a grudge against her dickhead father. Butt out, Joel. You're a very lucky boy. Tom Gower wanted to press charges. He could take legal action against you. And he'd win.'

I bit my lip wishing I could bite his lip, drank the vodka and put down the glass and the phone. I'd got a decent buzz on, fast. I needed it. I opened the glassine bag. Versions of her slid out on to the table. My daughter. My baby. Very pink. Very shiny. Sarah Grace Sorrell. Born 6 September 1999. In one of the photographs – presumably before Gower (or *she*, for fuck's sake) suggested she become fully naked – she wore a pale green T-shirt and black knickers. Her hair was swept back off her face and tied into pigtails. Her fingernails were blood red.

In the nude photograph she had a tattoo, some cursive text I couldn't make out, inked under her left breast. A navel piercing. Her right ear was punched through with half a dozen steel loops. No props. No clues in the backdrop: a featureless brick wall. There was nothing on the back of the photos, either. Except for one: a date three weeks ago and the words 'SLX sesh'.

What was SLX? A kind of camera? Sesh, presumably, was

session. I found myself praying to a god I didn't believe in that he hadn't just misspelled SEX.

Why did he have this set of photographs on him when he died? Was he on his way to meet Sarah, maybe, in order to show her? Or was he on his way back? Surely he would have let her keep these prints if he had the negatives. Maybe she hated them. I sure as shit did. But that would be another reason for Sarah to keep them. So if he was on his way somewhere – neatly dressed, man bag – why was he on some shitty track away from any of the conventional routes into the city centre? Which meant what? That Sarah lived nearby? Or that he was killed elsewhere and brought to this spot?

I checked my watch. Eight o'clock. I picked up the phone. Philip Clarke answered on the first ring. Clarke was one of a number of forensic pathologists used by the Met. He was the only one I knew well enough to share an occasional bottle of wine with.

As usual, his voice sounded brisk and bright though he'd probably been working over fourteen hours. I imagined him in his surgical gown, portly, dashing, with a nose broken and bent from a collision with an oar during a boat race when he was at university. Under his thousand-pound double-breasted sharkskin suits from Gieves & Hawkes he wore novelty braces. 'Joel, I'm about to get very red. Can't it wait?'

'Red with whom? Not the guy who looks like he shaved on a trampoline with a samurai sword?'

'He's only just landed on my plate, J,' he said. 'He's fresher than my lunchbox.'

'He knows... he knew my girl, Phil. I'm just looking for an in. Anything that might lead me to her. Ian Mawker's blocked me out of this one. I'm in the cells if I kick around in his dust any more.'

'You'll cost me my job, Sorrell.'

'Well, maybe, unless they catch you at your work-time hobby, necro-boy.'

'I'll email you if I see anything unusual. It will be anon. It will be unsigned. Got it?'

I fired up my Triassic-era laptop and stared at the winking cursor. I typed in: 'SLX sesh'. I got a bunch of surfing references. I tried 'SLX camera'. Bingo. There was a Rolleiflex SLX, a single lens reflex camera from the 1970s. Naturally it used film, which fit with Gower's Luddite work ethic. I typed in 'Martin Gower photography'.

Gower had a Tumblr account but he hadn't posted any candids here. Just more of what Mawker had described. Lone tree in a field. Rainy urban back street. Desolate beach. At the foot of the page was a badge with a cartoon camera lens sketched upon it and the words 'Swain's Lane Snappers'. I copied and pasted that into the search engine: an amateur photography group who met regularly at the Leopold Café, a little place on Swain's Lane. I knew that café very well.

'BLOODBiTCH'

12 MARCH – 15 MARCH 1985

There weren't many things that made him happy. Marilyn Monroe in *Niagara*, a full moon, the park on a freezing November morning, fish soup.

So when he found himself smiling at the young boy on the bus home one Friday afternoon, he was surprised. And when he realised he was smiling he was a little shocked, angry, and for some as yet unknown reason, more than a bit afraid.

His shopping list for Saturday demanded a small onion, a bottle of tomato sauce, a meringue base and a packet of rice. He came back with a kilo bag of Winalot dog food and a trowel from the market, which was strange as he despised dogs and didn't own a garden. That was when he sat down and began to worry. And think.

He decided that he needed a helping hand, so he padded barefoot to the drinks cabinet and liberally poured from a bottle of Teachers, watching the golden liquid swirl in hypnotic shimmers. He got back to the couch and slumped in one well used corner, glass in one hand, botle in the other, wishing he had put Mr Brahms on the stereo before he sat down.

Too late, he thought, and sipped his whisky.

So. What was up?

In a word, nothing. So why was he panicking?

It took half a bottle of TEachers before he got it. He hated children. And today he had been smiling at one of the little brats. He sighed and put his face in his hands, wincing at the raw smell of alcohol on his breath but keeping his position anyway. He had big hands that completely covered his face which suited him fine because he didn't relish the prospect of seeing his features in a mirror at that moment.

Now with the darkness absolute, he thought, dwelling upon his past and dreary present.

Okay, he thought, I'm thrity-three. No, come on, tell it how it is. What's the point of lying to yourself. Okay. Deep breath.

I'm thirty-seven. I'm lonely and single. I've got a stinker of a job. I hate my boss. I hate green peppers and Sunday mornings. I hate every morning. No TV, a crackly transistor radio that only receives Radio 2 in the evenings and static every other minute of the day. No friends. Well, Stan at the Tusk and Bottle, but I only see him when I feel like having a drink. I don't think he's even capable of seeing me half the time. No girl. Well, once. And then he stopped thinking and sighed. The sound was like broken, dead leaves on a quiet woodland path. The clock on the mantelpiece chimed twice. It was 2 am, he was drunk as you like and utterly depressed.

Her name had been Claire, and once, a million lifetimes ago, they had been engaged and he had been proud to take her out, his ring gleaming as big as an egg (to his eyes at least) on her finger.

They had fallen in love at university and his first year was devoted to her, sending her roses once a month, wining and dining and pining for her, showing her affection.

And everything was fine. He was happy and smiled a lot. Sometimes he smiled in lectures, for no apparent reason and he would walk through the streets to the shops with the same goofy grin on his face and the old women chatting on the poirches would smile and glance at each other, recognising his emotions and commenting on what a wonderful season summer was for love.

And then his mother died and his world fell apart.

It had been three years since Claire walked out of his life, four since Brenda, his mother, succumbed to the laughing black cancer in her stomach.

Claire had been everything to him in the months after Brenda's death. She had been a crutch and he leaned on her hard.

It had been April when she rang at his doorbell. A slightly overcast day, similar to the moods that had been sinking on him lately. She had smiled. And he knew then that it was over. He didn't need to look at her finger to know that the ring had been removedI didn't have to look at the eyes to see the determination in her actions. The smile said it all. A fleshy Pandora's box about to open and spill all manner of nasty things.

'Dont't say it,' he murmured, adn wandered off to the kitchen to make some coffee. That had been the frist time he had cried since his mother's death.

4

The balcony and the bottle were hitching their skirts at me but I couldn't relax now that I had another possible route to Sarah. I was over the limit so I trotted down to Seymour Place to hail a cab. I nodded and made affirmatory noises as the driver monged on about pit bulls and Chelsea footballers – I resisted the urge to ask what the difference was – all the while wishing I'd brought a hipflask with me. I kept my eyes on the human traffic as we swept along Marylebone Road and turned left into Albany Street, eyes boring into faces, same as always, just in case. It was a beautiful evening. People were flooding into and out of Regent's Park. I remembered picnics at the Japanese garden in Holland Park with Becs, and Sarah when she was little. She always helped to pack the hamper. She always brought Grapes, her teddy bear with her. Proper picnics, with steel cutlery and china plates. Real glasses. We'd drink chilled rosé and listen to the radio while Sarah turned cartwheels or made giant daisy chains. One time, Rebecca, she said:

Let's have another.

And I said: *Maybe… we'll see.*

I often wonder if I'd said yes we'd have moved elsewhere, and she'd have gone to a different gym. Maybe she'd still be alive.

'...and as for that French prong with his anachronistic Hoxton facking fin and his pink boots, he couldn't pass the facking parcel, the cahhhnt...'

The driver slowed up around the gnarly bit where Camden High Street feeds into Kentish Town Road. His invective faded too, maybe because he'd run out of things to say or more likely because the noises I was making didn't marry with his content any more. Quite possibly I'd chuckled and said 'yes' enthusiastically when he asked if he was boring the shit out of me. The tired, clustered Kentish Town thoroughfares became the slightly leafier, slightly more spread out streets of Gospel Oak. We hit Highgate Road and I readied my wallet. I tumbled out on to Swain's Lane a little more refreshed than I'd thought. I gave the cabbie his fare, and a tip to show him I wasn't the sort of cahhhnt he'd taken me for, and turned to face Leopold's. I'd been here a few times for a morning-after-the-night-before breakfast. They did great Bloody Marys and hefty full Englishes to sponge up all the undigested alcohol and regret in your belly. Now they were open for the evening crowd they sold artisanal pies and craft ales from a nearby microbrewery. It was all wobbly old tables and mismatched wooden chairs. The walls were plastered with ancient beer mats and sealed with varnish. Newspapers and board games. Candles melted into wine bottles. They played classical music, exclusively.

I went in and sat at the tiny corner bar. It wasn't too busy midweek, but it picked up on a Friday. I ordered a Czech Pilsner and a black pudding and wild venison pie. The girl behind the bar was dressed in a purple vest and denim shorts. A grey beanie kept her hair out of her eyes. She smiled as I handed over the shirt from my back; one of her teeth was decorated with a twinkling red jewel and there was a little silver bolt through the flesh just below her bottom lip. Her eye snagged on my scar; maybe she thought it was skin decor. Maybe she coveted it. She was Sarah's age. I had to restrain myself from grabbing hold of her throat and demanding she tell me where my daughter was. I wasn't so pissed to want to risk a night on one of Mawker's skidmarked mattresses.

A door to the rear led through to the toilets and the stairs to the rooms upstairs, which could be hired for private parties. A magnetic board fixed to the wall was covered in fliers and adverts and offers. Among them I found reference to the photography club, held in one of the upstairs rooms. They met on Thursdays, apparently, which was today. But I was too late. Their meetings finished at seven-thirty p.m. Presumably they had relocated to Hampstead Heath and were busy taking pictures of kites, muggers and flashers.

But no, there were a couple of women in one corner looking through a small album of black-and-white photographs. One of them clenched an ostentatious camera bag between her knees. I felt my heart smack against my ribcage at the thought that they must know Gower and, by extension, Sarah. I took my pint and sauntered over, pulled back a chair at the table next to theirs.

They both looked up at me. I smiled and sat down. I guessed they were in their early thirties. One of them wore a dark-blue sweater dress and knee-length buckled boots. The other was more formally attired in a grey pinstripe trouser suit over a white ruffle shirt, as if she'd just come from the office. The photograph album in front of them was opened to a page on which there was glued a photograph of a brilliant white jumbo jet framed by fat, leaden clouds, its landing gear down as it made an approach.

'Nice picture,' I said. 'Some contrast.'

'Thank you,' said Sweater Dress. Her voice carried that uniform media pitch, eager and bubbly but at the same time seen-it-all. 'I took that at Heathrow. Last flight in before they closed the runway for an hour. Massive storm.'

'Right place, right time,' I said.

'That's what photography's all about.'

Trouser Suit demurred. 'Well, you say that, but you have to make your own luck too,' she said. Her voice was tartan-edged. Glasgow, I reckoned. She picked up her glass of Prosecco. The blood-red ghost of her lips grinned on its rim.

'I suppose it depends what kind of photography you go in for,' I said. 'I don't suppose there's much luck in following a starving African kid around while a vulture waits for it to die, but Kevin Carter won a Pulitzer, didn't he?'

'You know he killed himself because he was haunted by his work?'

I thought of the bodies I'd seen over the past few years. I could buy that. 'There's a photography club here,' I said.

'Yes,' said Trouser Suit. 'We've just been. You a photographer?'

'Not to any great standard,' I said. 'Not to *any* standard, I should clarify. Is it good fun?'

'It's all right, isn't it, Cass?' Trouser Suit said.

Cass nodded. Her hand was rotating her half of black lager. 'There's a good mix of ability levels. People who just want to take better holiday snaps and those who know all about f-stops and white balance. A couple of semi-pros. Everyone chips in with feedback. There are no prima donnas.'

'Is there a Sarah that goes along?' It was hard to keep the desperation from my voice.

'Not that I know of,' Cass said. 'But I've only been three or four times. Loz?'

Loz was looking at me as if I might not be as random a stranger as they'd thought. Guardedly she said: 'There's a girl who turns up occasionally, but only to give one of the others a lift home. She's not a member or anything. Why?'

I couldn't make anything up. And I realised I didn't have to. Sometimes it was okay to just tell it straight.

'She's my daughter,' I said. 'I've been trying to find her for years.'

Loz and Cass traded looks. Cass said: 'I thought you reminded me of someone.'

I could hardly breathe. 'Thanks, but she resembles her mother more than me. Was she here tonight?'

'No,' said Loz. 'But then neither was Martin. That's her... well, I think he's her...'

'Squeeze? It's okay. I guessed that might be the case. I know Martin Gower.'

'Martin's always here,' said Loz. 'I've been coming for a year and he never misses a session.'

'Martin's dead,' I said.

I was getting used to being the bearer of bad news. It was becoming a doddle. Loz and Cass traded looks again, this time with larger eyes and paler skin.

'You're police,' Loz said.

'No, but sometimes my work sails me close to what they do.'

'And what? You think your daughter's involved?'

The question took me aback. 'No,' I said. 'I don't think so. I haven't thought about it.' I felt sullied, as if someone had offered me a box of chocolates that had turned out to be frosted cat turds. 'I just want to find her.'

'Why did you lose contact?' Cass asked.

'Problems at home,' I said, and then, to cut off any more prying, I did some of my own. 'These photography classes… anything else go on there, other than feedback?'

'How do you mean?'

'I mean, like artists sometimes do life drawings…'

'There's no mucky stuff goes on here,' Loz said. Her body language had all changed. Where previously she had been open, now she was half-turned away, her legs locked against each other, her arms folded across her chest. Her mouth had shrivelled like a salted slug.

'That you know about?' I asked.

'At all,' said Cass. 'If we do any photography here, it's portraiture, to demonstrate lighting with flash.'

'What about outside this venue? Did Martin ever invite you to pose for him at his house?'

Both women said no as if I'd invited them to paint my kitchen with their armpit hair. Cass narrowed her eyes. 'How about your daughter?' she said. 'Something happened to open this line of enquiry, didn't it? Something you didn't like seeing?'

At that moment Grey Beanie slipped my supper in front of me. I stared at the pie. I'd never felt so lacking in appetite. I asked if she wouldn't mind putting it in a bag to take away and she wordlessly removed it, but I heard her lip bolt clacking against her teeth. The modern-day tut.

'I have some photographs of her, yes,' I admitted. 'Candid shots. I believe Martin took them. I came here to find out if this was where the shoot occurred.'

'Do you have them with you?' Loz said.

'No,' I said. 'I was hoping to just take a look upstairs.'

'We can do that,' Cass said, after a couple of shared meaningful looks.

'We have the key,' Loz explained. 'Whoever's last to leave gets to lock up.'

They both stood up at once, and I followed suit. 'Martin used a Rolleiflex, didn't he?'

'I've never seen Martin use anything other than a DSLR,' said Cass. 'He was married to his Nikon.'

We were on the stairs now. I imagined Sarah's footfalls. I imagined her hand on the wall as she steadied herself. Somewhere in the dust and air commingling in this narrow space were Sarah notes. I was breathing my child in. I was close to her.

'Mind the equipment,' Loz said, as she stepped into the room and flicked the light switch.

There was a bar, but it didn't look as if it saw regular use. The beer taps were covered with towels, and there was no fresh boozy smell, just a redolence of perfume from the recent meeting. A small bookcase was stuffed with photography volumes: handbooks and manuals and aspirational tomes by Ansel Adams, Diane Arbus, Dorothea Lange, Richard Avedon. There was a small pile of camera bags, cables and tripods.

'This doesn't look like it,' I told them. 'The room where he took these photos was much bigger, and it had a bare brick wall.'

'Well, I'm sorry,' Loz said.

'Do you know of any other studios he worked out of?'

Cass shook her head. 'He certainly didn't own a studio. He might have paid for the use of one, for an hour or so. Unless he knew someone. I'll have a word with the others. But it probably won't be till next week now. We don't socialise. I only know them from this place.'

I asked Loz if she knew anybody. She wrote down the names of the half a dozen other group members, but she didn't have numbers for any of them.

'Who ran this thing, anyway?' I asked.

'It was Martin, really,' Loz said. 'He organised the shoots, the guest speakers. He decided what subject we'd discuss each week.'

'Do you know anything about... Accelerants? Or the Accelerants?'

'A band?' Loz asked.

'I think so, yes. I think Martin played guitar for them.'

'Jeez,' Cass said. 'You think you know someone.'

'No,' Loz said. 'I don't know them. Martin never said anything about it.'

'A man of secrets,' I said. Nobody agreed or disagreed.

I had nothing else to ask. I thanked them for their time, and handed them both a card with my number on it. 'If you should see Sarah,' I said, and they nodded.

I left Leopold's feeling sober and cold and anxious. I stood in the street, half-heartedly expecting a cab to turn into Swain's Lane, thinking about Martin and wondering if Sarah might have been similarly dismantled, left in a ditch or a wood, yet to be discovered by the early morning dog-walkers or joggers, an old picture of me trapped forever in the frozen meat of her brain.

'Don't forget your pie,' came a voice at my shoulder. It was Grey Beanie. She handed me a small carrier bag.

'Do *you* know the Accelerants?' I asked.

'No. But don't go accelerating *that* in a microwave,' she said, raising her eyebrows at the bag. 'You'll ruin it.' She tapped her teeth a couple of times against the bolt through her lip, winked, and went back inside.

5

I woke up early and Mengele was sitting a foot away from me, gazing into my eyes.

'It doesn't work if you try hypnotising people when they're asleep, fuckwit,' I said.

He showed me his teeth and I politely asked that he move to one side so I could get to where I needed to be. I was convinced he was putting on weight, and for a grown Maine Coon, that's impressive. Another kilo and I'd be able to ride him down Marylebone High Street, I reckoned, if it wasn't for the sneaking suspicion that he was packing on the timber in order to take over the world while carrying my head on a pike as a totem.

I took a piss-warm shower under a dribble from a scale-infested rose. Breakfast was a heel of bread that was a day away from spots of mould. I chased it with some water and made a mental note to get some shopping done or I'd be having Fishbitz and vodka for dinner. Then I sat and thought about what to do next. I no longer knew my daughter. I wasn't like the regulation parent who, when faced with a young teenager 'leaving home', can identify a number of likely destinations – best friend, relative, boyfriend – where they're likely to tip up. I had no idea who Sarah's best friend was when she ran away, six years ago, so there was no chance I'd be able to follow that line of thinking now. She could be anywhere, but I felt very strongly that she was in London, and the chances were that if she wasn't dead, then she knew about Martin's death, and she was scared.

What if she killed Martin?

I hissed at myself in disgust, and forced the thought down, much as I had done the previous night. But it wouldn't sit still. I couldn't accept that had happened, even if I no longer knew my daughter, had no empathy whatsoever with her. I wondered if she might try putting further distance between us, especially if she felt at risk, and part of me hoped she might, if it meant it took her away from the threat.

Though I was anxious to track her down, I knew my only chance lay in nibbling away at Martin's case, finding out why he died and who killed him.

I caught the Tube to Seven Sisters and walked to Bernard Road, a street of small businesses and properties gone to seed yet batting their eyelashes with For Sale or For Rent signs unlikely ever to attract anyone. Opposite a floor suppliers I saw an old electric guitar, shorn of its strings, glued and screwed to wooden battens outside a steel door. A sign above the door read LEX: LUTHIER. Most of the streetlamps were broken; target practice for the local street urchin marksmen. You never knew when you might be called upon to lump half a brick at a copper. Glass shards were set in the coping stones of a surrounding wall like the grin of a bare-knuckle boxer. The buildings huddled together as if for moral support. Television colours splashed against net curtains further down the street where the businesses gave way to a residential stretch.

I leaned on the bell and a kid answered. He was wearing a bobble hat with the Icelandic flag knitted into it. Beneath it was long, greasy hair. He wore a T-shirt with the legend THIS IS MY FAVOURITE T-SHIRT. Over it was an ancient biker jacket with one red sleeve.

'Your dad in?' I asked.

'Look, this is my place,' he said, with not a hint of irritation; clearly he was used to it. 'And we're closed.'

'You're the guitar tech?'

'I'm the luthier, yeah.'

'Lex?'

'Yes. Alex. Alex Turner.'

'Do you know the Accelerants?'

He gave me a look. I say 'a' look. I mean 'the' look. The kind of look all snoops receive before all of the cards are on the table.

'Listen… Who are you? Police?' He had a voice that made you want to ram broken champagne flutes into your ears. It dripped with arrogance.

'Why would the police come calling for you?' I asked.

'Well… *duh*,' he said. 'Sometimes there are raves in the abandoned factories and warehouses around here.'

'Have you heard of the Accelerants?'

'Leave me alone, would you? I'm busy. No time to talk to doorstepping nutters.'

He was going to shut the door on me so I took a chance. I blocked it with my foot and charged it with my shoulder. He flew back into the hall with a shout. I was in big trouble now with Mawker, and looking at three months in Sing Sing for using violence to secure entry. There would be more immediate grief if it turned out this kid was a karate expert, or used one of his guitars to brain me. I thought, *in for a penny*, and hooked my arm around his neck before he could right himself. He didn't try any sneaky self-defence moves, so I knew I had him. I frogmarched him up the stairs to his studio, following the smell of wood glue and solder. Once the door was shut behind us I let him go.

'Listen... what the fuck is your problem?' he yipped, like one of those snappy, nervous little dogs you see in the parks with prolapsed eyes, wearing cardigans or being carried by their owners. 'Look... you can't just do what you just did and expect to get away with it. I'm calling the police.'

'Okay,' I said. I gave him a number and told him to ask for Detective Inspector Ian Mawker. 'While we're at it, call an ambulance too. If I'm going down for forced entry I might as well go down for GBH as well.'

'Look... who are you?' he asked again.

'Doesn't matter. Let's just say I'm someone in a desperate situation. I'm trying to find someone who is very dear to me and I believe this person is in danger. The information you give to me could mean the difference between me finding where she is, or getting to her a fraction too late.'

'You're police then?'

'After a fashion,' I said.

'Look... why do you need to talk to me? I don't know anything about a missing person.' Behind the arrogance, and the fancy, arty job title, I could see there was more kid in him than man. I felt a twinge of guilt, and yet another unreasonable and irrational impulse to demand of him the whereabouts of Sarah because he was in London and she was in London and he seemed like the kind of louche prick she might like to hang out with (as if I'd know), so yeah, of course he must know where she was.

'Because of murder,' I said. 'Because of a lead.'

'What murder? Look... what are you talking about?'

'A client of yours – Martin Gower – his body was discovered yesterday on a patch of derelict ground in Enfield.'

'I know Martin Gower,' he said. He sounded as if he was about to be sick.

'Yes, I know you do. We've already established that.' The pressure was growing in him. You could see it, like the mercury expanding in a thermometer. Any moment now he was going to ask...

'Am I a suspect?'

'I don't know. I doubt it. What do you think? Should you be?'

'No!'

'Okay then. So Martin comes to you to get his strings strung or his pick-ups picked up, or whatever the fuck you do, and you chat about guitars and guitar bands and girls and chucking TVs out of hotel windows. And he mentions this band called the Accelerants. And you say—'

'The Accelerants?'

'And then *you* say—'

'I don't know of a band called the Accelerants.'

I took a deep breath. I needed a drink but this guy only looked old enough to have Tizer in his fridge. 'Did Martin Gower ever mention the Accelerants to you?'

'Listen, I'm not comfortable with this. You're getting angry. Angrier.'

'That's nothing,' I said. 'Keep up with this time-waste babble and you'll see I make Hulk look like Buddha. After "angrier" comes "hurt" and then "hurtier".'

'Look, you can't just do what you did. You broke in here. You assaulted me. You aren't the police.' The arrogance was creeping back into his voice. I was losing him. He could sense that I wasn't going to hurt him, seriously hurt him. Soon he was going to clam up, or call my bluff and ring the number and here would be another lead smothered.

'What's that?' I asked. I pointed at a sparkling blue guitar, a kingfisher against a muddy backdrop.

'It's a teardrop bass,' he said. 'A Vox. A replica of a Bill Wyman model. You heard of the Rolling Stones?'

'Yeah,' I said, 'they're all about the jazz too.'

I went to the guitar and picked it up by the neck. I heard air hiss through his teeth. 'Worth much?'

'Only about four grand,' he said. His voice was all *look, listen, learn, I must be important because I fix things your job can't afford.*

I pursed my lips and made appreciative sounds.

'You might want to put that back down,' he said.

'You fixing this for someone?' I asked. 'Bill Wyman, maybe?'

He snorted laughter. 'Guy who owns it wants it fretless so I'm stripping them out. He's a Jaco Pastorius fan.'

I nodded.

'Listen,' he said. 'I'd be careful with that. The guy who owns it plays bass for an outfit called Lettuce. He makes Lemmy look like Julie Andrews.'

'Well then, I imagine he'd be annoyed if it went back to him in pieces. So many pieces that a luthier even as rarely skilled as you would be unable to fix it. Especially with broken hands and severe concussion.'

'Look, I told you I don't know the Accelerants. Try the Dome in Tufnell Park. Try the Silver Bullet or The Lexington or the Union Chapel. Try the fucking NME.'

'Tell me something you *do* know. About Martin Gower.'

He flapped his arms in exasperation. 'Look, isn't that your job? Finding things out?'

'Most of the stuff I find out is a direct result of people answering my questions. Something you are singularly failing to do.' I'd had enough of his shit, his passive-aggressive posturing. I jammed the headstock of the bass into his desk drawer, pushed it until the edge was gripping the neck, then began to exert pressure on the body.

'No!' he yelled. He sounded like a kid who'd had his iPod confiscated. 'Martin Gower. Okay. Martin Gower. He played guitar but he wasn't what you'd call proficient. He wasn't one of Malcolm Gladwell's ten-thousand-hour freaks.'

'So what?'

'Well look, he was taking lessons. With an old friend of his.'

'Who?'

'Guy called Craig. Craig Taft. He lives in Mayfair.'

'See?' I said, rescuing the teardrop bass from the desk drawer. 'Smell, taste, feel, look, listen. See how reasonable you can be?'

I left immediately, quickly, knowing he was now in a strong position if he wanted to get in touch with the police. My best bet was if he got through to Mawker because it would just add to the long list of things to beat me over the head with; but it wouldn't go any further than that. The problem would be if Alex Turner passed on Taft's name. I had to crack on and find him now, before the plods started flat-footing all over my leads. If they got to anybody crucial to my search before I did, my chances for success would sink lower than the gusset of a drugs mule whose shoulder has been tapped in Indonesia.

I caught the Tube back down to Green Park and picked up an overpriced cheese salad cob and a coffee that tasted more of the plastic it was contained within. I didn't know this area of London too well; I've seldom popped out to Bond Street to stock up on four-hundred-pound shirts, or visit the upmarket barber's for a shave with a cut-throat razor. I wondered how Taft could afford to live here if he was teaching wannabes for a tenner per half hour. Maybe it was a sideline. Maybe he was teaching Bill Wyman.

I googled him and found a website, his grinning photo, and an address. Five minutes later and I was on George Yard, in front of a respectable-looking building made from handsome red brick behind the Marriott Hotel. I tried the doorbell and a clean, cultured voice came through the intercom. I guessed I'd not get away with the approach I'd tried at Alex Turner's.

'Mr Taft?'

'Yes?'

'My name's Joel Sorrell. I'm a private investigator. I'm here about Martin Gower.'

'What about him?'

'He's dead.'

Silence for a moment, and then the intercom clicked and our connection was lost. I rang the bell again but he wasn't answering. *Why do I always have to run up against the chatty fuckers?* I thought, as I mulled over the possibilities. Maybe he was crippled with guilt, or on the phone to Martin's parents to find out if – after all – it was true. Or Sarah? He might call Sarah with the same agonised request. My stomach filled with snakes; I tried the door anyway: locked of course. I began pushing buttons at random in the hope someone would just release the catch and let me in. But then there was a shadow in the hall and the door yawned open and I recognised him as Taft. He was pale and tall, his hair iron grey, tied back in a neat ponytail. He wore jeans and an orange jumper. He wore odd socks. The lines in his forehead seemed deep enough to store coins.

'A private investigator?' he asked. 'Why? What's going on? Who are you working for?'

'Do you mind if we talk inside?' I asked.

He considered for a moment, staring at my face as if he might better be able to read my intentions. Then, wordlessly, he pushed the door open wide and gestured with his head to come in.

He lived in a busy one-bedroom flat on the top floor, but though he owned a lot of stuff it seemed somehow less cluttered than Alex Turner's place. Like Alex, he had a lot of guitars, but they were whole, not piecemeal, and arranged on mounts bolted to the living-room wall. There were a couple of music stands in one corner of the living room, and copies of various guitar-learning books lying around: *The Guitarist's Friend*, *Rock School*, *Burt Weedon's Play in a Day*. I didn't need to see the CDs close up to know they would be heavy with guitar-led music.

'What happened to Martin?' he asked. He'd stopped in the centre of the room and stood facing me, his arms folded.

'Well, the pathologist is yet to tell us the results of the post-mortem, but he was attacked violently. Most probably stabbed to death.'

'Jesus Christ.' He put a hand over his mouth. He moved, and then paused, as if undecided about something. 'You want a drink?' he asked, eventually.

'Vodka. If you've got it.'

I followed him to the kitchen where he poured me an inch

of Stoli and after a moment's consideration, a brandy for himself. Then we returned to the living room.

'What can I do?' he asked.

Put another inch in there, I almost said. 'Since his murder, I've come across mention of something – a band, most probably – called the Accelerants. But I haven't seen any reference to them in the local press, or online. Have you heard of them?'

Again, he looked at me as if he was unsure about something. I guessed he was a drinker because he'd put that brandy away quickly so his hesitancy there perhaps had something to do with dependency. But this? Either the Accelerants was a band or it wasn't. I put my drink down and wondered if his guitar lessons were like this, his students attempting to extract an A7 chord from him, like blood out of stone.

'Accelerants isn't a band,' he said. 'But Martin did belong to them. As did I, for a while. It's a writers' group.'

'A writers' group?'

'Yeah. But a closed group. We didn't advertise for members. At least we didn't when I was involved. How did you find out about it?'

'I saw something at his parents' house, something written on a calendar. So Martin fancied himself as a writer? Is there anything he didn't fancy himself at?'

Taft raised his glass to his lips and gave a guilty start at finding it empty. 'Nothing wrong, is there, in having a broad range of interests?'

'No, of course not. But karate, writing, guitar, photography… These are subjects that demand a great deal of commitment and practice. How did he find the time?'

'He wasn't working last time I spoke to him.'

'Money… how did he pay for all his classes?'

'I don't know. If he still lived at home maybe he tapped his folk for a couple of quid. I only charged him a fiver for half an hour.'

'He had a nice guitar,' I said. 'Not that I'm an expert in these matters.'

'He did, yes,' Taft agreed. 'A Fender Custom Shop Strat.'

'How much would one of those go for, normally?'

'Couple of thousand, new. But he could have picked it up second hand for, what? Under a grand, say?'

'Still a hefty outlay for a novice.'

'He was all right, actually,' Taft said. 'He wasn't going to win any shredding competitions, but he showed some flair playing lead. He practised regularly. He was coming on, you know.'

'I suppose the guitar could have been a gift,' I admitted. 'His parents aren't short of a bob or two.'

'There you go,' he said. 'And anyway, it seems to me you're tackling this the wrong way. He was killed, after all.'

I ignored that. 'Why did you leave this writers' group?'

Another pause. I felt he was delving for the answer most likely to shut me up, rather than the truth.

'I was interested in songwriting,' he said. 'Nobody else was. No point in hanging around for feedback when everyone else was interested in fiction.'

'Where did you hold your meetings? Pub? Library?'

'No. They were always at a different venue every time. The location always had to have some kind of literary connection. The last one I went to was in St Leonard's Terrace, where Bram Stoker lived. We met and talked on the street for a little while. Swapped pieces of work. News. And then home.'

'Each to their own,' I said. 'Any idea where they'll meet next?'

'Why should I? I'm not a part of their setup any more. Other than Martin I had no contact with the others.'

'Who were the others?' I felt like going back to Alex Turner's flat and marching him over here to show him how an interview ought to go. Taft might not be completely transparent but at least he was talking to me. And he poured me a drink. *Register that, Turner, you arsehole.*

'Other than Martin... I don't know,' he said. He'd magicked a plectrum from somewhere and he twisted and turned it between his fingers. 'We decided not to share names. Real names. The writing was the thing. Not the writer.'

Christ. 'What about Sarah Sorrell?' I persisted. 'Or Sarah Peart?'

'I've never heard of those women.'

'It's just one woman. Did you ever see someone with Martin?'

'No. He came to Accelerants meetings alone. You kind of had to. It was... kind of necessary.'

I really wanted another drink but it was important I faced the coming days with a clear head if I was going to make inroads and beat Mawker to the early worms. 'Refill?' I suggested.

With Taft gone I gave his living room another look. He obviously lived for his music. As well as the CDs, his shelves were laden with well cared for LPs. A tower of scarily expensive-looking hi-fi separates – Naim, Cambridge Audio, Denon – was flanked by two mighty speakers that looked as if they'd tear off the whole face of the building if they were turned to full whack. They made my shitty little radio look like something found in a fossil bed. Like me, he didn't seem to possess a TV. There was nothing on show – diary, journal, photo album – I might snoop through as there had been in Martin Gower's bedroom. And still, despite his insistence to the contrary, I couldn't help but play the cruel game: Sarah might have been here once, with Martin. She might have been sitting where I was sitting. She might have talked about her sad, tragic father, who crumbled when she needed him most.

I'm different now, Sarah. I'm a changed man.

Yeah, right, Dad. You're only ever half a bottle away from falling asleep on the floor with your pants pissed, begging Becs to come back to you. Only her. You pursue me to keep your claws in her. She's dead. I'm gone. You're lost.

'No. No, that's not it.'

'Say again?' Taft said, as he returned to the room, my vodka in his fist. I took it and downed it and thanked him. I told him I had to go. I'd been on my feet all day. I couldn't believe that only the previous evening I'd been standing on derelict ground in Enfield staring down at pieces of Martin Gower.

I gave him my phone number and lurched for the door. I was tired to the bones and the drink seemed to have replaced the marrow within. I was sure something else was trying to rise from the spot on the sofa that I'd been occupying; some sooty presence, my slow shadow. A ghost.

I walked north through Mayfair until I hit Oxford Street. Sleet was in the air. First week of April and bloody winter still hanging on, or eager to make an early comeback. I could feel the cold move keenly in the livid, resculpted flesh on my left cheek. I stared at the buses and taxis as they shuttled east and west; all the shadows hunched behind those windows ghosted with condensation. Going home from somewhere; coming home to someone. Drifting.

Finally, the feeling that I was being followed went away. I couldn't understand why I'd invented such ugly invective from the mouth of a girl who had once loved me – and still did… I firmly believed that, or at least firmly held on to the hope of it. As a child she could not go to sleep until she had kissed my forehead, my cheeks, my lips, and recited a litany of reassuring exchanges: *night-night, sweet dreams, sleep well, I love you…*

I shook off the claustrophobia of those pampered, preening streets, where every other car was some precision-tuned penis replacement made in Germany, and every shop sold its own weight in silk or silver. I crossed the busy main drag and cut down Holles Street past Cavendish Square and then tiredness blocked the route out and the next thing I knew I was waking up on my sofa and Mengele was looking at me with an expression of feline disgust. I sat in the dark, looking out of the window at the Marylebone rooftops, and strange lights hung in the sky and it was only when I stood up to take a closer look that I realised it was the reflection of my tears in the glass.

6

I drank coffee and dressed against the chill. Frost had settled in the night, sealing cars and casting weird leaf patterns in the surfaces of puddles. No phone calls in the night. No visits from Mawker or any of his minions. Or maybe the telephone and the door had been rocking non-stop and I was too tuckered out to hear anything. It comes on me like that sometimes, fatigue. Oblivion at the end of a brutal sequence of late nights: my body's totting-up process. Pushing myself too far, too hard. Drinking too much, eating unhealthily or not at all. Shallow sleep or the endless, harrowing nights when I can't rest and all there is to do is listen to the couple next door argue or fuck, or watch the lights of the jets winking as they enter or leave Heathrow.

I opened the laptop and searched for her but she wasn't there. I knew her well enough, before social networking became the all-consuming monster, to know she would despise it. I remember she had been damning of any kind of look-at-me behaviour while at school. I tried to think of some of the friends she'd had but couldn't remember their names. I tried Martin Gower, but his Facebook page had been deactivated.

Though the sleet had not lasted long, freezing fog had fixed what had fallen into place with lethal glue. The main street had been gritted but all the smaller roads were glassy and treacherous. I skated and cartwheeled down to Marylebone Road and checked my phone as I did so, in a stunning act of accident defiance. There had been no messages from Craig Taft in the night; I willed them to come: *Joel? It's Craig Taft. I know where the next Accelerants meeting will take place. Joel? Craig. About Sarah. I said I didn't know who she is. Well, I was lying. I know who she is, Joel. And I know where she's staying. Joel? About Sarah. She's dead, man. She's dead. She's dead.*

'She's dead if she comes round mine with a gob on her again.' The woman jostled me as she pushed past, multitasking like a Swiss army knife: pushing a buggy filled with snot and pastry, vaping, jawing on her Nokia. A memory of Sarah in her buggy, and me getting used to pushing it, getting on and off buses, learning which Tube stations to avoid, understanding the cruel physics of trying to enter narrow shop doorways with wide wheels. I remember, at the start, how stressed I got; I couldn't understand the cool, urbane mums; how they glided around as if they were pushing little more before them than the warm air from their smiling mouths. And I remember Sarah picked up on this – she can't have been much older than three – and she reached back and patted my hand, and said: 'It's okay, Daddy. Look, here's a green Mini car.'

She lifted a load off me with that, and I realised it was no big deal. I was one of the many cretins pushing a buggy around a buggy-unfriendly city. There was no reason to let myself get annoyed about it. How annoyed could you allow yourself to be with a beautiful little girl in your charge?

Once off the ice I marched into the library and said hello to the woman behind the loans desk.

'Do you have any writing groups meet here?' I asked.

'Writing groups? Do you mean like reading groups?'

'Exactly like that. Only not reading. Writing.'

'We have a couple of reading groups,' she persisted. 'One meets every other Thursday, the other meets on the first of every month. Except for New Year's Day.'

'Right. Do you have any writing groups?'

'We have writers who live locally, who come and do readings. Do you mean like that?'

'I don't mean like that,' I said. 'What I'm looking for is a group of people who write. Who get together from time to time to do writing. Creative writing. In a group.'

'We don't have anything like that,' the librarian said. 'Were you looking to set something up, perhaps?'

'Any ideas where I might find a group like that?' I asked. I wasn't holding out much hope. She seemed to find the concept of creative writing as impenetrable as I did the Dewey Decimal System.

'Creative writing?' she said. 'You might try the universities. They all seem to have a course these days. But I guess that's not quite what you're after. How about... hang on.'

She collared one of her colleagues, a raven-haired woman wearing a fitted cardigan with a tissue balled up one sleeve. She was carrying a stack of books with the studied indifference of a waiter carrying mountains of crockery. 'Gill, this gentleman is looking for a creative writing group. Any ideas?'

'You could try the British Museum,' Gill said.

'Really?' I asked. 'You're not mixing up creative writing with Archaeological Studies of Ancient Greece?' I smiled my best disarming smile, but the pair of them rightly gave me a look that would have put lesser mortals in the grave.

'Would there be anything else?' she asked.

I thanked her and left, wondering after all whether a reading group was really all that different to a writing group. I had no idea. Presumably they both had the same priorities at heart. Presumably it was all about story. Did it work, did it not work? Did it entertain? Did it bore you rigid?

Though it was cold I decided to walk, at least until my feet turned to chunks of stiff wood. I reached the museum by mid-morning. I went inside and spoke to a guy on reception who confirmed that yes, there was a creative writing class that met regularly in one of the museum offices every Monday night. And not only that, but the co-ordinator was in right now.

'Could I speak to him? Her?'

'Him. Doctor Louis Ferguson. He's a lecturer at UCL. I'll take you up.'

He led me to the lift. We went up in silence to the second floor and he led me along a carpeted corridor flanked with wood panelling and unidentified portraits. We stopped outside a door bearing a plaque containing a mystifying combination of numbers and letters. He gestured grandly and I knocked.

'Come!' said a withered voice.

'I'll leave you to it,' the receptionist said.

I went inside. I thought for a moment that I had entered an empty office, and that I had been the victim of a pointless prank executed by a staff member who had a gift for projecting his voice. But then I saw how the pattern on a gaily upholstered armchair appeared to move, and a figure emerged from the pattern like someone who had given much of his life to the rare pursuit of total domestic camouflage.

'We aren't meeting now, are we?' he asked, looking at his watch.

'If you're free,' I said.

'We're meeting in twenty minutes. That's why I came in here early. To fix my head and relax first.'

'What is the meeting about?' I asked.

'You mean you don't know? Did you not receive the email?' He was unfolding from the chair and I was put in mind of spiders with long legs emerging from tunnels of silk. He was very tall, perhaps as much as six foot four, but he was painfully thin. I guessed I probably weighed much more than he did, and I was giving away the best part of ten inches.

'I'm sorry,' I said. I felt hollow, scraped out from too little sleep, and I didn't want to maintain this pointless bluff. I had no patience for it. 'I don't work here. I'm here to talk to you about your writers' group.'

He sat up straight. I noticed crumbs of pastry glued to a fledgling salt-and-pepper beard. 'You want to sign up?'

'Well no, not really.'

'A good thing, I'm afraid. The Knackers Yard is oversubscribed as it is, and anyway, you're a little too young for us.'

'The Knackers Yard?'

'I know, I know, it's something of a demeaning, self-defeating name we've given ourselves, but well, it's meant to be ironic. We're all over sixty-five, but afire, still, with ambition.'

'I wanted to ask your advice,' I said. 'About writers' groups in general. Do you have a minute?'

He consulted his watch again. 'I have fifteen,' he said. 'What is it you want to know?' He gestured to a chair.

'The Knackers Yard,' I said, sitting down. 'Do all writers' groups have names?'

He bowed his lips. 'I expect so, but I imagine it isn't crucial. I like telling my friends I'm off to the Knackers Yard.'

I bet he did. I bet it never wore thin. For him. I imagined his friends and colleagues with fixed grins.

'I suppose it lends everything a more professional air,' he went on. 'It gives you some focus, and you treat the two hours with some respect, with purpose. It codifies the whole thing.'

'What do you do, over that two hours?'

'It depends if anybody has submitted work for review. We might have a couple of WIPs to consider—'

'Whips?'

'Sorry. Works in progress. Members like to get feedback from their peers.'

'Really? Isn't that a bit too tempting? I mean, you know, you might read something and like the idea. Pinch it for yourself?'

He seemed genuinely shocked, and insulted. He narrowed his gimlet eyes at me. 'There is no magpieing in my group,' he said. 'Nor have I seen any in the industry in the thirty years I've been active.'

'You're published then?'

'Not these days, but back in the late eighties and early nineties I had three novels published by Fourth Estate.'

'That's quite some break,' I said. 'What happened? Did you retire?'

He smiled at me. I knew that kind of smile very well. If you could transcribe it into words it would say: *Aw bless, you fucking idiot.*

'A writer never retires. You can never *not* be a writer.'

'Really? I don't understand. Shelve the typewriter. Throw away the pencil sharpener. Watch TV. Make bread.'

'I'm writing all the time. Even when, especially when, I'm

doing something else. You don't switch off. It's pointless even to try.'

'You must be fun to live with,' I joked, but it wiped the smile off his face.

'I used to be married,' he said. 'But she was only ever the other woman.'

'You chose your writing over your wife?'

'Substitute the word "work" for "writing" and you'll agree that isn't such an uncommon occurrence. Anyway, I didn't choose one way or another. The choice was taken out of my hands. It chose me.'

'I'm sorry,' I said. I had a sense of the conversation sliding away from me; it was not unusual. 'I'm here to talk about creative writing. Not marital fuck-ups.'

'It's all grist for the mill,' he said, but he couldn't keep the bitterness from his voice.

'Anything else you get up to, other than peer appraisal?'

'We sometimes have a guest speaker. We can't pay, but we'll cover travel expenses, and take them out for a curry. Bottle of wine. You know… writers, agents, editors and the like. Or we'll talk about publishing trends, or recommend books to each other. And we'll always begin and end with a writing exercise.'

'A packed two hours, then?'

He nodded. 'Oh yes. We frequently go over. Sometimes the cleaners have to kick us out. If we've got a second wind we'll pop to the Museum Tavern across the road and continue over a nightcap.'

'What kind of writing exercises?'

'Well, it differs at the end of the night, but we always start with five solid minutes of automatic writing.'

'Is that like word association football?'

'No. Not word association. Nothing so structured. This is completely abstract, but quite punishingly regimented. So we write for five minutes using a medium we're unused to in order to keep it fresh, to take the brain unawares. So I might bring in a piece of wallpaper and write on it with a crayon. Or a piece of black paper and a silver outliner. No laptops. You need that direct contact between the paper and your brain. It must be physical. But it must be unconventional too. A shock to the system.'

He was hunched forward now, bristling with enthusiasm. 'No taking your pen off the page. No punctuation. No dotting of i or crossing of t. At the end of the line, a delicious scratch as you drag your pen back to the start of the next.'

'Sounds demanding.'

'If it was easy, everyone would be doing it.'

'I can assure you, that's not the case.'

'It's pretty tough at the start, but once you get into it, it can be quite therapeutic. You can lose yourself. I once wrote for an hour and I meant only for it to be a five-minute warm-up. And occasionally, if you can read back what you've written, you might find something, maybe one word, maybe a phrase or a sequence, that sparks an idea, and zoom! You're off.'

'Seems like a lot of work for little reward.'

He considered this for a while. Time seemed to have slowed down. He was one of those people who make glue of all that's around them. His slow, rich voice was part of it. The retarded blink of his eyes, which I realised with a jolt didn't blink all that often. Outside, the traffic on Bloomsbury Street was muted and far away; its aggressive murmur couldn't find its way in here.

'I suppose you've summed up writing,' he said. 'Perhaps

all art. But you tap away at the rock regardless, hoping to hit that slim seam of gold.'

I was attracted less and less by this job but who was the clown? My own career was hardly what you'd call stellar or interesting. If writing was a fool's job then I was scrabbling around underneath it in the great shit jobs pyramid.

'Anything else you get up to?' I asked.

'There are loads of exercises. But all the best ones, I think, involve cutting. Writing is mainly all about editing, really. Kill your darlings, and all that.'

Yeah, I thought. *Kill your darlings stone cold dead.*

A woman poked her head around the frame of the door. She wore glasses with circular lenses. I couldn't see her eyes through them for the windows' reflection. Her short hair was teased out in little flicks around her face as if it had been the origin of some mild explosion.

'Hello, Lou,' she said. 'Are we on?'

'Yes, yes,' he said. 'We were just finishing up here... that's right, isn't it? Or was there something else?'

'No, I'm done,' I said. 'Thank you for your time. I really appreciate it.'

He walked me to the door. The woman stood back, scrutinising me with naked suspicion. 'What's all this in aid of anyway? Are you looking to start a group of your own?'

I shook my head. 'I'm thinking of joining one,' I said.

I walked back to the main entrance. I was no writer, but I guessed that was kind of the point of joining a writers' group: to improve. I read a lot; I was halfway towards being moderately intelligent – how hard could it be?

All of which was academic if I couldn't find my way into the Accelerants. Maybe they'd be more receptive to me if I had a reference, from a real, honest-to-God published scribe. I hurried back to Ferguson's office. The door was open but he'd gone. His meeting had apparently ended, or was taking place elsewhere. But that open door suggested he would be back soon.

'Hello?' I called out. But this time there was no chameleon against the upholstery. I sat in his chair and waited. I thought, *Sod it, just make something up. It doesn't matter.* There was a bulging bookshelf in the room, adjacent to a desk cluttered with the paraphernalia of the habitually disorganised: coffee cups bubbling with mould, towers of paper, Post-it notes petalling a small PC monitor. I thought it couldn't harm just to check it in case there were any copies of Ferguson's novels up there. It would help if I could back up my pretence with some bona fide titles at least.

Here: ageing books with rubbed spines bearing his name. I pulled them out and checked the black-and-white author photograph on the back cover. His hair was dark, long, swept around his shoulders. He was resting his chin on the back of his hand, as all authors seem to need to do when the camera comes out. He wore the faint smile of someone who was looking forward to many years of good reviews and improving contracts and no idea that it would be over within the time it took to write a couple more novels. I thought about that for a while. Was it more painful to have tasted success, to have experienced the heady process of publication, than for it to be a tantalisingly unattainable dream, as it was for so many?

I admired the titles. *Suspense Motif. Ghost Notes. Zeloso.* A brief scan of the various blurbs taught me they were all part of the same series featuring his pet detective, a concert pianist called Gala Blau. It looked like a modern-day Modesty Blaise reworking, with faintly ridiculous plots and cartoon characters with Flemingesque names: the villain in the first book, for example, was called Sebastian Shrike.

I checked the dedication pages and acknowledgments.

For Katrin – my love, my love...

For Romy, Daddy's sweetheart for ever...

'A page-turner', gasped the *Daily Express*. 'Breathless, the year's best thriller', drooled the *Sunday Times*. 'Watch your back, Mr Deighton', warned the *Daily Mail*.

'Professor Ferguson?'

'Yes?' I don't know why I said it. Most likely it was because he was on my mind and I'm a bolshie bugger who likes putting himself in tricky situations and—

Sorry. That's a bunch of crap and you know it. You know exactly why I said yes. I mean, look at her...

She was tall and lean, with a long neck and long, straight black hair, the colour of India ink. Her mouth was a broad cherry sweep. Big eyes, such a dark brown you couldn't discern the pupil. She wore a knitted stone-coloured dress and knee-length black boots. She looked like Anne Hathaway, minus the flaws.

'Oh,' she said. 'I'm sorry. I was expecting someone—'

'Older?' I suggested, and raised an eyebrow. 'Yes, I get that a lot.'

'I'm here,' she said, spreading her hands to show just how here she was. She had small hands, slender fingers, no wedding band, no engagement rock. 'A little early, but better than being late.'

'Yes,' I said. 'Shall we get down to it?'

'Lead on. I'm starving.'

Right. Lunch. I could do that. I walked out of the office, retracing my steps to the exit, Ferguson's books padding out my jacket. I made a mental note to phone him and apologise but I doubted he'd mind if it meant someone showing an interest in his work. Outside I bit the bullet and headed towards the Museum Tavern, one of Ferguson's favourite watering holes.

'Professor? The bistro is this way.'

'I'm sorry,' I said. 'Force of habit. My, uh, club is in that direction.'

Bistro. Who went to a bistro on a Monday? If it was the one I was thinking of on Montague Street, then you were looking at a bill of at least fifty pounds and that was before you took a sip of wine.

She slid an arm through mine. I smelled the faint trace of her warm skin come at me from beneath that thick woollen barrier. Would she do that to a complete stranger? I thought perhaps she might. I'd heard enough of her voice to discern a faint accent – maybe French – to suggest a warmth and a boldness with strangers that doesn't seem to be shared by us diffident islanders.

'Was there anything in particular you wanted to see me about?' I asked, wondering if that warmth would go south should I come clean about my imposture.

'You asked me,' she said, and gave me a conspiratorial wink.

'How are things in your department?' I asked. The game was up. I could only hope she was stringing me along because she fancied lunching with me anyway.

'All good,' she said, 'considering I've been in that department for a grand total of—' she consulted her bare wrist, '—three and a half hours.'

'Ah,' I said, thinking, *first day*. Maybe she didn't know what the professor looked like after all. 'I knew that. Just wondered how you're settling in.'

A slight squeeze of my arm. 'I'm settling in just fine,' she said. 'Thank you for asking.'

The midday light was brittle, as if the fledgling spring days were having trouble leaving winter behind. Exhaust vapours lingered in the street. I watched a man carrying shrink-wrapped boxes from a van to a printer's shop door. He wore gloves of such an acid red it looked as if he had scalded himself.

We arrived at the bistro and I held the door open for her. Inside we were greeted by a tall, immaculate waiter who showed us to a table by the window.

'Could we perhaps take a table towards the back?' I asked. I blamed the cold, but really, I didn't want to risk being recognised by some off-duty plod, or any of the lowlifes I tended to find stealing oxygen from my personal space. I'd had a stomach full of innocent people suffering for the crime of knowing me, and being my friend.

I ordered a bottle of Sancerre and asked for bread and olives. Suddenly I was hungry. I hadn't eaten properly all weekend.

'It's good that we should have a little get-together like this,' I said. 'What with work and my involvement with the writers' group, I get precious little time for any kind of relaxation. Any kind of "me" time. Do you know what I mean?'

'I might, if I knew who you were,' she said, smearing a pat of cold butter on to her rustically sliced multi-seed snob cob.

'Ah,' I said again.

'Mm,' she said, and widened her eyes.

'When did you see through my cunning ruse?' I asked.

At that moment, Louis Ferguson came through the door. The woman stood up. 'Daddy!' she called out.

Right, I thought. *Immediately*.

Ferguson seemed perplexed to see me. His confusion

turned to glee when his daughter filled him in on my stupidity. I told him I wanted to just borrow some books and I seemed incapable of acting like a normal human being and I was ever so sorry, no damage done, lunch is on me and then—

Tears hit me. Hard as an April squall. I felt myself bow under the weight of them. I felt Ferguson's hand on my shoulder, lighter than air. There was only the mass of this sudden misery, sucking me down under the weight of its own gravitational force.

I calmed down after a while. There was a brandy on the table in front of me though I had not ordered it. Possibly it was meant for Ferguson. I downed it anyway.

'Are you all right?' she asked.

'I don't know your name,' I said.

'That's nothing to get upset about,' she said.

I laughed. I liked that. I liked her.

'It's Romy, Romy Toussaint,' she said. She gave me her business card. I gave her one of mine.

'Snap,' she said, perusing the text. 'Private investigations? How exciting.'

'Toussaint?'

'It's my mother's maiden name. I think it's a better fit than Ferguson.'

'Ferguson is a strong name,' said the professor, but there was a twinkle in his eye. They'd already had this argument long ago, you could tell.

'Romy. Like in the book,' I said.

She seemed confused.

'*For Romy. Daddy's sweetheart for ever.*'

'Ah yes. It doesn't take much to make you cry, does it?'

'That wasn't it,' I said. 'Although yes, I suppose it was,

in a way. I have a daughter I haven't seen in a while and watching you and your father together…'

'It's a scene you've yet to have,' she said, her fingers fluttering near her mouth in dismay. 'Unless you're lying to me again and it's really because your pants are too tight.'

I shook my head. 'I won't lie to you again,' I said.

Ferguson leaned towards me. 'I took the liberty of hailing you a taxi,' he said. 'I hope you don't mind.'

I thanked him and apologised again and said goodbye. I got in the cab and thought for a moment. I said to the driver: 'New Scotland Yard.'

7

I hung around outside, drinking overpriced coffee-flavoured piss. This was one of the downsides of no longer being on the inside. Half my time was spent skulking in the shadows waiting for someone, or for something to happen. The coffee seemed to be lasting longer than it ought but that was because the bucketing rain kept topping it up. My gaze darted around the windows where I knew Mawker had his office. If I was caught out here it would only give him license to tongue-lash me, the by-the-numbers prick.

A flash of colour on Broadway: Phil Clarke, aka The Kingfisher, cut across to where I was moping outside St Ermin's Hotel on Caxton Street, keeping the lion statues company. As I said, the pathologist had a bit of a thing for braces. I say 'bit of a thing' but it was more like an obsession. Or maybe even a fetish. I could well believe he'd wear them along with a leather thong and nothing else when he was back home in South Ken. These were emerald green, shining like wet electricity, beneath a two-thousand-pound Tom Ford suit.

'What are you doing standing in the rain?' he bellowed.

He gripped my elbow and led me into the hotel foyer. 'It's drink o'clock. And I don't mean that Styrofoam nightmare of yours. Lose the fucker. That's an order.'

He guided me into the bar, darkly lit with open fires and walls papered crimson. We sat opposite each other on expansive sofas. The cushions were patterned with little elephants.

'Thanks for agreeing to meet me,' I told him.

'Pleasure's all mine,' he said absently, trying to catch the barman's eye.

He ordered cocktails for the both of us – whisky-based, unfortunately – and he tucked into his lustily while I held mine at arm's length and eyed it suspiciously.

'What's this again?' I asked.

'Manhattan,' he said. 'Best cocktail there is.'

'I'll take your word for it,' I said, and slid it over to him. 'Too complex for me,' I explained. 'Too… brown.'

'Racist,' he spat, and gladly received it.

Good barman alert: he'd spotted this drinks awkwardness and stepped over to ask if I'd prefer something else.

'I'll have a Vesper Martini,' I said.

'Christ,' said Clarke. 'No matter how much you try, the call won't come.'

'What call? I'd accept any at the moment, to get away from you, the mood you're in.'

'Barbara Broccoli. Drink your fanboy drink. Bloody amateur.'

I looked at Clarke's hands while he drank. They were small and neat and very pink, like boiled crab claws peeled back to the meat. I wondered if he smelled of anything under that bourbon – of his latex gloves, perhaps, or the juices that invariably coated them.

'Shaken?' the barman asked.

'Stirred, actually,' I said, pointedly.

'Let's get to it then, Double-O Seven,' he said. 'I'm having one more of these then I'm catching a cab home for lamb chops and a blow job.'

'You know why I'm bugging you,' I said. 'Martin Gower. Anything you can tell me about him?'

'Well, should I tell you anything, of course,' he said, spearing olives on a plastic skewer, 'upstairs would carpet me so fast I'd have rug burns bone deep.'

'I know,' I said. The same old game. The ego massage. The long, slow waltz towards a back-scratch promise. We did all that, but the theatre wasn't over. He flourished a napkin and wiped his mouth with it, his eyes never leaving mine. He had slightly protuberant eyes that made him look perpetually surprised. He folded the napkin and placed it on the table. One more sip of his cough syrup cocktail and:

'Calling card. That's what you're after, isn't it?'

'Not necessarily. Just anything out of the ordinary. You know, anything exotic, anything that might give me some direction.'

'Guy gets carved like a Sunday roast and you want exotic.'

'You know what I mean. Why dismantle someone like that? It takes time. It takes effort. Was it done to disguise something? Conceal something? Or is the butchery its own message? A clue in itself?'

'A come on? You're assuming this guy wants to be caught?'

'Not at all. But it crosses your mind from time to time.'

'There's been nothing like this. This is a first. It won't be the last.'

'No,' I said, feeling a shudder work its way through my legs. 'I know that.'

I wondered if the business of the suits and the pricey

drinks and the bluster and blague were part of an act. I thought Clarke one of those people who had to inhabit a character. If he'd been a reporter he'd have met me in a boozer wearing a raincoat. Maybe he was lonely. He never volunteered anything about his private life, beyond the broadest of brush strokes. Neither did I, and I didn't because I didn't want people to know how utterly desolate my life was. My grim little cycle of vodka and cat food and photographs of ghosts. Maybe lamb chops and a blow job was code for Pot Noodle and a wank. Maybe he was really, really good at yoga.

'It's interesting what you said about disguise. Concealment.'

I narrowed my eyes at him. 'Why?'

'I found a puncture wound. Very small. Back of the neck.'

I had a vision of a body on a meat hook, and gave voice to it.

'No,' Clarke said. 'Nothing like that. This is smaller. Clean too. A meat hook would show tearing where the weight of the body has worked against it.'

'Fatal wound?' I suggested.

'Again, no. This was designed to incapacitate. Not to kill.'

'Incapacitate? How?'

'It's what's called a C2 complete. By which I mean the spinal cord was damaged at the second cervical vertebra.' He stuck two fingers against the skin on the back of my neck. 'Right there. Total paralysis.'

'Why not just knock them out? Use a cosh?'

Clarke drained his glass and stared at it as if wishing it was self-replenishing. 'My guess is that would have been too risky. You bash someone over the head and you could kill them. And this guy obviously—'

'Wanted to keep him alive.'

'For a while at least, yes. It would seem.'

He left then, but not before warning me again that this was strictly off the record and that if it should get back to his bosses that he'd been sharing delicate information I'd wake up short of a kidney or two.

Still no word from Craig Taft. I had to be patient. This was no ordinary writing group. This wasn't 'What I Did in My Holidays' or 'Tonight, boys and girls, we're going to write a poem about autumn'. Nobody in this group was over thirty-five, which meant it wasn't a thinly veiled lonely hearts club, or a support network for the romantically crippled. If you belonged to a gang of any sort at that age you were committed. There was a camaraderie, and a sense of competition; I remembered as much from my days playing Sunday League football as a teenager in the north-west. It was a savage kind of loyalty, a dangerous sort of love, even, existing for as long as the match lasted, or the training session. You felt, in moments of extremis – a goal down; the loss of a teammate to a dirty foul; a sending off – a kinship that went deeper than what it meant to be friends. You felt you might die for these people. You felt you might kill for them.

I felt an old, ill-defined rage come over me. It was too wayward to be part of what I had experienced after the death of my wife. That was tied up in complex emotions connected to frustration and impotence. This was connected – I was sure – to those trench warfare brothers of mine. I had not enjoyed that level of intimacy or involvement any time since; certainly nothing like it had existed at Bruche when I was undergoing police training, or at Walton Lane nick, my first and last posting after I'd passed out. Family engendered it – to some extent – but at a level of reserve. I missed it; pure and simple. I missed having someone in my life who meant something.

It was getting late; all day, for one reason or another, I'd been a coil of nervous tension. I needed to relax. Too often these days, no matter if I went to bed early, or – miracle of miracles! – without a drink in me, I'd wake up the next day feeling as though I'd been ploughing a field with a bent fork. I ached everywhere. My teeth ached. Once I'd decided it couldn't be Mengele beating the shit out of me with the cricket bat in the night, I realised it must be stress. I was going to bed with more knots in me than a sailor's practice rope. Sleep was failing to unpick any of them. Wake, angst, repeat. It didn't help, I suppose, that I had the posture of a wanking monkey.

I'd meant to walk home, but it was another beautiful London evening, so I strolled north-east, enjoying the warmth in the air, and the purpling sky. I wondered what Romy Toussaint was doing, and with whom she might be doing it. And a tender thought turned to a sour one and I remembered how it had gone with Melanie Henriksen.

Don't do that again, I thought. *You can't do that again.*

I was on the Strand, heading towards Aldgate. The sound of traffic had reduced to a murmur so I was able to hear the call of birds roosting in the buildings above me. Melanie had done nothing to deserve what had happened to her. Her only crime had been to be receptive to my overtures. She had become a target, a fulcrum for a bad person to lean on in order to get to me, because I cared about her. The monsters in this city are not stupid. They know the best way to harm you, or stop you from getting to them, is to find out who you love. Love is a killer, in this business.

Melanie was somewhere in Cornwall now, looking after animals, trying to bury the horror of what happened to her under whatever layers of normality would work. That and the love of her family, which was more robust than anything I could throw her way. You could only hope to bury it. You couldn't ever expect to forget.

My phone was in my hand somehow, my finger hovering over Romy's number.

I'd known her for what? An hour? I stopped myself from dialling; I wasn't thinking straight. Every woman I met was a rebound for me – no matter how long Rebecca was dead.

The phone rang and vibrated in my hand; I almost dropped it. Craig Taft.

'They're meeting tonight, well technically tomorrow morning,' he said. His voice sounded old, cold, disgusted. I wondered if he'd wrestled with himself over sharing their plans with me; whether he saw this tip-off as him selling them down the river. 'Two a.m. The Peter Pan statue in Kensington Gardens.'

I felt my heart lurch. A crazy moment when I wondered about what I should wear; what Sarah would be least unhappy to see me wearing; and then my voice, steady and confident. Autopilot: 'I'll be there.'

'I'm coming too,' he said. Now I could read something else in his voice, something I'd initially suspected was disdain. It wasn't; it was fear.

'I don't need my hand to be held.'

'It's not about holding anybody's hand,' he said. 'If the Accelerants are at risk, they need to be told.'

'If you go there and tell them that they will go to ground and I'll have no chance of finding my daughter.'

'With respect, Mr Sorrell,' he said, 'fuck your daughter. How would you feel if someone else died?'

I pulled hard on anger's leash. To lose it with Taft was to risk everyone's silence. I didn't want to have to return to relying on Mawker for crumbs. And anyway, I sensed that he wanted me to talk him out of it. He didn't have the belly for this kind of thing. He was looking for an excuse to lie low.

'I'm in this to stop whoever it is from killing again,' I said. 'I wouldn't put Sarah in any unnecessary danger now, would I?'

A long, shaky sigh rattled through the receiver.

'When you go tonight,' he said, 'you'll be expected to deliver my code name.'

'Code name? Are you fucking kidding me?'

'No joke. Prospective new members can only be referred by current, or ex-members. If they're not there in person to vouch for you, you have to provide a code name, to prove endorsement.'

'Christ,' I said. 'What is it? Tinker? Beggarman?'

'This isn't a game, Joel,' he said, and the warning was delivered in another voice; crisper, tighter. He was a regular voice-over artist, was Craig Taft. 'The Accelerants have been proved right to be suspicious. Their recruitment policy is necessarily thorough. It isn't just any old writing group. We don't do automatic writing exercises—' I felt a jolt, as if he had read my mind from earlier. 'There is... an agenda. They... skate close to the wind. I wouldn't be surprised if the police had files on us... them, or had kept one or two under surveillance at some point.'

'What the hell goes on at these meetings?' I asked. 'Shoplifting with added verbs?'

'You'll find out,' he said. Another voice change. Purring this time.

'Thanks for the tip-off,' I said.

'Not at all. One more thing. You'll need to take a piece of writing with you.'

'Great,' I said. I hadn't written anything creative since I pissed FUK OF into the snow outside the headmaster's office.

'Handwritten. Or use a typewriter,' he added. His voice had certainly warmed up a bit. He seemed to be enjoying himself now. 'They all use fountain pens. Or manual typewriters. Have you got one?'

'I have, as a matter of fact,' I lied, enjoying the sound of his bubble bursting.

'Right then. I hope for your sake your scrivening skills are as colourful as your telephone manner.'

I was about to ring off when I remembered the code name. I asked him what it was. He assumed his final voice of the night: tired, sad, perhaps at the knowledge that he'd never have any more use for it.

'It's President,' he said.

The shops were still open on Marylebone High Street. I found a fancy little gift shop and bought some nice paper. Cream. Textured. I spent the best part of fifty pounds on a fountain pen, and bought some violet-coloured ink with a fancy name (*Poussière de Lune*) to go with it. I sat in a bar with a glass of Reyka and defaced the first page with the words 'you pathetic twunt'. Screwed it up.

On the next page I wrote 'What I Did in My Holidays'. Screwed it up.

On the next page I tried Ferguson's automatic writing

exercisebutrealisedI'dreachedlevelfutilewhenallIcouldwrite was 'shitshitshitpissshitshitshitcockshitshitshitfuckshitshit'. Screwed it up.

On the next page I tried writing a haiku.

'Hello, Ian Mawker
Would you mind if I punched
Your punchable face?'

But I couldn't work out if 'punched' counted for one syllable or two. Screwed it up. By this time I had ink all over my fingers and the vodka was gone.

I covertly dropped the rest of the pages and the pen into the bag of a student who was making her half of Guinness and black last for as long as she was able.

I'd turn up and just scare some answers out of these exclusive pricks. After an hour of trying to force some kind of sense from my mind I felt twisted and hot, like a shorted wire. I got home and fed Mengele then had another vodka on the balcony. The guy in the pub kitchen opposite was doing things to a shepherd's pie with a piping bag. He had his back to me and he was showing off the crack in his arse. I remember Sarah telling me once that she'd seen a photographer at a pop concert she went to who sported a bum crack that reminded her of a fanny from the seventies. I'd laughed so hard at that – she could have only been eleven at the time – that I earned a hard rebuke from Becs for 'encouraging' her.

By the door was a plastic recycling tub where I put all the free newspapers and circulars and menus that were pushed through my letterbox. I plucked a circular from a cancer charity, one of the free gift mailings that include a biro. I felt a pang of regret at dumping the fountain pen, but this felt right.

I started:

Dear Sarah

Screwed it up.

I started again, on the back of a large envelope. I couldn't call her Sarah. And though it felt a little as though I was disowning her, it meant I could maintain a little distance, a certain perspective. It meant I could write the damn thing without having to reach for the bottle or the tissues or the razor blade.

A car went by; there was a short blast of music, but I nailed it, sad child of the eighties that I am. 'Rosanna' by Toto. Or maybe it was something else, but Rosanna it was that stuck in my head.

Dear Rosie

Or let's just go with Rosie. Cut the 'dear'. Dear is for nice old ladies who make pots of leaf tea and provide a plate of biscuits to go with it.

So.

Rosie.

I won't go on about what happened, and what I did or didn't do to make you leave. I don't want to bleat about how much I miss you, and how I regret my behaviour, and wish you were back in my life. I'm just going to write about your mum, your amazing mum, and the day you were born. I don't think we ever described that day to you (I certainly didn't) though I remember your mum once answered (truthfully) your query regarding where babies come from. You were five (I think), and you collapsed on the bed, you were laughing so hard.

You were born at exactly one o'clock in the afternoon on Monday 6 September 1999 I know this because we had music playing (we were listening to Classic FM) and I was determined to remember what was playing at the time you were born (I intended to buy a copy of it for you). You appeared at the exact time the news jingle was being played. Typical you.

Your mum was so beautiful in that moment, among the shit and sweat and blood. But she was tired; my God, you put her through the wringer. You should have been born in August (your due date was the 25th), but you were late. In the end, your mum had to be induced (you just did not want to come out). And the first thing she did, when you were born – the very first thing – was to ask that you be passed to me so that I could hold you before she did. She'd carried you all that time, but her first thought was not for herself. It never was. So I held you while your mum had a shower. I held you for – I don't know how long, but I cradled your perfect little head in my hand and stared into your eyes. I was with you in a small waiting room and there might or might not have been anyone else in there with us – I have no recollection – because I didn't, I couldn't look away. Your eyes wouldn't settle. They drifted and swirled, unfocused, the most beautiful blue I have ever seen. You sneezed and yawned and I was rapt. Just so fascinated by every tiny movement. This little person, suddenly there, formed, evident, in my hands. And I was overwhelmed because everyone else I had ever met that I cared for in my life, I had had to grow into the love that developed. It took time. I'd always been sceptical about this idea of instantaneous, unconditional love – but there it was. Immediate. Irrefutable. I would have died for you. I still would.

Rosie. Come home. Please come home. Rosie.

Sarah. Sarah. Please come home.
Sarah. Sarah. Sarah…

8

I only stopped writing her name when I got to the bottom of the envelope. You know how some words you say over and over seem to lose their meaning and become more and more alien? The more I wrote Sarah's name, the more real she became, the more sense it made, until I became certain I was upon the brink of writing her into my material surroundings, as if the persistent writing of her name was acting as some kind of invocation. I could smell the baby skin under the soap, the shampoo – something coconutty – she liked to use. I put the pen down and tore off the last lines containing her real name. I wasn't going to read it all back. If I read it I would not submit it. Which would mean absolutely no chance of an audience with the Accelerants. It was from the heart – as Craig Taft had warned it must be – and if they didn't like it, it didn't matter. I didn't want to be a writer. There were about a million other ways of becoming destitute I could try first, without any hard work involved.

But despite that... something had happened to me. It wasn't just this perceived proximity to Sarah (although that was part of it). That was an illusion, of course. No. The act of writing something down, an event I had thought about many, many times over the course of the past eighteen years, had somehow fixed it in time and also liberated me from the punishment I took whenever my thoughts turned to my dead wife. My mind felt unburdened to some extent. I felt great. For the first time in a long time I felt much the same way as I did in my late teens and early twenties when I went for a run. Back then I didn't run to keep healthy; I ran for the extraordinary buzz it gave me, that rush of natural opiates, the flood of serotonin and endorphins into the bloodstream. Usually, before heading out on some dumb-arsed mission – often involving the threat of bloodshed (more often than not mine) – I'd swallow a few healthy slugs of vodka. Now I didn't want it. At the risk of sounding like some big jessie writer, I'd exorcised a demon or two. I'd mined a seam of writing called therapy. Pass me my smoking jacket. Pass me my beret.

I was itching to get out. I stuffed the letter in my pocket and set off for Kensington Gardens.

9

I'd spent many hours in Kensington Gardens pushing Sarah around in her buggy. I knew which bits of the park she liked best; the Peter Pan statue had been one of them. She loved to wave at Peter, and always seemed certain that *this* time he would come to life and wave back.

I'd climbed the fence into the Gardens near Lancaster Gate, after an age waiting for the traffic to peter out so that I would not be observed. I was careful once I'd moved past the Italian Gardens at the head of The Long Water – I knew some of the guys who worked for the security firm charged with guarding the area; they were no slouches. The Gardens closed at dusk, but enforcing those hours was difficult, if not impossible. The police patrolled the Gardens and the adjoining Hyde Park but it was pretty easy to dodge them if you kept your wits about you. I saw some guys cruising for action, and sometimes you'd see the pickpockets and muggers who preyed upon them. It was dark but the night was made of that strange, summery, roseate grain. Tiny light sources – candle flames, lighters, cigarette coals – smouldered like fireflies. The air was warm and dry and bristling with energy. I hadn't noticed but I was almost skipping along the path; I felt new, excited. I couldn't say if that was down to the therapeutic benefits of my writing session, or the thrill of positive action. There was every chance Sarah might be a part of this group meeting by the statue – I could see a lantern up ahead, and hear male and female laughter – and if she was there, then my little charade would be over before it had begun.

I reined in my optimism; nothing was guaranteed. Danger was here. I'd do well to pay that heed even if it was hard to acknowledge in this soft, buttery air.

They had arranged themselves on blankets around the statue. Someone was pouring wine from a bottle into glasses. Jazz was playing through a portable speaker. Three figures. Two men. One woman. She was blonde, her hair cropped. She was short, petite. Silver glittered in her face. Her lips were chapped. It wasn't Sarah. It couldn't be Sarah. Can someone change so much?

'This is civilised,' I said.

Nobody responded just then, but they all looked my way. You get to recognise hostility churn beneath apparent calm, and it was coming off one of them like heat from a full-on radiator. I kept an eye on him, without making it too obvious. He wore a black jumper and black jeans. His brow had the look of permanent furrow, and his mouth was flat and broad, unimpressed, like a frog. His hair was a luxuriant scoop of shining black. You could smell the product in it from here.

The rest of them seemed curious, expectant even. One of them, the girl (not Sarah; voice coloured by the north-east), stood up and said: 'You police?'

'No,' I said.

'Reference?' This from ostensibly the oldest member of the group, in Taft's absence. He sat with his legs extended, his back ramrod as if he was demonstrating a yoga pose. The wine bottle was clamped between his thighs. He wore a Joy Division T-shirt over a long-sleeved top and a white knitted beanie from which salt and pepper hair sprouted.

'President,' I said, feeling faintly ridiculous, like a spy from the Cold War given a contact cue.

'Sit down,' said the girl. I wanted to ask where Sarah was, but I had to play dumb. She pointed at herself: 'Odessa,' she said. And then she pointed at the other members of the group. 'Underdog, Treacle.'

Great. More code names.

'Why Odessa?' I asked.

'You're in no position to ask questions, buddy,' Mr Hostile said.

'It's okay, Underdog,' she said. He didn't seem mollified by her intervention but he assumed a seething quiet.

'Odessa because of Jon Voight. I liked him when I was a kid. And I especially liked him in that film. *The Odessa File.*'

'What about the others?'

'Fuck off,' said Underdog. 'This is your interview. Not ours.'

'Interview? This is a writing group, isn't it? Not a job vacancy.'

Underdog stood up. Whenever he spoke he dipped his head forward like a heron trying to spot a fish in a stream. I'd seen that somewhere else. A boxer, maybe. An actor. Some tough guy. I bet he had seen it too. And rehearsed it in front of a mirror. He had five inches on me, and fifty pounds or so, but he moved like someone who had learned about violence from watching *Tom & Jerry* cartoons. I ignored him.

'We never use our real names,' Odessa said. She passed me the bottle of wine and I took a long, deep swig. Warm white. Christ.

'So what'll we call you?'

'Corkscrew,' I said, handing back the bottle and trying to keep the wine down. I suddenly realised I was so nervous my body was shaking. 'Is this it? A pretty small group.'

'And what if it is?' Now the other guy stood up, as if being the only person left on the ground meant that he was somehow emasculating himself. As if they all were incapable of speech unless upright. I thought it was a pretty good observation, the kind of thing a writer might put in a novel, but I didn't imagine it would go down well if I brought it up now. This guy – Treacle – was about the same height as me, but he looked as if he could back up any meanness in the way Underdog could not. Despite her relatively diminutive stature, it seemed that it was Odessa who called the shots.

'We're a small group because we need to be organised,' she explained. 'And the names thing... well, it's important we retain our anonymity.'

'You've lost me,' I said. 'I thought writers wanted anything but. Recognition. Sales. Awards.'

Underdog sneered. 'Do you know what a pseudonym is?'

And I thought, *Oh, you little cunt.*

'It's not just about the writing,' Treacle said. 'It's important. There *is* product. But the anonymity is there to protect us during the gathering of materials.'

'I hope you write with more clarity,' I said. 'Because what you're telling me at the moment is so dense it's bending light.'

'Did President not fill you in?' asked Odessa.

Underdog was flexing his fingers, making his knuckles

crack like a meathead minion in a Bond film. 'Did Prez not tell you about IN-IT-I-A-TION?'

'No he did not,' I said. I didn't like the sound of that. I thought of Sarah and whether she had performed an initiation. Why wasn't she here? Had she ever even met these people? I had to say something and I was on the brink of coming clean. But I felt so close to her, despite her absence. I couldn't bugger it up now, even though I was sailing into uncharted territory. I had to keep reminding myself that to refer to her was to lose her again. 'I brought some writing with me, if that's what you're referring to,' I said, knowing full well it was not.

'That's part of it,' Odessa said, hand held out.

I pulled the folded envelope from my back pocket. There was a moment of panic as she took it from me, when I was convinced my address was upon it. *Too late now*, I thought.

'How very guerrilla of you,' she said.

'You going to read that right now?' I asked.

'Nothing like the present perfect,' she said, and ostentatiously unfolded the envelope.

'Christ,' I said. 'It's like being back at school.'

'Who do you read?' Underdog asked.

My mind went blanker than an amnesiac's Christmas list. 'I tend not to read much when I've got a novel on the go,' I said. I'm a comfortable liar, but I was so far out of my comfort zone that I was sure they could see through me.

'A novel,' he said, and he couldn't have sounded more contemptuous if he'd been trying to get a charge for being in contempt of court. 'A novel about what?'

'I don't talk about works in progress. I'm sure you'll understand.'

'Precious fucker, hey?' he said, and I knew there was trouble up ahead with him. I wondered if he was the kind of person who was capable of the kind of determined dismantling of a body Martin Gower had been on the wrong end of, but I couldn't see it. Not quite. 'I talk about my work all the time,' he said.

Yes, I thought. *I bet you do. All the time*. 'Are you not worried about story thieves nicking your ideas?'

'Everybody steals everybody's work anyway. There are no original ideas left.'

'Speak for yourself,' I said. I meant it as a joke but it obviously stung him. I couldn't blame Taft for jumping ship if he had to put up with crap like this every time they assembled.

Odessa, though apparently absorbed by my work, must have been burnt by some of this friction developing between us. 'You'll forgive us for seeming a little testy, a little jumpy,' she said. 'One of our members. One of our founders – a friend – was found dead a couple of days ago.'

I almost said his name. Instead, I held my hands up. 'I'm sorry,' I said.

'We have a vacancy, as a result,' Treacle said. 'We are a six usually. Always have been. President leaving has made things difficult. Suddenly numbers are down, but we don't blame him. How do you know him, if you don't mind me asking?'

'How come there's only three of you tonight?' I asked. 'President, and your dead friend, that makes five. Who's six?' My heartbeat threatened to obscure any answer.

Treacle continued: 'We have a member – Solo – whose attendance is… irregular.'

'To say the least,' said Underdog. 'I'd be tempted to kick her out and find someone more reliable.'

Her.

Odessa folded the envelope shut. 'Treacle asked you a question.'

'I found him when I was looking for a guitar teacher,' I

said immediately. Treacle and Underdog might have been packing some muscle, but Odessa was the one to watch. She was sharp. 'I had some lessons, we ended up talking about books. About writing.'

'Some coincidence,' Underdog said. 'Another guitar-playing writer.'

'Like John Lennon,' I said. 'Like Nick Cave. Everyone's a writer. Are you telling me that's *all* you do?'

'That's all I do,' he said.

'And you live in London? I'm impressed. How many six-figure deals have you signed lately?'

'You don't need some cliché job to get by,' he said.

'No,' I said. 'That's right. So what non-cliché job do you have? Something criminal?'

'What if it is?' he said, his voice suddenly filling with venom. 'What are you? What is this with all the questions? You know what? You stink of copper to me.'

'I wouldn't mind having a copper on our side,' Treacle said. 'Especially after what happened to Needles.'

'Needles?'

'Martin Gower. Our dead… our murdered comrade.'

'I thought you always used code names.'

'A code name cannot help a dead man,' Odessa said.

'We seem to be playing twenty questions with each other,' Treacle said. 'Shall we just get on with what we planned for tonight?'

'You want to be a writer?' Underdog asked.

'I *am* a writer,' I said, trying to play the game. Trying to sound convincing. I could feel things slipping away. Anger was percolating.

'I mean… are you committed? Do you consider it your calling?'

I was annoyed by the question but I guessed it was him annoying me more than what he'd said. I didn't want to ruffle his feathers any more, or prolong this damned evening, which felt like a severe going-over by one of Mawker's IQ-deficient bumchums.

'He is committed,' Odessa said. I felt my heart again, causing ructions. I thought, *I'm too old for this. Sell up and move out. Live in a tent in the Quantocks*. But there was nothing to sell. I didn't know how to pitch a tent. And I didn't know where the fucking Quantocks were.

'There is fuel for his writing,' she continued. 'Inexhaustible, you might say. I think Solo would enjoy meeting you. You have much in common.'

She knows. She knows. She knows. She knows. She—

She held out the envelope and I made to take it but she did not immediately let go. A worm of sweat slid down the small of my back.

'I have a problem with this,' she said. Her voice was low and slow and sly. Up close I could see the gleam of light reflected in her eyes. She was tiny, but in that moment I felt I was looking up at her.

'I don't understand,' I said. I was ready to make a bolt for it. There was no physical danger here – not much, nothing I hadn't dealt with before – but I had never felt so naked, so exposed, so *vulnerable*.

'There are a lot of parentheses,' she said. 'I don't trust writers who use brackets. It suggests a great deal of concealment. A hidden channel of thought.'

'I'm sorry,' I said, snatching the envelope from her fingers. 'I wrote it fast, from the heart. I didn't plan it first. Maybe I should have done. Maybe that way there'd be less afterthought, fewer brackets. It doesn't strike me as that important.' I tucked the envelope into my pocket. I felt rejected. My face burned.

'Maybe it isn't,' she said. She smiled. 'It was a beautiful letter, I should say, once you forget about the technicalities. That's all that matters, I suppose.'

My palms were greasy. I resented having my feelings – still raw after all these years – picked apart by someone who was probably dealing in poo jokes at the time of Rebecca's murder.

Any other time and I might have argued the toss but this was a test of my restraint. 'I'll work on the brackets in future,' I said flatly. 'So what now?'

'We are called the Accelerants for a reason,' Treacle said.

'Are you sure President didn't clue you up about our selection process?' Underdog asked, incapable, it seemed, of concealing the disgust from his voice.

I shook my head, imagining that Taft enjoyed this trick he'd played; his way of getting back at me for wheedling information out of him.

But Odessa said: 'It isn't vital he knows. In some ways it is better he doesn't. No time to prepare. His responses will be pure. Human. Unrehearsed.'

I didn't like the sound of that. I said so.

Odessa smiled. She had an attractive, crooked smile. She was enjoying herself. 'As Treacle pointed out, we are called the Accelerants for a reason. We write from lived experience.'

'Write what you know,' I said.

'That's right,' she said. 'But you are looking at some very cosseted writers. Only recently have we managed to escape our cotton-wool prisons. Adults with no great history. Clean slates, to all intents and purposes.'

'Accelerants,' I said. I was thinking of Neville Whitby's

photographs taken in Archway the previous winter, of the pitched battle with police, a demonstration turned ugly and Sarah in the thick of it. 'You... manufacture experience.'

'That's one way of putting it,' Odessa said. 'Another would be that we throw ourselves at life, eager to catch up on what we have missed. We have become our own catalysts.'

'Throw yourselves at life how?' I asked.

'We have a manifesto,' Underdog said. 'You can read it if you like.'

'I'm older than you,' I said. 'Maybe I don't need to create experiences. I've lived much of them.'

'Then fuck you and good night,' Underdog said.

'What about you?' I said. 'You're what? Late twenties, early thirties? You're telling me you haven't lived? No travel? No girlfriends? You ever had a vindaloo? Gone to bed past midnight?'

'You think that's experience?'

I spread my arms. 'I'm ready to be enlightened.'

'Have you ever been afraid? I mean, afraid for your life? Have you ever been in prison? Have you ever meted out violence? Have you suffered pain?'

'Prison? No. But I can put a tick in all those other boxes.'

'You've never been in prison?'

Who was this Underdog? Early thirties going on ten? He seemed moments away from *ner-ner-ne-ner-ner*. 'There are hundreds of writers out there,' I said. 'Successful published writers' – a reaction to that, a barb that found its way under his armour – 'who have never been in prison. If they want to write about a prison, or a convict, they do some research, pay a visit, talk to people. Hey, maybe they *make it up*.'

'But you lose something,' Odessa protested. 'You must agree that authenticity is compromised if you don't possess the authority of lived experience.'

I was on a tightrope. I had to be careful. Treacle and Odessa seemed to be relishing the debate; Underdog less so. If he owned a suspicion gland it would be red and swollen and weeping by now. The others didn't seem to be paying much heed to his probing; maybe he was like this with everyone. Maybe they were sick of him. But if I kept arguing they'd show me the door. They were seeking an ally, not a dissenter. But I couldn't back down. Mawker would have recognised this cussedness in me; Rebecca too. It was one of the reasons I couldn't hack it as a policeman.

'But this attitude presupposes that your readership, such as it is, has the same level of experience.'

'We don't write for publication,' Odessa said, and there was triumph there in her voice. 'We don't crave readership.'

I snatched a glance at Underdog. *Bollocks you don't*, I thought.

'I like that,' I said; I had to throw a sop. 'There's an admirable purity to it.'

'We don't self-censor,' she said. 'Anything goes. There are no market forces. No editor to please. Peer appraisal only.'

It struck me that any writing, though pushed to the fore in this 'public' forum, seemed secondary. It was an excuse for criminal acts, it seemed. A way to make nihilistic behaviour appear justified. *Christ, Sarah*, I thought. *What are you into? Just you wait till I get you home, young lady.*

'What are you smirking at?' asked Underdog, eyes fast on me.

'As I said, I like it.'

'Yeah, well. You might change your tune. What are your fears?'

'I'm not good in lifts,' I said. 'Or with heights in general.

I don't like dogs. I'm not a big fan of aubergines. Pick something out of that lot. I'll write you a sonnet.'

Odessa seemed decided. Her movements had a finality about them, or at least the drawing of a line. She drank wine, finishing off the bottle, and tossed the empty at a wastebasket. It dropped neatly in. I resisted the urge to tell her to write about that.

'We meet twice a month,' she said. 'Nothing planned in advance. You come or you don't. But three absences on the trot and you're out.'

'Is that what is going to happen to Solo?' I asked, but I put too much sauce on it. Odessa didn't seem to notice, but Underdog certainly did. He was observant too; I had to give him that. Treacle was bored. I noticed he seemed put out that Odessa had drained the bottle. Maybe he was a drinker; maybe I could use that to my advantage at a later date.

'Solo's missed one session. But she has special dispensation. An unfortunate anniversary, I'm led to believe.'

Another lurch in the chest. I felt that I'd become utterly transparent; that Odessa, Underdog and Treacle could see the bruises on my heart, the fissures of suspicion like black splits in my mind. *Surely not. Surely not.* My mind struggled with dates and places. How could I forget? But of course I couldn't. I could block though. I could fight, subconsciously, to keep that terrible door shut.

'Shall we get a wiggle on?' asked Treacle. 'I've had too much bed lately, and not enough sleep. I need an early night.'

The mood seemed to have lifted where Odessa and Treacle were concerned. I'd miscalculated; obviously they had been nervous about this meeting too.

'So when will I know where and when the next meeting is?' I asked.

'We'll leave you a message. Once you've passed the initiation.'

'All needlessly Le Carré isn't it? You could just text me.'

'No phones,' she said. 'No emails. We go face-to-face or write letters. No printers. No computers. No word-processing packages. Typewriters, pens and pencils.'

The way she spoke made the words bounce around. It was like performance poetry. It was, I supposed; I was sure she had recited this litany before. For a nominally liberated group they seemed to be beset with a lot of rules and regulations and restrictions. I said as much as we began walking north-east, towards Marble Arch.

'A friend of ours was killed, Corkscrew. We suspect it might have something to do with the group. Do you think it would be wise of us to let all of our defences down? We have no idea who you are. The only way we can hope for an inkling of trust is to take recommendations. President was well-loved, but he couldn't stay.'

'Why not? His leaving looks a bit suspicious, doesn't it? If you were inclined to look at it dispassionately.'

'If he'd killed Needles, the stupid thing to do would be to draw attention by leaving,' said Underdog. His lip was so curled by disgust it was threatening to become a Möbius strip. 'He was scared. He's older than the rest of us. It was an experience he could do without.'

'You don't think you're being targeted, do you?' I asked.

'Christ,' Underdog said. 'You sound so much like a copper it's unreal.'

'Not a copper,' I said. 'Just nosy. Like a writer, you know? Sniffing out an idea, a plot. Maybe there's not so much difference between us and our boys in blue. Isn't writing all about finding clues? Solving problems?'

'If you say so,' Underdog said. Again, I was dismissed. He seemed cheated of something; maybe my reaction. If he'd been trying to get a rise out of me he needed to try a different tack. I was used to being pissed about by noisy, toothless mutts; I almost didn't hear them any more. Some of his earlier cockiness returned as we approached Cumberland Gate though. It was closing on three-thirty in the morning and it was quiet now, but for the odd taxi and a white van taking the corner into Park Lane more quickly than it needed to.

'It's interesting you should reference Le Carré,' Odessa said. 'You know, there's a line in *Tinker Tailor*, when he talks about the way some people live... God, how does it go now... something about a dozen leisured lives when someone else just lives a hasty one.'

'That's very interesting,' I said. 'I don't know what the relevance of that is, but really, it rocked my world. Where are we headed?'

'You'll see,' said Underdog.

I noticed Treacle had switched off. Maybe he'd seen this a dozen times and was bored of Underdog's postures. Maybe, as he'd intimated, he was just tired. I noticed too that his hand and Odessa's were interlaced.

10

We exited the park by a shuttered ice cream stall and crossed to Edgware Road. Underdog took a torch from his pocket and gave two short flashes and one long one at the cinema entrance. Two long flashes were returned.

'Quiller's back from Berlin already?' I asked. Odessa snorted at this but Underdog only scowled. We crossed the road and the cinema entrance was yawning open before we reached it. A security guard stood aside as we piled through.

'You have until seven,' he said. 'First staff on site today at seven-fifteen.'

'We'll be gone in an hour,' Underdog said, slipping him a note from his wallet.

'We watching a short?' I asked. I'd had a bellyful of Underdog's cloak and dagger.

The guard pressed some buttons on a door panel and let us through to a corridor. We moved in the opposite direction to the cinema screens. We took a lift to the top floor, then a short concrete stairway to fire doors that fed us onto the roof, eighty metres above the West End.

'One of the last times we'll get to do this,' Treacle said.

'The owners are going to knock this fucker down and replace it with flats. So enjoy the view while you can.'

It was a fine view, but all I could see was Treacle positioning himself between me and the exit. Underdog eased a leather cosh from his jacket pocket. He shook it out, enjoying the theatre, the sound of ball bearings as they shivered against each other.

'What the fuck is going on?' I said. 'What's with the menace?' My voice was all over the place but they didn't pay it any notice and ignored the question. Odessa and Treacle sat down on the flashing, which gleamed dully in the flat dawn light, and proceeded to explore each other hungrily beneath their jackets. I was forgotten. But not by Underdog.

'Initiation,' he said.

'But I wrote something. You can read it too, if you want.'

'It's not about the writing,' he said, shaking out the cosh some more. The leather was like the skin of something alive.

I looked around for another way down but there wasn't one, unless I chose to be my own express lift. But that was good only for a single ride.

'You'll walk the perimeter,' Underdog said.

'I'll do no such fucking thing.'

'You'll get up over that rail and walk the perimeter or I'll break both your legs with this cosh and there'll be no tomorrow with us.'

I knew I could prevail in a one vs. one with Underdog, despite his cosh, but so much was at stake that I was prepared to let him have his violent way with me. But the little coda, about being out, was more difficult to stomach. If I took a beating and they legged it, I'd have no recourse other than to hang out like some weirdo spotter at places of literary interest in the distant hope I might find them again.

I'd only have Taft to lean on, but he was none the wiser now; once you recommended a replacement, you were out of the loop for good.

'What did you do?' I asked.

'What?' The question appeared to jolt him from some kind of trance. He was gleaning a vicarious pleasure from this. He was welcome to it.

'Your initiation. What did you do? Drink beer out of a sock?' I swung a leg over the low railing. London swerved away from me far below. 'Streak through Piccadilly Circus?'

'I crossed both lanes of the M25,' he said.

'Piece of cake. Why can't I do that?'

'I was wearing a blindfold.'

'Kudos,' I said. And then there I was, twenty-one storeys above certain death, on a parapet that was only slightly wider than my size nines.

'Chop-chop,' he said.

A wind had crept up on us, unless it had always been there and only now was I noticing it because it was plucking at my clothes.

I stood utterly still, aware only of the path in front of me diminishing into darkness. Another ten minutes and the sun would break over the horizon, but they wanted me to do this in technical night. A bit of spice. An edge to the challenge.

I couldn't look to my left: that was the side with the sheer drop. To my right was Underdog slapping the cosh into his hand. If I concentrated on my feet I'd be too aware of the abyss screaming away an inch or so from my little toe. Straight ahead was somehow easier, even though I'd have to trust myself to walk in an utterly straight line. In the distance, Peckham maybe, the cherry and ice-blue stutter of police lights. Burglary in progress. Man down. More likely it was a couple of night-shifters bossing traffic so they could pick up their coffee and pastries. *Use that*, I thought. *Focus on that.*

I started to walk.

I'd never had a problem with heights when I was a kid. I could climb trees and leap from branch to branch fifty feet above the ground, where squirrels fear to tread. And then something happened – I don't know what – and I was afraid of heights, to the point where my mouth would turn tinder-dry and my knees would become crucibles of molten metal. Maybe it was as simple as becoming an adult; more likely it was because I became a father. It might have had something to do with the fight I had on top of the railway shed at St Pancras four months previously. That kind of behaviour does nothing for your sense of mortality, believe me.

But this was going well – as well as I could hope – to the extent that I was building up some speed. Get it over with. Get home. Get vodkaed. But of course it's when you're feeling at your most confident and comfortable that something comes along to welly you in the bollocks.

Part of the parapet shifted underfoot.

I felt myself sway sickeningly to the left and my hand instinctively reached out for a counterbalance that was not there. I heard, very clearly, Underdog say: 'Shit.'

I knew I was dead if I didn't move, and the only move I had was a jump, off my right foot. But because I was already tilting left, unbalanced, there was a strong chance I'd only propel myself into dead space. So I had to keep right, which meant launching from my left, which meant little purchase because there was hardly anything below my left foot any more but concrete dust. All of this went through my head in the time it took for that syllable to fly through Underdog's

114

teeth. I pistoned my foot down and the parapet collapsed completely, but there had been some purchase there, enough to lift me a foot in the air, so that I could get my fingers on the railing. My face connected with the abrasive edge of the brickwork and took off a layer of skin. I felt a fingernail fold back from the flesh of my finger; the dawn air was shockingly cold against the exposed meat. That, and the cold mask of lymph and tears, kept me aware, and I clung on, hearing the chunks of collapsed masonry smash into windscreens on the street below.

I felt hands on me, lifting me over the rail: Treacle and Odessa.

'I've not finished,' I was saying, over and over, babbling it like a mantra.

'You don't have to prove anything else,' Odessa said.

'Where's Underdog?'

Treacle lifted me upright and gently drew me towards the exit. 'He bailed. I think he's expecting some sort of police presence off the back of that, um, structural failure.'

Shock was crowding into me. That and exhaustion. And pain. I winced as the flapping nail on my finger caught on Treacle's jacket. I rammed my hand into my armpit, relishing bitterly the nausea apparent on Odessa's face.

'I'd have thought Underdog might have embraced some new experience like that,' I said.

'It isn't new,' Treacle said. 'That's the thing. He's been involved with the police before. Suspended sentence. Another strike and he's in clink. Again.'

'Again? He's done time?' Talking helped keep my mind off what had just happened. Vodka would help even more. But I knew I wasn't going straight home this night... this morning.

'He did a stretch when he was in his teens. Fell in with the wrong crowd. Fencing stolen goods. He was in and out of institutions till he hit his twenties.'

'Grist for the mill,' I said. 'What happened in his twenties?'

'He met a woman. He started writing poetry. He went right.'

'Or went wrong. Poetry?'

We were inside now, descending the fire escape stairs just in case the police had been summoned. We'd left no evidence of our occupancy of the roof. We could hide out in a dozen different places while they hitched their belts and pressed buttons on their walkie-talkies and thought about what frostings they were going to have on their breakfast doughnuts.

There was no sign of the security guard; we let ourselves out, pushing against fire doors that emptied us on to the side street. I stared at the tarmac, at the hard gleam of it. I wondered if you could hit something so hard there'd be some sort of molecular exchange; if it was possible to become the thing that slammed the life from you. And then the streetlights went off and the road lost its morbid glamour. No banter, no exhilarated recap – Odessa and Treacle were preparing to leave.

'You want to go for breakfast or something?' I asked. My legs and arms were jangling, as if I'd just been electrocuted.

'We don't fraternise outside of meeting hours,' said Treacle. His face was straight when he said it.

'What about you two?' I asked.

'Same,' Odessa said. 'It's too risky.'

'So you don't know each other's real names and you don't know where you live? But you play gusset puppeteers with each other?'

'Chef's perks,' Odessa said. Treacle laughed.

I was shaking my head but I had to accept it. Maybe it was

bullshit and they were just protecting each other from me, the unknown quantity. That I'd proved to them I was insane was certainly no reason to disburden themselves of personal information. I bit my tongue again when the instinct was to say that Solo and Needles knew each other, probably intimately, and had done for years. Had they hidden that from the other Accelerants?

'Okay. Well, I've got to go and run this off. Or eat something. Preferably while also mainlining a bottle of Smirnoff.'

'Okay,' Treacle said. 'Knock yourself out.'

Odessa put her hand in her jacket and pulled out some sheets of paper. She pushed them into my hand. 'I read you,' she said. 'You read us. Maybe tell us what you think. Next time.'

I had a gander at the first page. Handwritten. Fountain pen. Green ink. *Twenty feet from sanctuary, a SulciCam swam up out of the soul mists and pricked the back of Nuland's head. He knew it was a SulciCam because the anaesthetising balm that preceded its sting was anathema to lice, and here they came, pouring off his scalp like black sugar from a scoop. So forget sanctuary, for now.*

'Next time,' I said. 'How do I find you next time?'

'There's a tree on Birdcage Walk, near Cockpit Steps,' said Odessa. 'It's got a blue cross painted on it. We'll leave you a message, pinned to an exposed root. Tomorrow. After nine p.m.'

'Okay,' I said. I didn't know how to close proceedings. Handshake? Group hug? A tribute to J.G. Ballard via the medium of Bharata Natyam?

Treacle solved that problem for me. '"Risk anything! Care no more for the opinion of others... Do the hardest thing on earth for you. Act for yourself. Face the truth."'

'Beautiful,' I said. 'Who wrote that? You?'

'I wish,' he said.

'Goodnight, Corkscrew,' Odessa said.

I said: 'Good morning.'

I followed them.

It seemed less important to find out where they lived than to quash this silly charade about anonymity. I was so sure I'd see Treacle and Odessa disappear through the same door that it was a genuine shock when they separated at a bus stop on Oxford Street. Treacle headed north along Berners Street and Odessa watched him go, so I had to stick with her. I hung back under an awning until I saw Odessa move towards the road as a bus approached. Just as the doors were about to close I hopped on, relieved that she'd headed to the top deck. I stayed downstairs. I'd had enough of heights for one night.

Odessa disembarked in Tufnell Park but she loitered at the stop, hunting in her bag for something. The bus moved away. I bolted to the door and begged the driver to let me out. When he started quoting company policy I triggered the emergency release and hopped off. He was swearing at me now, using words that were unlikely to be found in any company policy handbooks and would be considered extreme on the oil rigs off northern Scotland, or the terraces of underperforming football clubs.

Odessa caught wind of it too and looked up just as I ducked behind a Range Rover parked on the street. Some more hard-earned experience for her Moleskine. I heard her footsteps moving away – thank God; I didn't fancy playing 'edge around the 4x4' – and gave cautious pursuit. She moved north, along Dartmouth Park Hill. Behind us, the Tube station was coming to life. I could smell bacon and coffee, and that reminded me what time it was. I felt my blood sugar levels slump. I needed food. I needed sleep. Probably both. At the same time if at all possible.

Odessa still seemed appallingly perky. She had the kind of gait that made you think there were springs in her shoes. Tokuzo called it 'The March of the Tit-Jigglers'. That was what youth did for you, I reasoned. And as we turned off the main drag into a series of leafy streets, finally emerging on Laurier Road, I thought: *that's what wealth does for you too.*

At the foot of the road she turned into a house with an aubergine-coloured front door. I gave it a glance as I flashed past; not sub-divided into flats like many other big houses around here. A three-floor semi, with a converted basement. Newly clipped privet guarded a small front garden of fuchsia and beardtongue. Some other climbers I couldn't identify – honeysuckle maybe. Maybe deutzia too – all assiduously pruned. I tried to remember if I'd checked out Odessa's hands, but it meant nothing. If she worked on gardens she would probably wear gloves. The house was worth three, three and a half million, easy. *What do you do, Odessa? Who do you know?*

Eventually I turned left on Highgate Road and traipsed down to Kentish Town. Cold sweat clung to my temples like blisters of hardened wax. I stopped at a café opposite a shabby kebab shop and bought a couple of bananas, a croissant, a bottle of orange juice and a large coffee. I scarfed the lot on the pavement outside and felt myself spiking away. It wasn't quite on a par with Popeye plus spinach but the fear and the nausea were pressed back into their cages for a while.

I sank into the London Underground and burned smells sank with me – old, overused cooking oil, tar and tobacco – until I was in the sweaty world of scorched diesel and black snot. A woman on a seat, head down, was three bites into a green apple and had been overcome by tears. A paper bag shook in her other hand. Monsters and victims everywhere. The night crawlers go back to their pits and the unabashed day shift takes over. I stared at the headline of the newspaper opposite me as we chuntered down to King's Cross where I caught a Circle Line Tube to Edgware Road. Somebody missing. Somebody dead. Somebody heartbroken.

Mengele yelled at me when I got home. His litter tray was like a horror scene filled with severed gorilla thumbs. I cleaned it all up and saw a note from Tokuzo. Away for the rest of the week at some reclamation yard or other in Barcelona and I was welcome to use her place if I needed to as long as I took care of the plants, you bastard. She had left me some cold chicken and salad and half a bottle of Sauvignon Blanc.

I'd been on the go for a day and a half. I made myself a cup of green tea and drank it on the balcony. The girl in the back bedroom at the pub was playing guitar and I could just hear snatches of it when the wind drew the notes my way. Slow and sad. Pretty. Then I went to bed, willed sleep into me. And it came, but it was not pure. It was not undisturbed.

You write. You cut and shape. You rewrite. You wipe the blood and sweat and tears from the page. You rewrite. You get the rhythm correct. You find your voice. You know your characters. You believe in your story. You cut and shape. Edit. Revise. Ten per cent inspiration. Ninety per cent perspiration. The pages stack up. The characters develop. They change. They take over. They dictate. The story thickens and splits. You control the strands. You rewrite. In a windowless room you stand at the lectern sharpening pencile. The ream of paper. You will not finish until those twenty pointed leads are worn down to the wood. Four thousand words, give or take. And then to the typewriter. Hone. Polish. Commit. You stand there shirtless, covered in sweat. In perspiration. When you write you go to war. And you write every day. Its a story that needs to be told. Its a narrative that needs to be dug out of you, like a canker, something raw and bloody and painful. You pay back. You layer. You accrete. I beheaded him because he beheaded me. I will behead you because you beheaded me. The inspiration. I rewrite. You rewrite. You go on. I cannot go on. I go on. The pages stack up. Ten per cent. Ninety per cent. The characters come alive. Chapter and verse. Dedication. Acknowledgment. Beginnings. The end. I cut and shape. I redraft. The end. I polish. I rewrite. Perspiration. Inpsiration. Ninety-nine per cent. The end.

PART TWO

...AND MANY OTHERS

11

I didn't want cold chicken and leaves. I didn't want white wine. I wanted a greasy, hot burger with everything on it, and a frosty beer to help it down. I stretched and looked out upon Marylebone, wondering how long I'd been out. The day had a glow to it, suggesting dawn or dusk, and I guessed evening because I had a cocktail pang in me and, screwed though my body clock undoubtedly was, I never yearned for vodka first thing. Much. So that meant I'd been out for nine hours or thirty-three hours. And I guessed the long haul because of the rasp of my chin. And the fact that Mengele had been creating more satanic effigies in his litter tray.

I showered and dressed and went out into the balmy evening. My mind was full of blue crosses. Edgware Road was its usual polyglot scrum of charcoal and shisha and crawling, honking traffic. A little rain and neon and it would pass for *Blade Runner* country. I sated my meaty needs at a bar and grill where I was tempted to plant my flag and stay until closing: it was beer-drinking weather and there were pleasant-looking women walking by that I could watch while I drank, but Sarah. But Sarah. She kept me moving.

I studiously avoided looking up at Marble Arch Tower, but noticed that the roads around it had been closed off; the reason for the slow traffic. A sign warned against falling masonry. Another spoke of unstable structures. I could have worn that one.

By the time I got to Green Park it was dark and I'd bypassed any number of bars and pubs but I was a good man, a considerate dad, and I did not waver. Of course, I had chosen not to bring the Saab with me because once my mission was accomplished I intended to turn myself into a human cocktail shaker.

I reached Birdcage Walk around ten minutes later. I found the tree with the blue mark – I felt like a spy in a Cold War drama; I felt like Quiller, like fucking Smiley – and I leaned against it for a while, watching the traffic, looking out for Max von Sydow or Patrick Stewart. Then I pretended to tie my shoelace and had a grope around between the roots. A piece of paper was thumbtacked into the wood. Many holes told of many previous messages. I felt a strange resentment that this had been going on without me for so long. I imagined Sarah bending here to retrieve, or plant, some code of her own.

Quaint. It had been typed:

```
corkscrew. you're in.
51°28'59.58"N 0°10'11.63"W
09.04. @ 0200
```

I pocketed the scrap, realising it should have gone in an evidence bag straight to Ian Mawker, realising too late I should have picked it up with tweezers, or worn latex gloves, and I nipped over to the Westminster Arms. A pint down and I was feeling twitchy. Usually I'd be settling in for a long session; there was often a couple of Met officers with their beers and whisky chasers whose backs I could scratch, but now I just felt kettled. I wanted to be out in the night-time again, prowling.

Something else was bothering me too, but I couldn't put my finger on what it was. It was perhaps just the combined triple whammy of adrenaline, hope and frustration. The Accelerants had... well, they had accelerated me. I felt the need to run, to fly. And yet. And yet.

Another meeting? Tomorrow night? It didn't sit well with their ethos. Yes, they forced experience but they wrote too; and they shared. There was a reason for a gap between meetings. A chance to let off steam. An opportunity to take stock, recover. And to read the submissions.

Which reminded me of the papers that were still in my jacket. I spread them out on the table. Three single sheets of different quality paper. No identifying marks. All pages handwritten.

Before I'd properly thought it through I was on the phone.

'Romy? It's Joel. Are you busy? I was just... would you like to be? Well, no. I meant busy in a fun way. Well, that's great. I'm in town. Victoria way if that helps. Yes, yes I like beer. Yes, yes I like football. Okay. Okay. See you there.'

She was sitting in a corner booth of a sports bar in Haymarket and there was a fresh pitcher of lager in front of her. Two glasses. The place was crammed with men wearing pastel-coloured polo shirts and placing in-play bets on their smartphones.

'I didn't interrupt anything, did I?' I asked, looking around.

'I was about to leave,' she said. 'A friend stood me up

at the last minute. And then your call came through so I bought this.'

She poured and I drank. She held her glass with both hands, like a child, and closed her eyes when she took her first mouthful.

'Oof,' she said. 'That's good.'

'That was the drink of a person who has just walked out of the desert,' I said.

'Feels like it. Had a tough couple of days.'

'I know how that feels.'

'So I watch football to unwind.'

'Really?' I said. 'It doesn't relax me. I end up swearing at the set.'

She took another drink, leaned back in her seat. On the screen, ex-players in panic-inducingly expensive suits and fuck-me haircuts bantered around a pitch-side table.

'That's because you're partisan. You're invested.'

'You're not?'

She shook her head. 'Itinerant upbringing. Didn't stay in one place for long enough to swear allegiance. I'm as neutral as it gets. I just like to watch. The patterns. The shapes. The flow.'

'So what's on tonight?' Screens upon screens. Giant screens. Tiny corner screens. Personal screens on tables. So many screens you'd be hard pressed not to catch the match at all, even if you were a dwarf with cataracts. In a different bar.

'Champions League semi-final, first leg.'

'Who's playing?'

'No idea.' She looked at my clothes. 'Red versus blue. France versus England. Expansive versus cautious.'

'You could be describing us.'

'Experience versus youth.'

'Very good,' I said. 'Very funny.'

'So how come you're out on a school night?' she asked. 'Adult education class in professor impersonation?'

On the screens overpaid, oily-haired prongs stood in the tunnel. And that was just the match officials. Smoke from a flare turned the stands into a ghost-red battle zone. The bar management ramped up the volume and the Champions League theme shook our glasses.

'No more professors,' I said. I'd gone through my beer as if it were water. I realised I was nervous. She poured me another glass. 'I've been looking into a death. Someone was murdered a couple of days ago. In Enfield. He knew my daughter.'

'I don't know what I can do to help.'

'Possibly nothing. It doesn't matter. But I was wondering if there was someone at the museum who could look at some documents for me.'

'You mean me?'

'Of course I do. I'm rubbish at being direct.'

'What sort of documents?'

I pulled the pages from my jacket and handed them over. She took another deep drink and studied them.

'My uncle would have been all over this,' she said.

'Your uncle?'

'He was involved in the Zodiac killings back in the sixties and seventies.'

'No kidding.'

'Yeah. He was one of the team who studied the notes Zodiac sent to the *San Francisco Chronicle*.'

'And you got into palaeography because of him?'

'Kind of. But I'm more involved with manuscript dating.'

'You just haven't met the right man yet.'

'Very good,' she said. 'Very funny.'

'So maybe you can't help.'

She licked the ball of her thumb and winked. 'Let's see what we can do for you,' she said. 'I happen to have a deep interest in the utterly pointless science of graphology.'

I drank. I watched players roll around on the grass as if the pitch was littered with landmines. Spittle arced. Arms swarmed with tattoos containing more ink than a David Foster Wallace novel.

'This is pretty rough handwriting,' she said. 'Probably written by someone who doesn't sleep enough. It's jittery. Slants to the right, which suggests confidence, assertiveness, perhaps even a level of insensitivity. But pressure is light, and that is linked to people with low emotional energy. The ink colour – blue – is conservative; I imagine this is a person who is not at all showy, who probably dresses without flair. Someone who sees clothes and food as essentials, chores even. This person has no interest in putting forward any kind of image; this person does not eat for pleasure.'

'You can tell all this from the loop on a "g"?'

'Oh yes,' she said. 'And much more besides.'

I was thinking of Treacle. He cared about his appearance: that strategically positioned tuft of hair that peeked from under his beanie was evidence of that.

'Like what?' I asked.

'Sex.'

'You can tell the gender from the handwriting?'

'Well, yes – this is a guy, for example. Obvious because of the content too, of course, but I was referring to *sex*. Fucking.'

I choked a little on my beer. On the screens the referee ran backwards away from a bearded, shaven-headed footballer clearly screaming that *I never fucking touched him, ref, you shithouse.*

'This guy, he holds something back in bed. He won't give

himself completely. Unlike our footballers here, he doesn't give a hundred and ten per cent.'

I thought of Underdog and his perpetual pout. Maybe he was wanting in the generative organ stakes. Maybe he had a cock like a tube of damp macaroni.

'He's emotionally stunted. Prone to violence. Has a victim mentality.'

'Hang on,' I said. I reached across and took my letter to 'Rosie' from her; I'd forgotten to separate it from the other sheets. I folded it and placed it in my pocket. I gave her a painful little smile. She gave me a painful little smile.

'Like you said,' I said. 'An utterly pointless science.'

She nodded. Bit her lip. 'Her name's not Rosie, is it?'

My head snapped up. 'What makes you say that?' If I was so transparent maybe the Accelerants could see through me too. It's not as if you get a chance to rehearse this shit, to test it on an audience before the real thing.

'Little clues. The tip of the pen did a tiny dance at the point where you started writing the name, as if you'd hesitated. The name didn't flow with the same loose action that serviced the words surrounding it, which suggests it's not as known to your fingers as the name of a daughter ought to be.'

'Right,' I said, and rubbed my face. Utterly pointless... I gestured at the other pages. 'What can you tell me about those?'

On the screens, a footballer wearing an Alice band pressed his fingers against one side of his nose and blew a gout of snot from the other. How long before someone pissed against a corner flag or took a shit in the penalty box? How long before somebody rubbed one out in the centre circle?

'Her name's Sarah,' I said.

* * *

It was interesting, what she came up with, but it was an inexact science at best. Also, because the pages were anonymous I didn't know who it was that had perhaps suffered a hand injury as a child, or who was likely to be unfaithful, or who was on medication, probably for a disease of the digestive system. Or whether any of that was of the slightest relevance or importance.

We'd moved on from the sports bar after the match was finished. I'd been impressed by her reading of the game – she understood the tactical switches better than the commentator or his ex-pundit sidekick.

'You'll get yourself sacked,' I said, as she let herself into the staff entrance of the British Museum.

'Nonsense,' she said. 'I have clearance. I also have a very nice bottle of cognac in my office, a gift from a friend when I got this job.'

'A friend,' I said. 'Would that be code for a man? A boyfriend? A husband?'

'No code,' she said, walking ahead of me up the stairs. I heard the shush of nylon. Her hair shook: ripples in molasses. 'But what would it be to you if it was?'

'Nothing,' I said. And I meant it. She was beautiful and spirited and kind-hearted; all the things I was not. I was not in her league. If she was a Premiership footballer, I was a crocked sub in a Sunday pub team. If she had a thing for foul-mouthed fuck-ups, that was nice. But I couldn't allow what happened before to happen again.

She let us into the office she shared with a colleague and retrieved the bottle from a desk drawer, along with a couple of collapsible plastic wine glasses.

'Tres posh,' I said, sitting on her chair.

'*Bien sûr*,' she said, pouring us a couple of generous

measures. 'Only the best for our professors.'

She was right; it was good. If you like that sort of thing. I craved ice and clarity. But it was smooth and warming. There was enough cold in me to keep me going.

Her desk was disappointingly barren. Apart from a PC and an in/out tray, there was nothing of note. No framed photographs, no notebooks bearing her own no doubt inscrutable handwriting, no nick-nacks or gee-gaws. Maybe she just hadn't been in the job long enough. Or maybe she was one of those psychopathic minimalists who are obsessed with clean surfaces and masters of storage fu.

We spent an hour in her office sipping XO while she showed me – wearing latex gloves – a fragment from an eleventh-century manuscript written on palm leaves found in Nepal, and I tried hard to concentrate, but I noticed a button had worked itself loose on her blouse and I could see the firm sweep of her tummy within the gap, the eggshell-blue curve of her bra. I couldn't tell her, obviously, and a little while later she noticed and fastened it and gave me an indulgent smile as if she realised I had been leching but that it was no big deal because it probably happened all the time and middle-aged men were no threat, especially when she could go home each evening to her ridiculously chiselled Adonis whose name was Garth or Grant or Alpha-fucking-Male Almighty.

'Penny for your thoughts?' she asked.

'Oh, I just realised I'm out of Fishbitz. You know. Cat.'

'You have a cat?' she asked, excitedly. And so we spent the short walk to the Tube talking about my cat ('What's his name?' 'Men... um... Mencap... after the charity...' *Christ...*) and how much Romy loved cats and how she was planning to get one as soon as she could find a place

133

of her own because her dad was allergic.

'What now?' she asked.

'I go back to the hunt.'

'Does it frighten you? Digging in the dark? Is it difficult to do what you do? Difficult to find who's responsible?'

'Finding who's responsible isn't about psychological profiles, or clever detective work. It's about talking to people. It's about pulling the lid off the tightly closed ones and getting them to spill what's inside. Sometimes it's very messy. Ugly work. And it's a process of unearthing truth. It's about walking whatever dark path you can expose. All the way to the end. And I'll go anywhere.'

She kissed me on the cheek and I felt her hair brush against me and her breast press for a maddening instant against my arm. Then she was gone into the throat of Tottenham Court Road, on her way back to Professor Ferguson's house in Hampstead.

I walked back along Oxford Street and angled towards Marylebone once I hit Selfridges. On Marylebone High Street I saw a guy trying to kiss a girl who was laughing so much she could hardly stand up straight. *What utter dicks we make of ourselves*, I thought.

I got back to find Mengele had eschewed his last bowl of Fishbitz for a pigeon he'd caught on the balcony. Feathers and blood everywhere. He placed the pigeon's head on my pillow and had somehow managed to get it upright. It regarded me with its haughty expression as if to say, *Well, what are you going to do about this?*

I cleaned up as best I could, having to risk Mengele's claws when I teased the pigeon's feet from his sphere of influence. It was a half-hearted swipe – he must have been stuffed fuller than the gimmick crust on a high street pizza

– but a claw caught my knuckle and sank in and blood rose from the skin like a ruby on an invisible engagement ring.

'Shitweasel,' I hissed at him. He yawned and narrowed his eyes at me.

I washed my hand and turned out the lights. My heart was racing. I saw the gap in Romy's blouse widen, the separating of silk and skin, and I fell through it into a nightmare sea lashed with combers of red foam, and sharks finning through a churn created from all the people I'd loved and lost, and the few I'd finished by my own hand. I was afraid to touch the bodies lying face down on the surface for fear of what they'd reveal when rolled over. I could feel the currents changing beneath my feet. Pressure rising; something nosing through crimson fathoms, hunting me. Something hungry and determined and massive and ancient.

And nothing, including the sharks, including me, had any life in its eyes.

12

I woke to bright sunshine but I couldn't loosen the feeling of grey from my bones. The dream had stuck in the base of my brain like a layer of grit in a standpipe. I couldn't shake it.

I washed in a basin of blistering hot water and breakfasted on a single shot of ice-cold Stoli. It didn't make me feel better, but it didn't make me feel any worse.

The gods of misery had decreed I should be up at the same time as the parents of small children and the poor souls completing ten-till-six shifts. A better man than me would have jogged around Hyde Park for an hour, or read philosophy, or gone for a swim, but all I could do was stare at the clock and count down the hours until I saw the Accelerants again at two a.m.

Two a.m. What did they do all day? Did they have jobs, or did they enjoy some sort of private income, rich kids who held sway over their parents, privileged, entitled. Spoilt twats. I thought about heading over to Odessa's house and keeping watch, but I couldn't decide what it would achieve. Either she worked – in which case I'd follow her to her job location – hairdresser, City worker, barista, rocket scientist

– and be none the wiser about what made her tick, or she'd remain at home, writing presumably. Either result was a pointless waste of my time.

I contemplated playing back my answerphone messages but there were over thirty of them and nobody but Ian Mawker knew my home number. And suddenly I was thinking about the great weekend I'd had with Adam in Northampton, and then I was thinking of what he'd said about Mum and before I realised what I was doing I was on the phone to Jimmy Two.

Jimmy's a friend of mine who looks after my Saab. He wants to buy it off me but I'll never sell it. My girls have sat in that car and so nobody else will. He keeps the engine tuned and ticking over and I keep him in bottles of single malt. I hardly ever see him though. He picks the car up and stows it at his garage on the Cally Road or he drops it off when I need it. And then he goes back to doing Jimmy Two stuff – whatever that is. I'm guessing it's above board though, unlike the antics of his twin brother, Jimmy One, who is on bread and water in Wandsworth for decidedly below-board behaviour.

I wasn't worried about waking Jimmy Two – he sleeps less than a lidless insomniac pulling an all-nighter – and he promised he'd have the Saab outside my flat with a full tank within twenty minutes. I made a mental note to treat him to a bottle of Talisker, and went to the bedroom where I packed a small bag with a change of clothes.

I chucked Mengele under the chin and poured him an extra big bowl of Fishbitz. 'Sorry it's not pigeon flavour, you ruthless, cold-hearted bastard killing machine,' I told him.

The car was where Jimmy Two said it would be. I got in it and pointed it north.

* * *

I arrived four hours later. I sat outside her house for some time, watching the smoke curl from the chimney, watching the birds and the squirrels duke it out for supremacy over the peanut feeder hanging from the laburnum in the front garden. I saw a glimmer of movement in the kitchen and my heart pitched. I saw her, fifteen years younger, perched on an armchair reading a book to Sarah while her granddaughter nestled in the crook of her arm, a tired hand playing with the curls in her hair. Crystal clear – so real I could reach out through time and touch it. The smells of the kitchen. The music on the radio. My mother's perfume, unchanged in all the years I'd known her. I set myself: there is an acute agony in going home, doubly so if you haven't been back in some time. It's a form of time travel. You will see things that will pierce you, especially if you're a nostalgic old cockmuffin like me.

I got out of the car and stretched, listened to the tick of the cooling engine like the second hand of some infernal clock.

I walked up the drive and rang the bell. I heard the same two-tone chime I'd heard when I was a kid waiting for Dad to come home. She opened the door and gave me an instant scolding – 'You might have ruddy well warned me!' – before she ghosted back to the kitchen, calling over her shoulder: 'And take your shoes off… the last time you were here you walked ruddy dog muck into my carpets.'

She asked me if I wanted my old room and I said no, I couldn't stay, that I had to be back in London that night. She called me a bloody fool, told me I'd do myself a ruddy mischief driving around all day. And then she stopped flapping around the kitchen like a trapped bird, put down the tea towel, sighed, and drew me into her arms. She was crying and I was crying and I couldn't have foreseen any other outcome. I'd dreaded it, but it was an immense relief too.

Once we'd recovered somewhat, she pressed me gently back into a chair and set about making breakfast. Everything in the kitchen was as I remembered it. Wallpaper patterned with sunflowers. Mustard-coloured floor tiles. A spice rack containing dozens of little pots of sun-faded spices and dried herbs that she never used. She stored the cereal boxes in the same place. The tea and coffee were in old jars both labelled SUGAR, next to an old tin of biscuits that would contain only ginger nuts.

'Have you heard from her?' she asked, and I hated that she'd asked, but I was relieved it would be out of the way so soon.

'I would tell you, immediately, if she got in touch. You know that.'

'But you know she's all right. You saw her. That photograph at the exhibition. You told me about it when you called. For a ruddy change.'

'It was just a photograph. I'm guessing she's all right.'

She poured hot water into a teapot and stirred it a few times before popping on the lid. 'If I was you I'd be raising holy hell... I'd be walking holes into the pavement looking for her.'

'What makes you think I'm not, Mum?' I asked, trying to keep the exasperation from my voice.

'Because you're up here, farting around CA12 for a start,' she said.

'Trails go cold,' I said. 'Dead ends where you'd think the road was clear and long and wide.'

'Adam told me you went to see him recently.'

It wasn't quite a question, not quite a statement. But there was the stench of rebuke all over it.

'I'm allowed some down time, aren't I? Jesus Christ. I'm switched on all day. Every day.'

'Not for her you're not.'

'What do you know?' I yelled. 'You know nothing. This talk, this is all just born of frustration. You want to be a part of what happens every day but you can't.'

'I know other sons who let their mothers in.'

'You were never left out,' I said. 'I never imagined you'd want to be a part of her absence.'

The same old cups and spoons. The same old jug of milk. The way she tipped a frying pan to spoon hot oil over the egg yolks rather than flip them.

'It's not just about her. It's you as well.'

'*My* absence?'

She slapped my wrist as she set a steaming plate in front of me and sat down. There was the smell of Fairy Liquid and vanilla essence under the perfume. 'I'm not bothered about that, though yes, it wouldn't hurt you to call once every ruddy ice age, would it? No, you. *You*, I'm talking about. You've not been the same, and before you tell me "no shit, Sherlock", yes, I understand, how could you be the same? But it's like you had the stuffing knocked out of you when it happened. When Rebecca... and then when Sarah... I'm just saying that you never quite put the stuffing back. If you see what I mean. You're empty. You think you're moving forward, and you might be for all I know. But you're empty while you do it.'

'I can't stop if she's out there, Mum,' I said. 'And she is out there. I'm closer than I've been in five years.'

She was nodding but her eyes glistened and pain was folding all around them. 'What if...' she said, and could say no more.

'What if she doesn't want to be found?'

She held my hand in her own and I was aware of the age that was in it: the skin dry, thinning, blemished with liver spots and the tracery of blue veins, like routes on a map that it was unwise to explore.

'Could you live with that, if you found her?'

I shrugged. Her pulse shivered in the delicate webbing of skin at the base of her thumb. I picked up some bacon and dipped it in the perfect yolk, knowing that eating with fingers made her shit hang sideways. She didn't admonish me. 'I have to know,' I said.

I went up to that old room of mine after I'd washed the breakfast dishes. The view – of the old school I had attended – was more or less unaltered but for an additional smudge of new housing up by the railway bridge. Boxes of my stuff were lined up against the wall, covered in my handwriting from twenty years before. A different life, a different person, before my two girls came and went. I opened a couple of them. Old vinyl albums. *The Unforgettable Fire*. *Meat is Murder*. *In Utero*. *Heaven or Las Vegas*. Books I'd read that I'd signed and dated: *A Dream of Wessex*. *The Ice Monkey*. *Concrete Island*. *Fahrenheit 451*. There were diaries from the nineties containing names of people who had remained there, for whatever reason. Claire. Amanda. Paul. John. Little deaths, these. Everyday corpses. Forgotten friends who took different paths. I felt a strange ache for them all.

I stopped myself from going through the boxes of

photographs; I'd had my fill of nostalgia. You're led to believe nostalgia is a good thing, a harmless appetite for what went before; little more than a strange kind of embarrassed pride regarding the TV shows we used to watch, the sweets we used to rot our teeth with, the music we danced to, the clothes we wore – a kind of time panic. You found yourself craving a you that didn't exist any more, that didn't exist in the first place. Younger and fitter, yes, but that was just cosmetics. Your memories and perceptions were formed by a stranger. Reconciling yourself with that schism was difficult, if not impossible. Or at least it was for me. Part of the problem of being human was being aware of one's own mortality, but this was tied to something even more tragic, the awareness that you were no longer the person that looked back at you from those photographs. And it was an ongoing tragedy. It was like a series of bereavements.

Christ, I needed a drink.

I went downstairs, trying to remember what my mother's tipple of choice was – God, was it *perry*? – and found her watering a burly hosta.

'I was thinking of nipping out for a walk, for a drink. You fancy it? You must be gasping for a red biddy.'

'Some of us have work to do,' she said. 'Go. Go on. Pick me up some milk and butter on your way back. I'll have lunch on the table at one. On the dot.'

I left, thinking of Romy and how much easier, how less painful this would have been if I could have somehow convinced her to make the trip with me. The thought released, I suppressed laughter. What was I thinking? I'd known her a day and I was imagining introducing her to my mother. There was something wrong with me. I couldn't work out if it was healthy to crave some kind of normality again, to be with someone living rather than a ghost, a wish, or whether it was creepier than an uncle with roving hands when his young nieces come to stay.

I walked through Keswick in the direction of Windermere. Eventually I reached the edge of the town and headed away from houses and roads, walking a bridle path with the hill of Latrigg to my left. I crossed the A66 over a footbridge and veered left at a fork in the path, which would take me around Mallen Dodd. I'd walked these roads with my parents and, later, with flings and friends so many times that even though I hadn't been back for years, I could follow the route without thinking.

I slipped through a gate and walked a fenced path alongside a plantation of Sitka spruce. Up ahead was a ridge called Saddleback. It started to rain, which gave me pause – I was wearing jeans and Converse and a light jumper over a thin-as-skin T-shirt – but I thought, *Sod it, it's April. I might get wet, but I won't freeze to death.*

I turned left and passed through a kissing gate into a field populated with sheep. They all watched me as I strode through the tall grass, the denim darkening with every step, past a stone cross and on to a gravel path leading towards Skiddaw mountain. Things got steeper, but that's mountains for you. I felt my heart rattling in my chest like a brick in a tumble dryer. My breath came in huge whooshing noises and I was put in mind of the three sucking chest wounds I'd heard in my life, all of which sounded like small beer compared to this. After a while the incline eased off and I plodded gamely on, kind of enjoying it, kind of not, the rain increasing in intensity, my clothes increasing in weight, until I reached a row of cairns that led me to the summit ridge.

At the top I crouched and concentrated on levelling

out my breathing. It wasn't cold by any means, but I was shivering like a shitting poodle. Out of shape. Ten years away from heart attack country, if I wasn't already there. I felt a shiv of fear stab me in the chest at the thought of suffering some sort of attack out here. I hadn't told Mum where I was going. If she called 999 she'd tell the ambulance service to check all the pubs in the town before she thought of any of the walking routes.

But I calmed down, and the wind calmed too, even if the rain did not. I stared out at Helvellyn and, further afield, the Yorkshire Dales and the Forest of Bowland. On clear days you could see as far as the Mourne Mountains, and Goat Fell on Arran. But the sky was torrid, skeins of rain drifting down like barrage nets, and visibility was failing by the minute.

I turned to leave, and I heard the whistles and frenzied cries of an osprey – *kareek, kareek* – the sound it will make when its nest is under attack. I searched the sky and peered into the black ledge of trees further down the ridge but could see nothing wheeling. The sound was not changing in tone or consistency, either, which confused me until I skipped around a thin ledge of rock and saw the fish hawk snagged on a length of barbed wire.

It was a juvenile – that much I knew from the streaked feathers on its head – but I couldn't tell its sex. If Romy had been here we could have got it to write something down and worked it out that way. It was clearly in distress. The blue cere at the bridge of the black bill was torn, and blood coated much of the plumage. It was trapped fast by the teeth of the metal; one of its wings was broken, the primaries drooping like long-fingered hands. I couldn't tell how long it had been here, but the blood had dried, and the nictitating membrane across its eyes seemed dry too, or reluctant to peel back fully. Its golden brown irises fixed on me, and it flapped in extremis, trying to get away as I approached.

I didn't know what I could do. I pulled out my penknife but the blades were blunt and it was adorned with nothing so grand as a pair of pliers. Even if I could have cut it free, there was no flying left in this poor beast. It was thin. It was dying. It didn't try to attack me when I reached for it. The black talons dimpled my hands, nothing more; no strength to drive them into me.

I wrenched its neck and shut off the pathetic cry.

It was still raining when I turned into Mum's road. I was exhausted. A little wander through the town had turned into a four-hour hike. She let me in and didn't say anything about the lunch I'd missed. She handed me a fresh towel and congratulated me on my intelligence regarding the change of clothes I'd brought. She shooed me into the bathroom and I took a long shower under water as hot as I could bear while she fixed me something to eat.

I dressed and seated myself at the table, feeling better. I fell upon the food when it landed and I ate it so quickly I couldn't be sure what it was, but it was hot and good and filling. She'd accompanied it with a glass of milk and I almost laughed, but I drank it and that was good too. I don't think I'd had a glass of milk in thirty years.

I washed the dishes and checked the time. It was getting on for six o'clock. I found Mum in the living room, flicking through a magazine, though her eyes were fixed on the window, where the sky seemed unsure of what to do. It seethed and boiled, but the light was such that it wouldn't have appeared strange had the clouds separated to allow some early evening sunshine through.

'I should go,' I said.

'You should,' she said. 'But I'd rather you had a nap first. You've been on the go for over twelve hours. You'll fall asleep at the wheel.'

I felt an impulse to tell her about the osprey, but Mum was about as squeamish as it gets. There was a good reason why she had never asked me about the details of my pursuit of the Four-Year-Old in the winter. She couldn't cope with the violence of it. She couldn't watch a butcher cut the pork chops she ordered. Whenever we cut ourselves as kids, we had to clean the wounds ourselves and apply our own sticking plasters.

'I won't fall asleep,' I said. 'I seldom fall asleep when I'm meant to, so don't worry.'

'Your dad could fall asleep anywhere,' she said. I was a little taken aback. She rarely talked about Dad. Certainly not since I was a teenager, not with me anyway. Maybe age had oiled her hinges. 'I saw him fall asleep standing up once, leaning his head against a pebble-dashed wall. He fell over and scraped half his cheek off. The ruddy daft get.'

'I don't remember that,' I said.

'It was when you were very small. I think I was pregnant with Adam at the time.' She sighed. 'You think you've got all the time in the world. You think nothing will go wrong.' She touched my hand. 'I love you,' she said.

I hugged Mum and I was surprised – shocked, even – by how insubstantial she felt. She had never been a large woman but now, underneath the padding of the large knitted cardigan she liked to wear, she was like a bundle of sticks. Age was settling in her where it had never dared show its face before. I struggled to remember how old she was, but I knew she'd been born in the year America entered the Second World War – so 1941. You do the maths.

'I love you too.' I got in the car and started the engine, buckled up.

'You got breakdown cover?' she asked, jutting her chin at the vibrating bonnet of the Saab and hugging her elbows to her chest.

'Very funny,' I said. 'Take care.'

'Be in touch,' she said. She waved once and went inside.

I was on the M6 within twenty minutes. The motorway was uncommonly quiet, just a smattering of lorries and cars, maybe a dozen or so in total. It was getting on for seven o'clock. Clouds were piled like wet grey towels.

My dad died when I was five years old. He dropped dead in a car park in Southampton while he was attending a conference, some work-related training course; he was an office manager for a stationery business based in Penrith. Aneurysm. The technical name for it – subarachnoid haemorrhage – gave me nightmares. I thought his head had split open under the weight of a skull filled with spiders. I bore the fear of that for years; a time bomb in the brain he had carried from birth.

I remember little things about him, although I suspect I've also dreamed some of them into perceived reality. The way he drank instant coffee exclusively with hot milk and lots of sugar; his penchant for big coats with big pockets so he could line up his pens in a row; a love of Dylan and Mitchell (I remember singing along to *Blue* in a Christmas living room smelling of vinyl seat covers and tangerines and

Harveys Bristol Cream). I remember going to the swimming baths with him, and clinging on to his shoulders in the deep end, where the water was always colder. He would buy me crisps and chemical-green pop from the vending machines afterwards, and we'd sit on plastic chairs while I ate and he tied my shoelaces.

What's the difference between a duck?

I don't know, Dad.

One leg's both the same.

My foot on the parapet. The crack of stone. The drop. How fast you'd go. A sense of freedom, of flight. Shackles off. A release forever from worry and fear and responsibility.

I bore down on the accelerator.

70... 80... 90...

I lifted my hands from the steering wheel and closed my eyes.

13

I got back at midnight. I went to the bedroom to take a nap, my body beginning to scream at me from a million overused junctions, and Mengele sank on to me in the dark. *Here it comes*, I thought, and braced myself for a savaging. But his claws were sheathed; I felt a soft, warm paw press against my cheek. He was purring fit to raise the feline dead (or his many victims).

'Maybe I should change your name to Gandhi,' I murmured, my voice thick with fatigue. And one claw dimpled my skin, as if to say, *Don't push your luck, cuntychops.*

Whatever I dreamed, I don't remember, but I woke up feeling disoriented and scared. A layer of sweat clung to me like a cellophane wrapping. Mengele had relocated to the sofa. He watched me as I shuffled about the room, trying to find my phone. I switched off the alarm and stared out, bleary-eyed, at the night. It was one a.m. I took a shower and dressed, then punched the co-ordinates from the scrap of paper into an online map. The location was on Cheyne Walk. A street-level view showed a building: Carlyle Mansions. I looked that up and it seemed there had been writers across the years stumbling over themselves to live there: Ian Fleming, Henry James, Erskine Childers, T.S. Eliot, Somerset Maugham. There were probably more blue plaques than red bricks on the damn thing.

Sarah – Solo – would be there tonight, I was convinced. She had to be. They'd said that she would jeopardise her chances of remaining a part of the Accelerants if she was absent again.

Like she'd give a shit.

I checked my messages – nothing from Clarke… nothing from Romy… plenty from Mawker, his voice becoming more and more animated with every recording he left (I imagined his uvula shaking and shivering like a beached fish) – then grabbed my keys and went out. I drove down to Chelsea. I held the wheel at the recommended ten-to-two position. I observed the speed restrictions. I didn't try to jump any amber lights.

What had I been thinking? I shook my head and swore at myself every mile of the way. I was disgusted with myself that I'd acted so irresponsibly. I could have killed not just myself, but any number of poor, innocent motorists. But I swore at Jimmy Two as well. He'd balanced the car so efficiently that there was no danger of the Saab veering off the road. When I'd opened my eyes, twenty seconds later, I was still in the left-hand lane, and the requisite stopping distance (and then some) behind the car in front.

The thrill though.

Until I opened my eyes, I'd felt the same as I had at the top of Marble Arch tower. I'd felt scared beyond words, but also weirdly improved. Attuned. It wasn't a sense of immortality I felt, although I could understand how some people who had survived what seemed like certain death might reach such a belief; this was more like a heightening of the senses beyond anything I'd known before. I felt young and electric. But in control too. Measured. Capable.

My heart leapt at the thought of what might happen tonight. I wanted to be a part of this forced experience. Fuck the writing. I just wanted to drench myself in adrenaline, enjoy the spike of danger that, for once, was something that was mine to sculpt. And it wasn't just a follow-the-pack mentality; I was having ideas of my own. Experiences I wanted to suggest to the group. I wondered how they'd react to a storming of New Scotland Yard in order to leave drawing pins on Ian Mawker's office chair.

I reached the river at around one-thirty. I parked the car on Lawrence Street and walked back, keeping an eye out for any of the others who might have arrived early. It was a little on the cool side, but you could definitely feel the change in the air from winter to spring. The river glittered with reflected light from the extravagantly illuminated Albert Bridge. Across the water lay Norman Foster's design lair, and his curvy Albion Riverside building with its shops, art galleries and million-pound one-bedroom flats. I sneered at the penthouses and the Porsches and any other expensive things beginning with P.

I stood under the trees on the river walkway and watched the road. It was nearly two a.m. now. I felt a frisson at the thought I was the only one keen enough to get here on time. All the other Accelerants were decelerated. And then a convoy of taxis: three of them, as if in formation, pulling up outside Carlyle Mansions. I felt pierced, cheated, left out of things: they must have been in touch with each other to organise that choreographed rendezvous, giving a lie to this charade about not fraternising outside of 'office hours'.

I trotted across to meet them, anxious to intercept before they could gather on the pavement and begin their incestuous whispering.

No Solo. Christ.

'Corkscrew,' said Underdog, the first to notice my approach. 'Nice of you to join us. Maybe we should change your name to "Tardy".'

'I've been here for half an hour,' I said, hating the wheedling tone in my voice.

'Whatever,' he said. 'I've already moved on.'

'You know, it's only been a couple of days, but I'd forgotten just how charming you are.'

'Oh, you don't know the half of it.'

'I know you're a cunt, and that you legged it sharpish when I was a gnat's chuff away from death.'

'It's all grist, isn't it?' he said, but he'd been stung by that *cunt*. I'd given it some extra spice.

'Enough,' Odessa said, and I stepped back immediately. My shoulders had tensed up and my fists were balling. I didn't realise how far my appetite for aggro had been ratcheted.

Treacle and Odessa were standing next to each other. They weren't touching, but you could see the closeness in them. You could see how they wished for their arms around each other. Something wasn't right.

'What's on the agenda?' I asked. 'Have we got a room in this gaff, or what?'

'It's just a meeting place,' Odessa said. 'It's known as Writers' Block.'

'I wonder why so many writers ended up here,' I said. 'Something in the water. Twenty-four-hour concierge has a pocket full of ideas for stuck scribes.'

Underdog snorted and turned away.

'Where are we going?' I said. 'What are we doing?'

'Somebody has been following me,' Odessa said. 'All of us.'

'Really?'

Underdog turned back, his eyes intent. 'How about you?' he asked. 'You been followed?'

'If I have, it was by someone better at it than the ones who followed you. I haven't noticed anything.' I clenched my teeth, wondering if Odessa had felt the heat of my pursuit the other night. But I'd been careful. No noise. I hadn't drifted too close, and I hadn't hung around outside her door once she'd arrived. And anyway, even if it was me that had spooked her, who had done the same to Treacle and Underdog? Both of them were rattled. It had affected Treacle by clamming him up and freezing him. Underdog was hopping around like a kid with a full bladder outside an engaged toilet. And his lips were flapping as if he'd just learned how to use them.

'I don't even know what we're doing here,' he said. 'Why not just step outside where we can play sitting ducks?'

Even Odessa was twitchy, on edge. She kept rubbing at her chapped lips with her forefinger.

'I'll tell you this,' Underdog said. 'If I see who's doing it… if I catch the wanker, I'll punch him into the Stone Age.'

He went toddling off again, and then turned on his heel – the sharp sound of his sole on the concrete shockingly loud at this hour – and came back.

'We weren't like this before you turned up,' he said.

'Underdog.' But Underdog was no longer paying heed to Odessa.

'Even before Needles died, there was no suggestion of any ripples in the water. But then he was gone, and suddenly here you are. With your copper speak. With your eagerness to please.'

'President backed me up. You know—'

'President is a loner,' Underdog said. 'All he does is write Springsteen-lite ditties in his inherited shag pad. I don't think I heard him say a dozen words…'

'Why would anybody want to say anything within earshot of you?' I asked, not unreasonably. I was getting jittery. It was late. I wanted to get to where we needed to be. I wanted to do what we were intending to do. I wanted to know what was going to happen to Solo now she'd missed another meeting.

'Never mind that,' Odessa said. 'We're here to decide a course of action.'

'What about the experiences?' I asked.

'This is an emergency meeting,' Underdog said. 'Feel free to go off and do something you've never done before. Sex with a grown-up, maybe. Have a pint.'

'We need to lie low for a while,' Treacle said.

I didn't know what to do. I hated not being in control of a situation, but there was nothing I could do to push this in the direction I needed it to go. A direct mention of Solo would have Underdog screaming accusations of badge. A suggestion we all pile back to one of their houses, even if it meant safety in numbers, would be greeted with derision. I had to just play it out. I had to feed off whatever crumbs they threw my way.

'But isn't this kind of thing exactly what you crave?' I said. 'Shouldn't you be embracing these emotions? Spinning them into gold ink?'

'None of us want to die for our art,' said Odessa.

'There's no guarantee anything dodgy is going on,' I said.

I couldn't keep the desperation from my voice. 'Needles might have been a one-off. There's nothing to suggest that he was the first on a shit list that has your names on it. You're anonymous. You cover your tracks.'

'It didn't help him though, did it?' There was a sudden yield to Underdog's voice, as though, even if his expression suggested otherwise, he was eager to hear reason.

'Random acts of violence,' I said. 'They happen all the time.'

'All three of us were followed,' Treacle said. 'That doesn't happen all the time.'

'You can't be sure, though, if that was the case. Odessa didn't see anybody.'

I don't know why I felt compelled to play devil's advocate. I ought to just shut up, play the nodding dog to whatever they said to each other.

'It doesn't matter what I saw,' Odessa snapped; the first time I'd seen her lose her cool. 'Something is going on. Treacle's right. We need to go to ground.'

'What about this other member? Solo? She doesn't know your plans. She's exposed.'

'He's off again,' Underdog said. 'What do you care? You don't know her. Butt out.'

I was this close to admitting that, actually, I did know her, and where the hell was she? But again, I could not convince myself that any good would come of it. They didn't trust me, or at least Underdog didn't. If I was transparent about my motives for being among them, they might clam up completely. I had to bide my time, such as it was. I had one avenue of hope: I knew Odessa's address. Keep an eye on her and she might lead me to Solo unwittingly.

'But she's a part of this group,' I said. 'What if someone *is* following her? What if there *is* some kind of shit list, and she's next on it because whoever it is doing the following can't find you lot any more? I don't know her, but you do. How would you feel if something happened to her? You'd be indirectly responsible.'

'Fuck off,' Underdog said, but I could see the cogs turning behind his eyes.

'We'll leave a warning, at the drop,' Treacle said.

'But what if—'

'Nobody knows where anybody lives,' Underdog said, as if he was spelling it out to a dim child.

'This isn't right,' I said.

Odessa shrugged. 'There's nothing we can do.'

They left then, wordlessly, as if they were part of a play they'd rehearsed but neglected to give me my lines. I watched them go, dispersing along separate streets, moving like dead leaves in a gusting breeze. Hesitant. On the edge of frantic movement.

I was clenching and unclenching my hands. I don't think I've ever felt so frustrated. But it wasn't so much their intention to bow out of public life, or their resistance to my probing about Solo. I realised I'd come here wanting to taste some more of the danger they'd tested me with at Marble Arch. I felt like the child who has been promised the moon on a stick only to end up with a pre-sucked lollipop.

I started after Underdog, but he was casting nervous glances over his shoulder every few steps. I wouldn't stand a chance. As soon as he hit the King's Road he was going to hop on a night bus or hail a cab. Or maybe they'd reconvene to discuss how likely it was that I was their stalker.

I thought about Odessa. Maybe she was going home with Treacle. Back to her place. Back to his place… She'd probably catch a bus again, wherever she was going. Which meant she'd not get back for quite some time.

I got in the car and tore off towards Tufnell Park.

Half an hour later I was on Laurier Road. I'd parked the car around the corner in Dartmouth Park Road, closing the door as softly as possible. This was London, a city that never sleeps, but someone had obviously forgotten to tell the residents of NW5. Curtains closed. Lights off. Do not disturb.

I found Odessa's house and studied it for a while but there were no obvious signs of anybody being at home. Conscious of spending too much time standing on the pavement, no matter how sleepy the rest of the street seemed, I pushed through the gate and walked up to the front door. One bell, which seemed to confirm my earlier suspicion that this place hadn't been carved into flats. I tested the door but it was rock solid. Around the back was a garden with stone steps down to a patio and French windows. I peered through the glass into this basement level and saw the gleaming curves of accoutrements on a shelf, suggesting it was a kitchen. What looked like bi-fold doors separated the space from a front room. I put my ear to the glass for a while and heard voices. But they were space-filling voices. There were no lulls. These were voices being paid to talk.

I broke in, tensing myself for an alarm that never came. The kitchen was immaculate. Nothing had been cooked here for some time. I moved through to the front room to find an impeccably made bed and a small TV. It had the feel of a spare room. The whole basement, in fact – there was a shower under the stairs – was a self-contained living area. Maybe Odessa kept it for guests.

I ascended, wary of the voices, but suspecting that they

belonged to a radio somewhere, the kind of low-level security effort that people made who didn't have fancy motion-detecting alarm systems installed. Yet she did: I saw them tucked into the corners, flashing red whenever I moved. So they had been deliberately switched off. I paused on the stairs, wondering if my incredible proclivity for shit timing had struck again. Wouldn't it just be sod's law to be in this building at the exact same time that Gower's killer had decided to bone up on his slashing technique?

The hallway gave on to a larger kitchen and here there were ghosts of what Odessa had eaten this evening. Something spicy, apparently. Smoked paprika was in that, and something meaty, a garlicky sausage maybe. *Gutsy Dinners*, by Odessa Scribbles. Lived experience. Write what you know. More separating doors and a big living room with scuffed old leather furniture. Dimmed lighting picked out the spot varnish on the spines in a bookcase. A vase of tulips past their best. No notebook. No diary. No laptop.

More stairs. A master bedroom containing a huge bed that was topped with a mess of blankets and pyjamas. Wardrobe with opaque glass doors. I stared at that for a while until I saw faces in the sweep of clothing that hung within. Spooked, I checked the bedside table but there was just a fat novel on top filled with dog-ear folds, perhaps to remind her of choice phrasing she could steal.

Next door I found her study, and the radio (one voice saying '...this day and age it's not videogames and TV that's distracting our children, it's social media...' and another saying '...but there's no evidence to show that children can't multitask...'), and the reason why the alarm system was disconnected: an old cat sitting in a basket. This raggedy chap wasn't up to any more outdoor adventures. Odessa couldn't put the alarm on because it would go off every time Tiddles decided to plant his face in a bowl of chow.

He only reacted when I was within stroking distance. No twitch of the ears. No inscrutable stare. Deaf and blind. I scratched his ears and as he began to purr, his whole body shook. He was drooling like a dental patient pumped with novocaine. A tag on his collar told me his name was Gatsby. Fuck's sake. What a great name for a cat.

I poked around Odessa's things, expecting to find something with her name on it, but her anonymity extended to her own four walls, it seemed. I couldn't find an envelope, passport or cheque book to illuminate me. More books, all of them research volumes: *A Dictionary of Surnames*, *A Dictionary of Architecture*, Joachim Berendt's *The Jazz Book*, Lawrence Block's *Writing the Novel: From Plot to Print*. I saw a piece of paper sticking out of that. Not a bookmark. A list of names. At the top it said *Acc. Wannabes Thru the Ages*. The first of the names – Rory Melling – was next to a date three years back. There were half a dozen other names yoked to dates that drew closer to the present day: Yvonne Gibson, Scott Dennis, Veronica Lake, Ben George, Barbara Parker. All of them had been marked with a red cross. And then, suddenly, from about eighteen months ago, presumably the change to anonymity had been made, because the list progressed with code names: Indigo, Renfield, Hawksmoor, Ransom, Odessa, Treacle, President, Underdog, Solo.

I copied the names into my notebook and returned the paper to the Block. I resisted the strong temptation to stick around with Gatsby until Odessa returned, convinced we could thrash out the whole mystery if she could give me the addresses of the people on that list. But I knew that was unlikely. This was London and people don't necessarily stay in one place for long. And just because she had a bunch of names didn't automatically mean she had a bunch of addresses. Instead I gave the old soldier another chuck under the chin and wished him well. Then I was out and in the car and driving fast, the smell of garlic and paprika in my clothes.

I got home and slung a few back and went to bed with a buzz on and a rage on. Somehow I fell into a shallow sleep and Becs was there, as beautiful as the day I met her and the wind was in her hair and she wore that maddening half smile and a long, cement-coloured knitted dress that clung everywhere. She gently picked the strands of hair from her green-brown eyes and I reached out for her. As soon as my fingers touched her she exploded into the red jigsaw puzzle I'd discovered in my house that night. I tried touching her again, craving some dream logic that might reverse her disablement, but my fingers only made tracks through the blood filming what remained of her face.

The sun was beating in the sky behind me, casting hot, pulsing shadows over the woman I loved. But that can't have been right because I found her in raining dark. I cast a glance over my shoulder and the sun was in the room, fierce and red and small. And it beat like a heart, burning, hotter than the breath of the devil.

I woke up in the airless stove of my bedroom and all I could smell was the bitter, spiced fug of cheap Nicaraguan cigars. I opened the windows and leaned out. Close your eyes and – early morning W1H – you could taste a sweetness in the London air... although at that moment I'd have tasted sweetness with my face inches above the quivering meringues of filth found in Delhi's most virulent hovels.

I swilled down a couple of painkillers and wrote my mother a postcard. She'd love it: I hadn't sent her a handwritten note since I was a homesick school kid on a weekend trip to Shropshire. She'd hate it: I only had one postcard in the flat, an H.R. Giger of a creature with a drainpipe for a penis blowing mucus-covered deformities out of the end. I think that one must have been from Giger's rose period.

I flipped open the laptop and went hunting for new names. Ben George: nothing useful. Rory Melling. Used to live in Camden Town. Long gone. Yvonne Gibson. I found a dead one, zonked by an aortic dissection. Same person? Who knows? Scott Dennis. Thousands of the fuckers. North, east, south, west. Veronica Lake. Dead Hollywood actress. Barbara Parker. By then I'd lost the will to live. London. I remembered the first time I'd arrived here. I thought the city was laid out for me. I thought I *was* the city. You've not seen my like before. *I'll tame you. I'll change you.* Yeah, right. You're a temporary skidmark. You're an immediate ghost. At best. Everyone drifts through this place, this eternal processing zone, this grand old charnel house. Fast turnover. This place ate you up and spat you out. Moorgate. Isle of Dogs. Strand. Weialala leia, Wallala leialala.

Madness descending. I had to talk to someone. I pulled my phone out and quick-dialled.

His voice, thick with sleep. 'Sorrell.'

'I've got a favour to ask,' I said.

I heard the flapping of duvet as he failed to maintain any vestiges of calm. Feet thumping on floor. Magazine pages sliding off the bed. I shuddered to think what he'd been reading.

'Favour my bollocks,' he snarled. 'Do *me* a favour. Get

yourself down to the copshop so we can put some irons on you.'

'I've done nothing wrong, Mawker. Come on. If you were that serious, you'd have put a foot through my door.'

'You need to wind your neck in, Sorrell. Let us do our job. You're muddying waters.'

'What *is* your job?' I asked. 'I don't remember "being a cunt" on the list the careers advisor brought to school. I'd love to know what you've been up to since Martin Gower was found.'

'Ditto,' Mawker said. Now I could hear his feet on the stairs, slapping on lino in his Ealing misery hole. The tinkle of cornflakes in a bowl. A radio snapping into life: Deacon Blue.

'You know what depresses me?' I said.

'Loyalty?' Mawker suggested. 'Honest work? Human decency?'

'When DJs refer to the music of my youth as Golden Oldies,' I said. 'I mean, I use the stairs whenever there's a lift option. If I kick a football, it stays kicked, and I remain upright. I don't have any problem pulling my socks on. I don't have any grey pubes.'

'Thanks for sharing,' he said. I heard a kettle whistling. I heard something launch itself from a toaster. It all sounded like domestic bliss but I couldn't shake the image of him sitting in his own filth in a rat-infested dump playing breakfast SFX through a tape recorder. We all have our favourite fantasies.

'Do you know what you and Deacon Blue have in common?' I said.

'Well now,' he said, equably. Track six: butter scraped across a pikelet. 'I'm not Scottish. I don't play any musical instruments. So I can only offer conjecture that you believe

164

we share some level of cuntdom as yet unattainable by the common man.'

'You seem unusually relaxed,' I said. 'What happened last night? Did you fuck something living for a change?'

'What do you want, Sorrell? Some of us have got real lives to lead. People will start to talk. You can't stay off the phone to me. People will think you've got a crush on me.'

'I'd love to have a literal crush on you,' I said. 'Don't forget to pilot your ship called *Dignity* into the nearest harbour of shit.'

'I'm putting the phone down.'

'I want to see Graeme Tann.'

'Oh, fuck off. You are kidding me.'

'I was offered the chance to see him once, remember? To spend some quality time with him, when you brought him in. And I couldn't. I couldn't do it.'

'Well you won't get any quality time with him now,' Mawker said. 'That horse has bolted.'

'This is my daughter we're talking about, Ian,' I said.

'No it's not. And it never was. Do you understand? Your daughter is incidental to all of this. As is Graeme Tann. She knew Martin Gower, a guy who was murdered. That's it. I told you because I wanted to help. To give you a lead. It was a favour. It was not a fucking invitation. Not to have you impersonate the police. Not to have you disappear and walk your muddy footprints all over my fucking case.'

'If my daughter is involved in all this... If my daughter dies—'

'We'll end up picking up the pieces. We'll be the ones who catch her killer. You'd better hope you don't get in the way any more. You don't want this on your hands. You don't want to fuck up, here, Sorrell.'

'I just want to talk to him.'

'Walk away from it, Sorrell. Forget about him. He's rotting in a cell.'

'I need it.'

'Why?'

I started laughing. It was hard, spiky laughter, razoring through my throat as if I was pulling out yard after yard of barbed wire. I didn't think I could stop. In the end I was able to put a cap on it. A headache was caroming around my head; I wasn't even sure if Mawker was on the line any more.

I said: 'For the experience.'

'BLUEBOTTLE JAM'

1 OCT 1988 BY RONNIE

MAIN CHARACTERS

Alexander Fox: 'Ali'
Brian Grey: 'Moon'
Gordon Thomas: 'Thommo'
Stephen Spence: 'Croc'

SUB CHARACTERS

Joanna Gifford
Henry Shetton
Robert Fox
Melissa Fox

Part One – Rumours
Part Two – Reality

CHAPTER 1

I lie asleep in bed, but only sometimes. Mostly I'm awake, struggling with my fear of the dark, conscious of the sweat on my forehead. Conscious of the cruel silence. After ten years the dreams still bother me. Ten years.

Sometimes, when I'm awake, the sheets becoming oiled with perspiration, I hear a dog barking in the night. Sometimes I want to scream when I hear that. When I hear a dog barking, it takes me back. Like tonight for instance. The dog barked and that was it. Sleep stays away.

So I'm sitting here. Looking out on to my street. It's quite chilly, and all I have on is a pair of shorts, but I'm sweating.

It is a cold February night. It has been raining; I can see puddles of water on the pavement and the road is shiny and wet. The streetlights are dripping and tears of rain runnel the windows.

The moon is full, the colour of ice that has strong light glinting on it. Almost blue in its brightness.

I can't see the dog but I can hear it. I think it belongs to number 27 or 29. I'm not sure. It sounds like a big dog. Not necessarily mean. But big. An alsatian. Or a doberman. A rottweiler.

I can feel the cold now. My arms have become covered with a layer of goosepimples. A car crawls past my house. I've got a notebook in front of me. One of the thick ones with the large spiralling metal rings that keep the paper together. I'm doodling.

I read what was on the cover and managed a smile. I don't smile much these days because there is nothing much to smile about.

The notebook is an old one, intended to record the events that happened ten years ago. I haven't written in it. Until now that is.

The cover is full of messages from my old friends. They are old messages. Stuff like: 'Bri85' and 'Skool stinx' and 'Johnno is a geek'.

The one that made me smile was directed at me, written

by a girl in my class in the last year of school. 'To Ali, we were ships that passed in the night. Love, Joanna.'

I can conjure up her face in my mind if I try hard enough. Sometimes I wonder what happened with her. Where she went, what she's doing with her life now.

Sometimes I wonder what became of all the school friends. It's natural.

Only, I know what happened to some of my friends, my close friends.

And that's part of the nightmare.

I've started writing. I knew that I would have to get this down at some stage or another. That time has arrived.

I sit here. A cold, February night. The wind has become strong and clouds – angry, charcoal-coloured ones, have shut out the moon's light.

The rain has started again. Spitting lightly on my windows like fingernails tapping softly.

I hope the dog doesn't bark again.

I'm writing faster.

And the memories are flowing.

Shelton Farm. Autumn.

My friends. Moon, Croc and Thommo.

And Midnight at the start and end of it all.

14

I nipped to the cigar terrace at the hotel on Manchester Street and bought a box of Nicaraguan cigars, the best I could afford. The guy I bought them off said the Oliva Serie V Melanio Figurado had been the previous year's winner of *Cigar Aficionado* magazine's top smoke. He kept talking about nuanced leaves and notes of coffee and leather as he wrapped them in gift paper. It all went over my head. I'd just as much inject bleach into my eyeballs as suck on something that would turn my lungs to kippers.

I got on the motorway fast. I came off the M1 at Aspley Guise and drove through the countryside along ever narrowing B roads until I reached a long approach road to the ten-metre electrified fences around HMP Cold Quay.

Graeme Tann. I had not seen him since the trial. I had not read the papers or watched the televised bulletins; none of it was news to me, and I didn't want to see photographs of my wife. I hardly knew anything about him, other than he was a janitor at the leisure centre near where we had once lived, and that he had hidden a camera in the female changing rooms. Out of the hundreds of women who passed through those doors he developed a fixation for Becs. Part of me wanted to know, *Why her?* But most of the time I was saying, *How could he not?* I remember a couple of bottles of guilt I drank off the back of feeling more disgusted that his taste in women was impeccable over the horror he had visited upon her.

And what did I know about him now? Incidentals. Prison life detail. He slept on a mattress that was two inches thick. He now owned three pairs of prison clothes consisting of a dark green shirt displaying his surname and identification number. Someone clipped his finger and toenails once a week. Everything he owned – and none of that was from his life outside – could fit inside the five foot by fifteen inch locker that was kept under his bed. He was in C-wing, unofficially known as Red Row, where they kept the meat-heads, the serial killers, the psychopaths. I knew that his day began at six a.m. with breakfast. There were 200 men on Red Row – nobody ate until every man had arrived at the canteen. Once seated you had ten minutes to eat what had been dumped on your tray. After that came Punishment 60, an hour of 'free time' in the quadrangle – the outside communal area. You could exercise out there: they had a cinder running track, they had a stack of free weights, they had batting nets and football goals. There were no cameras here: security was afforded only by a handful of guards on each of the corner towers. If convicts were going to dole out any pain, this was where it happened. I understood that Tann had received a couple of beatings during his time at Cold Quay.

At eight a.m. everyone returned to their cells for the count. Anyone not sitting nicely on their bunks was red flagged. Three red flags and further punitive action – usually a ban on free time or curtailing of other privileges, sometimes a period in solitary confinement – would follow. Then the wait for the doors to unlock for the next plate of slop, the next hour in the Quad – rain or shine – and lights out at nine p.m.

I crossed the gravel forecourt to the gate. There were two guards with Armalite rifles slung loosely across their shoulders; one of them was stroking the barrel as he watched me progress. The car that had shadowed me through the Bedfordshire countryside since I slipped off the M1 at Aspley Guise had parked a little distance back; a pair of blank faces tracked me from the front seats. Nobody was taking any chances with this gig.

Mawker had wanted to accompany me, but I told him I wanted to go it alone. Publicly I explained it was because I didn't want Tann to have the satisfaction of seeing somebody holding my hand; it was a rite of passage, an exorcising demons process, something I had to do to try to propel me to some halfway normal life path, especially if Sarah was bent on never being reunited with me. Privately it was because I didn't want him to suffer any fallout were I to launch myself at Tann and try to chew through his carotid artery.

I was met by the governor's assistant, a guy called Furniss who had chunky hands with squared-off fingers and doe eyes with long lashes. His body language was professional and warm, but his mouth couldn't disguise his distaste of me or my reason for this visit. It was curled as if he'd just taken a lick of something rotten. Disdain dripped through his words like venom.

'Welcome to Cold Quay,' he said.

Outside the visiting area I was halted in front of a desk, behind which was seated a thickset man with close-cropped silvering hair and damp blue eyes. He looked as if he had worked out a lot in his youth and then let everything slide. He wrote my name down in a ledger and gestured at the box.

'What's in there?'

'Cigars,' I said. 'For Tann.' I knew full well that he wouldn't be allowed such luxuries and that they'd be confiscated before I got near him, to be returned to me on my way out. The desk jockey said as much.

'I know,' I said. 'But let me tease the bastard, just for a while? It's a cheap shot, but I don't have anything else.' The desk jockey smiled, his lips peeling back to reveal tiny pebble teeth set in broad gums. I was frisked before they opened the doors for me. If the officer who did it noticed how wet the back of my shirt was, he didn't let on. A buzzer sounded, the door unlocked. I went in.

All the tables and chairs were bolted to the floor. Each set of furniture was accompanied by a steel pivot loop. I sat down and waited. The air was heavy with the smell of Doublemint and Juicy Fruit. The fluorescent tubes arranged across the ceiling bleached the skin and chased away all shadow. One of them was on the fritz and it buzzed and popped erratically, scattering chancy light like a strobe.

I'd thought about this moment a lot in the years since Tann's arrest, but I'd never rehearsed it, despite my conviction that I'd meet him some day, face to face. I just never imagined it would be while he was still incarcerated. It was always in some dark alley, or in the kitchen of whatever squalid backwater he found himself in were he to be granted parole. I remember when the life sentence was passed, thinking, *Good. I hope he rots in jail. I hope he contracts Hep B. I hope he overdoses on bad gear. I hope someone tears his eyes out and wears them for earrings.* But pretty soon after I was fantasising about a day he was allowed to go free so that I could find him and do something to him that would secure a long custodial sentence of my own.

Buzzers sounding in muffled distance. Bars sliding open and ramming home. I tried to relax. My fingernails were jammed into the tops of my thighs. A shadow falling through reinforced glass and lengthening across the floor towards me. I wondered if my nails were long enough, sharp enough. I wondered if I was quick enough. Would I have time to tear his throat open before the guards fell on me?

I kept my eyes on the cigar box, even as the shadow stilled, and he sat down before me. I heard the slither of chains as they were fed through the pivot loop. I concentrated on the words:

Oliva Serie V Melanio... Gran Reserva Limitada

'Hello Joel...'

Figurado...

Tabacalera Oliva SA

'Joel... how have you been keeping?'

Esteli, Nicaragua

'Are those for me, Joel?'

I lifted my head and my first thought was, *How could someone so small do what he did?*

'No,' I said. 'They're for your jailers. I bought them for you, but, you know. Rules.' It was puerile. I wish I'd never picked them up in the first place. It was an expensive way to try to hurt him, but all I'd done was make myself look a dick.

'Pity.'

'Yeah, after all, these could have been the cigars to finally give you cancer.' *Keep it up, dick. Keep it up with the petty jibes.*

'One of the things about not being able to smoke in here... at least it's meant I've become fitter now, Joel.'

His words came at me as if from far away, from a dream

zone I was unable to access; something remembered, or a hit of telepathy from a distant mind. The shape of his head was curiously beautiful now that it was shorn back to stubble: petite, fragile, all neat angles and planes and blue shadow. He barely blinked those ash-grey eyes of his. He barely moved his mouth when he spoke but he licked his lips a lot. His tongue was broad and thick and purple; it was crimped white at the edges like the top of a pie. I imagined it clamped between his teeth as he masturbated on to the dead body of my wife. I hated how he kept using my name.

My stomach performed an oily roll.

'Are you okay, Joel?'

'What do you fucking think?'

'Joel, I think you need help.'

'*I* need help? I'm not the one who killed in cold blood. I'm not the one who took photographs of naked women in changing rooms and then tossed off over them back in his sad pad.'

'No. But it's a sunny day. And you chose to come and sit in a cold room in a prison miles away from where you live. Shepherd's Bush, isn't it? Or did you move? I'm guessing you would have moved. Somewhere smaller. You'd have been rattling around that old place, wouldn't you, Joel? You and perky tits... what was her name?'

I'd stood up without realising it. The guards in the room stepped closer. One of them rested his hand on the Taser in his belt. I'd come in here determined to control myself, to control him, to control the situation, and within seconds he had the upper hand. He was playing me like a knackered trombone.

'What did you think you could do, Joel? Why did you even come here?'

176

I was shaking my head. I was digging my nails into my palms. I could feel the adrenaline from my kidneys, a hot liquor that was slowly poaching me from the inside out.

'May I offer a hypothesis?'

A peeping Tom. A guy who scraped shit off toilet bowls. A coward. A thief. I remember word for word how the judge had referred to him just before passing sentence: *a pathetic, tragic alien living among us, the antithesis of everything good in his victim.*

'I think you came here because you consider me the strop that keeps your edge keen. You came to see me because you're losing your grip on who you are and what you feel your point in life is. Rebecca was your anchor. She kept you grounded. And now you've been cut adrift, there's nobody to steer you into safe waters, is there?'

He licked his lips. His face hosted boles of deep shadow, like the cross-hatchings in a bleak political cartoon. His eyes were pale crucibles of cold flame. In the dock he had stood bowed, like an S, like something defeated, burdened with a weight only he could feel. A grey man, his hair thinning, apparently being eaten away by something more deleterious than the most aggressive of cancers. Now he was loose-limbed and lissom. Muscles shifted like oiled rats against each other under his clothing. His skin was pink. He gleamed.

He rubbed his hand over his mouth. His nostrils flared. His fingernails were like polished slivers of almond.

'So Joel, how's the search for your daughter going?'

The guards picked me off the floor thirty seconds later. My nose was bleeding heavily – I think it was broken – and my eyes wouldn't stop watering. Pain strummed rhythmically across my face. A guard was standing over Tann, his Taser drawn. Tann himself was sitting upright, his chained hands as far above his head as he could raise them, and he was slowly, calmly talking the guard down.

'It was self-defence... He attacked me... You saw it...'

One of the guards leaned in and suggested it was time to leave. I nodded. I apologised.

'Apology accepted.'

Now the thought was in my head, I couldn't wait to get outside. I felt stifled. I felt, in a sudden blaze of panic, that I was the prisoner, and Tann was free to go.

The buzz of the door. As it swung open, he slid his stiletto in, between the ribs: 'She offered to fuck me, if it would save her. And later, she begged for her life, at the last... when most of it had ebbed from her anyway. She—'

But I couldn't hear any more because I was screaming. I was trying to tear my ears from the side of my head.

15

At first I drove in search of a drink, but getting pissed out here meant staying in my car overnight and I didn't fancy that, comfy though the back seat of the Saab was. Furniss was all for getting the Cold Quay medic out to have a look at my face – he was worried that I had suffered a concussion and was in no fit state to control a vehicle – but I shrugged him off. He seemed happy enough with his £200 box of cigars.

I drove until I found myself on a narrow road called Cobbler's Lane. It took me through a tunnel under the M1. Out of the other side I parked on the grass verge by a pylon in a field of cut logs awaiting collection. I could smell hot tarmac and petrol fumes, scorched wood where blades had slid through boughs, willow herb and dried haycocks sealed in hot black plastic.

Big rabbits around here, I used to say, on family days out, whenever there was a field full of those large packages. That always used to tickle Sarah. Becs would tut in disgust—

No I didn't.

Yeah, you did. Whenever I came out with that joke.

Mock disgust.

It's still disgust. Seeded with real disgust. At least twenty-five per cent.

It's a relief, I have to say, not to have to listen to your shit jokes any more.

Don't. Please.

What are you doing out here? In the middle of nowhere?

I need some peace and quiet.

What the fuck happened to your nose?

I was defending your honour.

You should have tried defending your nose.

Who's coming out with shit jokes now?

Where's Sarah?

You know I haven't found her yet. Nor her me. Not that she's looking.

She's old enough to look after herself now. Maybe it's time to back off.

Five years, Becs. Five years without you. Without her. I can measure that five years in nothing but vodka and blood.

And cat food.

Becs. Five fucking years.

We talked about when Sarah had been conceived. Well, I wanted to talk about that. She didn't. She never did. Sex was something you did. Not talked about. But I persisted.

I remember it was – at the risk of sounding like some Hollywood ponce – perfect. You were warm and soft and it was as if you'd been overtaken by your hormones. It was the optimum moment and that shone in you. Your skin was golden. You engulfed me.

Oh, Christ. That's not how I remember it.

We were on the living room floor. Joni was on the stereo. Your hair. Your eyes. There was no awkwardness, remember.

Everything fell into place. Everything was so soft, so perfect.
There were no missteps. No pratfalls. No elbows in the guts.
No trapped hairs. No cramps.

Didn't you fart?

No.

I'm pretty sure you farted.

No. I didn't. And when we spoke—

Oh yeah, I remember saying: is it in yet?

That's not what happened. You're thinking of your ex.

Which one?

How many were there?

Hundreds. And they were all hung like blue whales.

When we spoke—

It was the tremulous voices of a choir of heavenly angels.

Something like that.

You Hollywood ponce.

Why are you being so disruptive?

This is an imagined conversation, you fanny. If you can't even control a conversation in your own head, you should get help. Get help anyway.

I could never have controlled you. Nobody could.

First sensible thing you've said all day. Now move, otherwise we'll be having the rest of this sparkling exchange in person. You don't want to check out under the wheels of a fucking Nissan Micra, do you? And a lime green one at that. Not a great way to die.

She had come to me at times before, when I was at a low ebb, when I really needed her, but now it didn't seem right. I panicked; it felt as though I was forgetting her. I couldn't remember her voice, or the way she laughed. I couldn't remember the smell of her skin or the way her hand felt under my fingers. The rhythm of her speech was too much like mine. I reached out to the seat next to me, convinced she was there in the corner of my eye, but I touched nothing but leather. She was nowhere now. I had failed to keep her alive in my mind where I thought she could exist, untouched, unspoilt, for as long as I drew breath. But visiting Tann had tarnished that, put a maggot in the fruit. I could feel her shrinking inside, and Tann, with his lizard-lick mouth, was filling in the spaces she vacated. I clenched my eyes shut and tried to recall those days that had really mattered. The blue riband memories.

Rebecca's face, the first time we made love, in a bedroom drenched with spring sunshine, her body above mine, hair across her face, breathing ragged, my hands full of her breasts. Her pale skin sprayed with freckles like a shake of cocoa over a milky drink.

Tann raised his head and ash fell from the sockets of his eyes.

Our wedding day on an August day of apocalyptic rain. We'd raced out of Westminster Register Office to our hired Rolls – no umbrellas – and laughed and kissed and fussed at each other, damp in the back seat, muddy water up the back of Rebecca's beautiful mermaid wedding dress. Her hair soaked, limp.

Tann in the driver's seat, wreathed in smoke, taking us somewhere we'd never be found.

Sarah's birth. Rebecca implausibly beautiful on all fours, snarling at me, whimpering. Tensed. Animalistic. Me feeling like a spare part. Blood and shit everywhere. A high beast scent of distress. A mealy reek of butchery. Classical music playing like some ineffective, inappropriate soundtrack. The speed of Sarah's arrival. Her utter silence. Her utter stillness. Enough time to register her sex. Enough time to register the cord wrapped around her neck.

Tann carrying her out of the room. A nod. A wink. *Back in a jiffy.*

He was as invasive and pervasive as the smoke he held in his lungs.

I've become fitter now, Joel.

The way he'd moved. The speed of him. His body was like a taut ship's cable. He hadn't broken a sweat. He'd hardly made his chains jangle. But he'd decked me with an efficiency and ruthlessness that wasn't in him at the time of his trial.

Tann had controlled her. Tann had controlled me.

Christ. This was fear.

I was shaking in my seat as if someone had suddenly run a high voltage through it. I needed Becs but she wasn't here. She wouldn't respond.

What was happening to me? I had to get a grip. Sarah needed me. The Accelerants needed me; they just didn't know it yet. Romy. Mawker. I had responsibilities.

I got out of the Saab. The sound of car engines up on the M1 dopplered north and south. I walked to the embankment fence and climbed over it. I moved up through the plastic drinks bottles and silver birch trees to the top of the rise where the motorway stretched towards the horizon. I stood behind the crash barrier and watched the weaving tons of metal as they came and went. It was busy. The road created its own micro-climate: warm air buffeted me at each passing car and lorry. It reminded me of my fear of train platforms when I was a child; the way the fast locomotives would come barrelling through the station at first pushing the air before them like a wall, and then sucking it away. I'd had to hide behind my parents, or cling to the drainpipes, convinced that

I'd be whipped into the air by the vortex it created.

Now I was excited by it. A black Audi flashed past in the outside lane, doing at least ninety. A horn sounded. In the distance lights flashed as an HGV indicated to a van that had overtaken it that it was now safe to merge with the inside lane. Sun beamed on the cellulose roofs like the shining crests of waves on a fitful sea.

I climbed over the barrier and moved on to the hard shoulder. The hum of tyres on tarmac. The brief snatch of a song from a convertible. I was six feet away from certain death. I had seen footage of people hit by cars travelling slower than this: a catastrophic dismantlement, as if they were waxwork dummies. The tarmac bore a petrol-blue sheen. I thought of the motorway at night, with the intermittent explosions of sodium orange.

I waited for a lull and then I closed my eyes. *Van Gogh would be painting motorways if he was around today*, I thought, and stepped out into the road. I was not nervous. I did not hurry. I heard horns blaring on the opposite side of the motorway. I could hear traffic rushing towards me on this, and it sounded like the skirl of loose grains over a beach of impacted sand. More horns. I reached the central divide and waited. Traffic blasted past me, rifling my jacket. I did not open my eyes. The horns stopped.

I walked back.

A foot away from the hard shoulder I heard the deep groan of an articulated lorry. It missed me by inches, but its wake floored me. I rolled over and over, thankfully away from the lanes. I heard someone raging through an open window:

'Stupid bastard!'

And then I was on my feet again and Tann was vanquished; there was clean air in my lungs and a tart clarity in my head and Becs was in my periphery once more and she said, *Get a grip you idiot. What are you playing at? I'll ask you again. What are you doing out here?*

I told her it didn't matter, and I was smiling, laughing as I cantered down the embankment, past the used condoms and bottles of piss. I got to the car and vomit fountained from me in a sudden, unexpected arc. I felt my legs give way and I sat down in my own waste until the shudders left my body. Cleaning myself up as best I could, I got back in the car, gunned the engine and drove to the junction. Once I'd got up to eighty and saw the roadside verges blurring to fast green, I felt my hackles rise and my mouth turn bone dry. I don't remember anything else about the drive back to London but I know she was with me every mile that slipped beneath the wheels.

16

The answerphone was flashing like a Christmas tree. I listened to them all, tensed for bad news, but it didn't come. Unless you were related to Treacle, whose real name (I learned in a tip-off from Clarkey, who had been summoned to deal with another piece of wet work) was Malachi Dawe. He lived in a house on Ellerslie Road. I knew Ellerslie Road. I'd lived near it once upon a time. According to Clarke, he'd been found in his bath, as dead as yesterday. Not only that, but there was a photograph of Sarah in his possession. No, nothing quite so gnarly as the packet that had been found with Martin Gower. This was the kind of snap that a dad would be proud of. He told me to stay put, that he'd arrange to get a facsimile of the picture to me. That there was nothing I could add to proceedings and that my physical involvement was not required; more: actively dissuaded. That Mawker would have both his and my bollocks on a cake stand under a glass-domed lid if I didn't do as he asked.

Fuck that.

Fifteen minutes and I was on Bloemfontein Road, slowing

for the turn, right on the doorstep of QPR's football ground. It turned out he lived right opposite Turnstile Block 1. Mawker was meant to be there to greet me, much as he had been when I'd gone up to Enfield. I was surprised to find a PC in his stead. Perhaps Mawker had called in sick. Perhaps he'd handed in his resignation and gone off to commune with aliens. I wondered if he actually did any proper police work or just stood around in his mac looking like a shifty wank-addict all the time.

I pulled up and got out. I recognised the uniformed constable standing by the door in his hi-vis gilet. He'd been with Mawker up in Enfield. I stepped past the flowers that had been stacked on the pavement outside and went up the steps towards him.

'Nice motor,' he said.

'You can take her for a spin if you like,' I said.

'Nice try,' he said.

I nodded at the flowers. 'Popular guy.'

'Actually, those are for an old woman who died in the house next door a few days ago. A pillar of the community, apparently. Charity volunteer. Rescued dogs. That sort of thing.'

'He who must be obeyed. Is he inside?'

'Chief Superintendent Mawker? He isn't here yet. We sent a squad car but there's been a bad accident at Hanger Lane. He was snarled up in it.'

'Could be his monumentally distracting shitstache *caused* it.'

No sign of a smile from PC Suckup. 'He'll be here in ten minutes,' he said.

'I talked to him this morning.' Truth. 'He told me to go on ahead; there might be some more photos of Sarah. I was to help myself. They weren't a part of his investigation.' Lie.

'Before forensics get here? I don't think so.'

'Come on,' I said. 'I know the ropes. I won't touch anything and I'll put a good word in for you at the promotions circus.'

He looked up the street and licked his lips. He seemed to be willing Mawker to appear, to absolve himself of having to make any decisions. But then he said: 'He warned me about you. That you might turn up. You're Joel Sorrell. Oh, he told me all about you. Who told you about this?'

'I couldn't possibly betray my sources,' I said.

'You really ought to scarper.'

'You got kids?' I asked.

'A boy.'

'Lovely,' I said. I wanted to whip the kid gloves off and choke him with the iron gauntlet – Mawker would be here soon, he hated being the last one to a butcher's scene – but I clearly had to play the long game with this one. He went home at night and polished his pips, probably while reading *Police* magazine from cover to cover. He wrote letters to *Police* magazine. He filled in all the quizzes: *Are you police enough? Which Z Cars character are you?* 'How old?'

'Three. Four next month.' He bit down on the end of each word; he knew what was coming. 'Let's leave it at that, shall we?'

'Magical age,' I said. 'I remember the first time my daughter – Sarah – said the word "Daddy". She must have been around three. You never forget a moment like that. Even when—'

'I said leave it,' he said. 'Carry on like this and I'll arrest you for wasting police time, aggravation, whatever I can nail you for... You are not getting in that house. Now piss off.'

I turned my back on him immediately. Dead end. No point in trying to push on through him. He was textbook.

189

Good thing too, really. The force needed some backbone in it. And so. Plan B.

I got back in the car and made a play of leaving in a huff. I got to the top of the road and turned right on to Loftus Road, where I parked again outside a small block of purpose built flats. I scooted down the side of it and saw that I'd have to do some serious fence-hopping in order to get into the rear of Dawe's property. At least it meant that the back entrance was unlikely to be guarded by another PC. I got over the walls and through the back gardens of most houses without being spotted. Well, I wish I could say that. I was spotted twice. Once by a dog lying by its kennel (reaction: tail wag) and once by an elderly woman standing at the kitchen window maybe washing pots or peeling potatoes (reaction: she waved… I kid you not). I waited for a short while at the rear of Dawe's building, mainly because I was trying to work out that it *was* Dawe's building. I slid over the wall and crept across decking to the back door. Tried the handle. Locked. I took off my jacket and wrapped my fist in it and punched the glass in. I waited for reaction from within, without. Nothing. I got myself through the door and did my job.

Nice place. Maisonette, I think they're called, though I didn't know for sure. A pretty way to say 'small place to live'. I could remember the place I lived in when I first came to London. It was punishingly small. Not so much a studio flat as a studioette. A studioette flatette. A cubbyette holette. A fucking toiletette.

I moved through the hallway, recognising the beanie hanging from a coat peg, into a living room that was spare and neat and very white. No signs of any struggle here. I had to battle with the urge to tear through the flat until I found him. There might be footprints forensics could work with so I had to tread carefully.

My eye was drawn towards a stack of uniform journals because they were a different colour to the room's stark white theme (Picador spines, ivory candles, a white ceramic bowl of white ceramic apples); Moleskine cahiers with red covers lined up on a bookcase. Post-it notes stuck out from the pages. I flicked through a few using the end of a pencil, careful not to touch anything. I recognised the handwriting from one of the pages Odessa had given me on the night of my initiation. Jagged and inconsistent. Short sentences. Lots of physical words. Lots of aggression. I'd guessed it was Odessa's handwriting, but that just goes to show what an astute judge of character I am.

The kitchen was similarly neat and minimalist. Orange was the predominant colour here. An early hardback of Nigel Slater's, some Penguin paperbacks, a Bugatti Diva coffee machine. A bowl of take a wild guess. No sign of forced entry here either. So what? He knew his killer. Most of us do. I went up the stairs. Treacle was in the bath. He'd been chopped up like a tree at a blind lumberjacks' Christmas party. I put a flannel around my fingers and gently tilted his head forward. There it was: a neat little puncture on the back of his neck, just beneath the occipital bun. Cold water. Wrinkles in abundance. Limbs flexed: decorticate posturing, a sure sign of damage to the spine. He'd been in here for a number of hours, I guessed. What expression was discernible within the slashed ribbons of facial tissue reminded me of a weary traveller who's just been told his flight has been delayed. A book on the floor. Maybe he'd been reading it while he soaked. Probably not. I didn't want to touch it so I craned my neck to read the title: *Green and Pleasant Land:*

Valentines to a Dying Planet. The same anthology of short stories that had been found near Martin Gower's body. That was interesting. I'd have to do my own research into that.

I went to Treacle's bedroom. No signs of a burglar rifling through belongings; not that there was much to rifle. A nice bed with some comfortable bedding. A glass-fronted wardrobe. A bedside table with an iPod Touch, a book of Raymond Carver short stories, a glass of water. Nothing on the walls. No personal touches. I checked in the wardrobe. Just clothes. I checked the iPod; he wasn't using it for email correspondence. Music. A GTD app. A golf app. I didn't know what I was looking for. I could hardly consider him a killer – *the* killer now. I suppose I was hoping to find something to do with those names I'd found at Odessa's place, or something that would incriminate Underdog; I wanted the unpleasant bastard to be true to type.

I found a laptop and a bunch of lever arch files in a small study that was also a repository for all the junk a person sworn to a minimalist life will hide away. Boxes of envelopes, Christmas decorations, tubs of bulbs, batteries, fuses and screws. A Hoover. A deckchair and a dismantled free-standing hammock.

I opened the laptop and saw a folder marked 'Dosh'. The files hinted at what Treacle... what Mr Malachi Dawe did for a living. It seemed he owned a property in Nottingham, a detached house in well-to-do Amber Heights that he was letting. The folder contained correspondence with his tenants and the letting agency, invoices from plumbers, electricians, cleaners and so on. Whatever profit he was making was keeping him in spaghetti down here while he cultivated his cheeky haircut and courted Odessa.

I went downstairs and there, framed and standing

alongside a telephone on an occasional table by the door, was the photograph Mawker had been so kind to tell me about. Odessa, Taft, Gower, Dawe, Underdog and… Sarah. They all looked as if they were trying to stifle laughter. Sarah was failing, her eyes crinkled, her hand raised to her gloriously wide mouth. It was a great picture, and I wanted it, I wanted the *her* part of it, but I couldn't touch it. I had to go. I opened the front door and the PC was standing in the road with his hand up. I hoped he might be hailing a taxi or trying to get the attention of the ice cream van rather than acknowledging the arrival of his superior officer.

No such luck.

'Ian,' I said, as he peeled himself out of the squad car. The PC wheeled around, shock on his features. Ian's face was damp and red. He hitched his trousers up and showed me his best waddling-duck-with-piles walk. I continued, enjoying everyone's aghast expressions. 'How utterly butterly it is to see your puce face gurning all over le fucking shop. I—'

I said no more because he got hold of my lapels and butted me. There was no great conviction behind it though. It was the headbutt of a man who has spent more time trying to extract it from the arseholes of the people who sign his monthly pay cheques. I was more shocked by its arrival than I was hurt by it. At least he'd steered clear of my swollen, purple nose. Maybe that had influenced the severity of his attack. He wanted to talk to me; he'd get no sense out of me if he compounded my earlier injury, or knocked me out.

He did some more hitching of trousers and straightening of shirt cuffs. His eyes were watering; there was every chance he'd hurt himself more than me. I remember at Bruche when we were doing our training we had a day of basic self-defence: pepper spray and baton use, restraint and escort techniques. Piss-poor and insufficient, but there it was; the need to balance the need to neutralise a threat with the proportional amount of force. The police were often hamstrung by this question of reasonable force and what it constituted. Mawker had been ineffective to say the least. To me, reasonable force was whatever I could do that would break the relevant bone supporting the weapon that was being pointed at me. Ian Mawker had moved like something freshly trapped in glue. He was no more able to deflect a strike to the head than he was likely to dress in a way that was appropriate to the current decade.

I touched my nose and checked my fingers. No blood. His face was tight with rage. He was rendered inarticulate by it. He looked like something pumped up beyond its natural capacity, like a bicycle tyre. He needed deflating. I didn't have a pin on me, so I told him he was a cock, oh, and while we're at it, a cunt.

'You are shitting in my bed, Sorrell,' he said. 'You are causing grief. You are putting people at risk with what you're doing.'

'What am I doing, Ian?' I said. 'Enlighten me.'

'You're stepping on my toes. You're impersonating a police officer, you're causing people distress. I could arrest you. I could tuck you away in a cell for a couple of days and have you cool down.'

'Do it,' I said. 'But I'll be in for a hell of a lot longer after I send your head up your arse.'

'You don't scare me, Sorrell,' he said. 'I deal with all manner of shitizens, every day of my life. You don't rank anywhere near the ugliest of them, unless we're talking looks.'

'Oh, I'm stung by that, Ian, I really am,' I said, hating the wheedling, riled-up voice in me. 'My daughter's at the centre of this and I'm not backing down. If you arrest me and she dies, you'll regret it, I fucking promise you that.'

He pushed me and I skipped and tripped and skidded down the steps. He joined me on street level and I shoved him back. PC Suckup was wringing his hands by the front door, checking the road again.

'The trouble with you, Ian,' I said, digging a forefinger into his ribs, 'is that you're so by-the-book, you're so chapter-and-verse that it wouldn't surprise me if you were made from recycled paper.'

'It's called *the law*, you fuckwit,' he said, grinding a fist into my shoulder. 'You are operating outside it. I am doing you a massive favour not arresting you. But you push me too far and—'

I got hold of his lapel tight, and then just as quickly dropped it. This was escalating. If *I* headbutted *him* I'd be locked up, despite his provocation. 'And what? You will bring me in? I've got a mate on a paper. Works in Liverpool but he's written for all the national dailies. I think he might be interested in the story of a man trying to save his daughter, and blocked at every turn from doing so by the rusty cogs of bureaucracy.'

'It's not red tape, it's the law. How many different ways do you need that pounded through your skull?' He thrust his thumb into my forehead. I slapped it away and steepled my fingers against his breastbone, pushed him back. His arse hit the squad car and the driver got out.

'I got some heat after that business with the Four-Year-Old,' I said. 'Offers of interviews. TV appearances. I turned them all down. Didn't want Sarah to see me injured, lapping up the praise. But it's banked me some column inches, Ian. I'll use them if I need to.'

'This is your final warning,' Mawker said. 'Stay out of it.'

I was walking to the Saab. 'I can't,' I said. 'You wouldn't, if it was you.'

'The difference is I've got the law on my side.'

'I've got the law too,' I snapped back, and slammed the door on him. I dragged down the sunblind; I keep a photograph of Sarah – a nice photo of her when she was eleven or twelve, before she discovered tattoos and piercings and boys and candid shots – in the little pocket up there. I took it down and stared at her pigtails, her gap-toothed smile. Rebecca shivered beneath her skin.

I whispered to them both: 'My law.'

17

That evening I drew a bath and settled into it with the book I'd bought that afternoon. I put on some music loud enough to drown out the couple next door who were either smashing their bed to bits with lump hammers or going at it like knives.

The book was a copy of the same book I'd found planted in Treacle's blood-spattered bathroom. The same book that had also been found at the murder site of Martin Gower, some distance away from the body. It was only now, armed with that knowledge, that I thought the book must have something to do with the killer rather than what the victim had been carrying around for his commute, or for a quiet half hour at lunchtime.

I leafed through the book, while the water – I always made my baths way too hot – lobstered my flesh and caused sweat to prickle in my hairline. It was an anthology of speculative fiction. The cover was of wind patterns in a sun-burnt desert. *Green and Pleasant Land: Valentines to a Dying Planet.* The publisher was an independent company called Leopard Books based in Crouch End.

Five of the contributors were listed on the cover: big names from the genre.

I flipped to the contents. Over twenty stories. I wondered if one of these authors was the person responsible for the deaths of Gower and Dawe. I imagined Mawker was thinking the same thing. I found myself wishing I could ask Romy what she thought, but it seemed even less relevant since there was no handwriting to study. I read the first story, a mildly diverting tale of scavengers sifting in post-apocalyptic dust for children's teeth; the currency of the future, according to the author.

I got out of the bath and moved – like some pink, steaming eructation – to the living room where I flung the windows wide open and tried to cool down with a heavily iced glass of Reyka. I picked up the phone and called the offices of Leopard Books. It was just this side of six p.m. so I was hopeful a slush-pile reader was still in the building. No response, but an answering message kicked in suggesting urgent calls be made to their on-call editor, a woman called Tula Barnes.

On-call editor... I liked that. A nice gimmick. But I bet the on-call editor didn't like it much.

'Hi,' she said. Her voice was deep and rich and sonorous. Plummy to the extreme. It couldn't have been plummier were she being teabagged by Christopher Plummer.

I told her who I was. I asked her if she'd had any difficulties with the writers who had submitted to the anthology. She sounded immediately guarded.

'What sort of problems?'

'You know... syntax difficulties, spelling errors, grammatical bollock-dropping... psychotic tendencies. Do any of your writers hold any grudges?'

She laughed. It sounded as though her jaw had been oiled by a few glasses of Chardonnay. She told me that there were more grudges in publishing than there were in any other profession. And probably in the criminal world too. I couldn't get a word in.

People wanted to be published, she went on. They saw the big deals and didn't appreciate how rare they were, how difficult it was to make any money, even if you were a seasoned professional. They thought that you only needed a pencil and some paper: there was no high cost outlay for specialist equipment. They saw the appeal of working from home. In your pyjamas. In bed, if you wanted to. The launch parties, the five-star reviews, the adulation. All that to produce what? A new book every two years? Money for nothing.

'Do—'

'But it's nothing like that,' steamrollered the publisher. 'Unless you're a bestseller. There are a hundred thousand books published each year, across all genres, shared between all the publishing houses. There are probably a hundred times that number of manuscripts that land on the desks of the publishing houses. The vast majority of people will be disappointed. Most people will never be published, unless they do it themselves. And they'll still not really be satisfied because, as pretty as you make it, it's still DIY. It'll cost you money. It's vanity publishing.'

'I just wanted to ask about the anthology. The Valentines to a Blah-blah Planetoid job.'

Her voice had grown spikes. 'The title is *Green and Pleasant Land: Valentines to a Dying Planet*. And I've already spoken to the police,' she said. 'I've helped them, fully, with their enquiries.'

So I was on the right track. But there was a tickle in her

voice – possibly that qualifier *fully* that seemed so eager to please – that suggested she was holding back on something.

'So you know there's a murder inquiry?'

'I know that much. I don't know any details. I don't want to know any details.'

'Did they take any materials away with them?' I asked. 'I'm presuming they came to see you.'

'They did,' she said. 'They asked to see files. They wanted our computers, our hard drives. We said no. They told us they could get a warrant. Our legal team reckons that's so much hogwash. Who are you anyway?'

'Suffice to say that I'm in with the local constabulary – Ian Mawker ring a bell? The guy with the lip ferret who wears macs in the hope of a Columbo vibe but ends up looking like Frank Spencer – and they'll not take kindly if they know you weren't fully co-operative.'

'I kept nothing from them,' she said. 'And you can't prove it.'

'I don't need to. I just need to sow the seeds of doubt in Mawker's brain. You don't know him like I do. He's thorough. If he thinks he's missed something, he'll take it as a personal affront. Do you want police cars keeping watch on you? Pulling you over half a dozen times a day for spot checks?'

'He'd never dare—'

'Okay. Well, my life is time sensitive even if yours isn't, so I'll get on the blower now and tell him you're playing hide the evidence.'

'It's not evidence. It's just the Valentines folder.'

'Why doesn't Mawker have the folder? What's in it?'

'Original manuscripts. Correspondence. Contracts.'

'It sounds as if that's the kind of thing they'd like to see.'

'And they will. But I need to copy it first. I can't risk it becoming lost. We're going to sanction a second printing off the back of this.'

'No such thing as bad publicity, eh?'

She seemed stung by that. 'It wasn't my idea, if you want the truth.'

'I don't care whose idea it was.'

'Patrick Simm,' she said, like the kid caught red-handed in the playground, desperate to pass the buck.

'Who's Patrick Simm?'

'He's an agent. One of his writers submitted to the anthology.'

'Where's he based?' I said.

'Albemarle Street,' she said, super-fast, all too happy to get me off her back. 'Patrick reckons we can all come out of this like cats in the cream.'

'There'll be stuff in that folder that the police can use. Evidence that could put somebody very dangerous away. Every minute you keep hold of that, with your thoughts full of cash, is another minute this lunatic is free. And another minute closer to another body. Let me come and take it off your hands.'

'I don't know who the bloody hell you are. You're not police. You could be him for all I know. This killer. This lunatic.'

I lost my temper then and started yelling at her. When I calmed down I could hear that she'd killed the line.

I wanted bed and Radio 3 and mano-a-cato wrestling bouts laced with vodka and bowls of wasabi nuts. But my free time had fucked off again, like a thief with a swag bag.

18

Patrick Simm was based on Albemarle Street, a pleasant road off Piccadilly filled with art galleries. He worked on his own and had garnered something of an aggressive reputation, working late when everyone else had bunked off, refusing to take no for an answer where his clients were concerned. He was known as the Honey Badger. I'd assumed he wouldn't be enamoured of this title, or at least be indifferent about it, but there, on a table after he'd buzzed me up to his first-floor office, was a stuffed honey badger in a glass case. The floor of this diorama was littered with bones, spectacles, bow ties and swatches of tweed. A shredded piece of paper with the word CONTRACT written at the top.

'Come in, young chap,' he said. 'My PA, Polly, is off shedding babies or some such. So I'm making my own tea and answering my own calls. Right. So, how can I divest you of your shirt?'

'Sorry?'

'Apologies... force of habit. It's my ice-breaker at meetings. What can I do for you? You mentioned on the phone something about cranks?'

'It's a little more serious than cranks,' I said. He gestured to a Windsor chair with a comb back. I sat down and refused his offer of tea. I wanted to get out of here. I didn't like his honey badger; it gave off a whiff of something chemical – formaldehyde, perhaps… naphthalene, I don't know – that hung heavily in the stuffy room and turned my stomach. I didn't like Simm either. I didn't like his pinstripe shirt and white collar, nor the way he didn't seem to blink at all, like a lizard.

'How do you mean?' he asked.

I didn't like his questions either. There was something… compliant about them, as if he was indulging me. As if he knew exactly what was going on.

'Two people are dead. We are assuming they were killed by the same person. The people who were killed were members of a writers' group.'

'A writers' group.' He couldn't keep the disdain from his voice.

'That's right,' I said. 'Based in London. A committed bunch of writers. What, that doesn't please you? There could be a future literary star in their midst. Someone you could play sycophantic parasite to.'

The shutters lowered on those unblinking eyes. 'It's not all about money, my job, you know. I offer a certain level of pastoral care to my clients, all of whom, it should be said, are very happy with the services I provide.'

'My apologies,' I said. 'I went for the theatrical perception of a ten-percenter, and I was wrong to do so.'

'You were,' he said. 'I charge twenty per cent.' The smile returned. It was like black poison spreading across his face.

'I think the person who did this has got some kind of

204

grudge. But it's become this twisted, personal thing. Obviously the killer is a psychopath. If you'd seen the bodies...'

'Spare me, please, Mr Sorrell,' Simm said, holding up his hands. 'I read a lot of unsavoury material during office hours. I don't need to hear about the real-life unpleasantness.'

'Something was found in the vicinity of both victims. A book. We don't yet know if it was something in their possession, or whether it was planted by the killer.'

'A calling card.'

'Maybe,' I said.

'The same book at both locations?'

I nodded.

'Seems unlikely to be a coincidence, wouldn't you say?'

'Unlikely, yes,' I said. 'But possible. People read.'

'Yes, but... what was this book?'

I told him.

'Hmm,' he said, and steepled his fingers, rested his bottom lip against them. His fingers were thin and long. 'You've spoken to Tula Barnes I take it?'

'Yes, she told me to speak to you.'

He smiled. It was the smile of a shark before it bites your leg off. 'Delightful woman. Pissed as a nappy half the time, mind.'

'Anyway,' I said. 'This book.'

'Commercially speaking, short stories aren't the thing these days,' he said. 'Novels are where it's at. Most people don't read short stories, more's the pity.'

'So you're saying it's probably a plant. Because of current tastes.'

'Well, a big name can sometimes carry what otherwise might be seen as a niche product.'

'I think the killer might be one of the writers.'

'Why?' he asked. He was smiling. Again I got the feeling he knew more than he was letting on. I wanted to jab a finger at his face and get him to blink. I had the fear he might only do so when alone, and then with some kind of third eyelid.

'I have no idea. But two of these writers in this group evidently did something to piss off this maniac. Maybe he was a member once upon a time. Maybe, when he asked for feedback, they gave it to him. And he didn't like it.'

'You think he killed people because his ego was bruised?'

'Happens all the time.'

'And he left a copy of the book with them to show that he had the last laugh? Difficult to enjoy that kind of victory when the reader is no longer capable of reading.'

'It's my understanding that he spent some quality time with them before he ended their lives.'

'Ah,' Simm said. 'How pleasant.'

'So I just wanted to talk with some industry professionals and see if they might have heard of any... strange goings on. I'm guessing you all have fingers in each other's pies... You go to the same book fairs, you know the same people, the same names in the same publishing houses bid for your writers... Have you heard anything on the grapevine?'

'No,' he said. All too quickly. And with that little smile on his face. His stare dared me to contradict him.

I sighed and sat back. His desk was one of those beautiful old things with a leather top. Way too big for anybody, apart from maybe generals and majors pushing plastic tanks around a map. There was a penis substitute fountain pen, and an ostentatious bottle of violet ink. A letter opener. A tiny red laptop that was probably just blushing at the ridiculous proportional contrast. A handwritten note that was half concealed by a book on top. It was signed *Pol*. My eye lingered on what text I could read:

tand, Pat, I'm not
ed to come in under
ances. I fully accept
ind another PA. I need
hink things over. I had
shock, you must see that.
y mother's until next week.
mber (only in emergencies) is

And then he must have noticed my scrutiny because he casually slid the book further over so that the entire letter was obscured. I'd seen the number, though. A Brighton number. I feverishly repeated it in my mind until I had it fixed there. I had no idea what I intended to do, but I knew Simm wasn't sharing his sweets with me and I needed some leverage from somewhere. This so-called baby machine Polly – who had clearly been scared out of town by something – might provide it.

'You're always on the lookout for a fresh angle, I'd have thought. Is that right, Mr Simm?'

'I'm always on the lookout for impactful writing. A strong voice.'

'But the zeitgeist exists, and you must have an eye on its coat-tails, if you're a successful agent.'

'Is there a point to this? Christ, *you're* not a writer are you? If you are I hope you can spin a story better than you vocalise one.'

'My point is that this hack… if he is a disgruntled writer, you might be able to make some dirty coin off the back of his arrest. If, say, there was a manuscript that he'd written. If, say, he'd submitted it to an agency with a view to securing representation.'

Simm blinked at last. It was a slow blink, the kind one affords an imbecile just before one explains what it is about them that is so imbecilic.

'We get a lot of manuscripts every week,' he said. He indicated a pile four feet high in one corner of the room. 'Those are submissions I received just this month. I'd say maybe one manuscript in every fifty is worth reading to the end. All those hundreds of manuscripts… I might take on two or three new clients a year. How many of those tomes are written by whackos? All of 'em. Some of my best clients are utter fruit bats. Writers, Mr Sorrell. All of them self-obsessed, paranoid pricks. They magpie feelings, emotions, episodes witnessed in other people's lives, rehash it all and serve it up as original fiction, framed in a nice little plotty world. It's all lies. Badly written lies at that. I polish turds for a living. That's ninety per cent of what I do.'

'So nothing out of the ordinary?'

'Define "ordinary".'

'Never mind,' I said. 'I can find my own way out.'

I resisted the urge to kick his stupid glorified weasel display across the room. I said, 'Any more bloodshed it's on your hands. And I will come for you. I'll staple your eyelids to your fucking forehead and then you won't be able to blink even if you want to.'

I called the number as soon as I was at street level. I walked towards Bond Street and shot a glance at his office window. He was there, behind the net curtains, like an etiolated revenant in a black-and-white horror film who did his own stunts and didn't need make-up.

She picked up and she sounded raw, on edge.

'Is this Polly?'

'Yes,' she said. 'Who are you?'

'He's killed twice, you know. Martin Gower in Enfield and Malachi Dawe in Shepherd's Bush. That one was just today. He'll kill again. How do we stop him, do you think?'

'Are you police? Did you speak to Patrick?'

'He told me you were having a baby.'

'He what?' There was a knocking, and a muffled thump; I thought she'd either dropped the phone or hurled it across the room. 'The bloody bastard,' she said, eventually. 'The bloody fool bastard.'

'What happened, Polly... may I call you Polly? What happened to get you riled up? Why did you leave work and go to your mother's?'

She sounded guarded and scared. But also, it seemed, on the brink of gushing, as if she'd been desperate for the opportunity to divest herself of some onerous burden, or shackles that had been locked around her wrists by a *Mellivora capensis* with an overactive thyroid.

'I open his post. All the letters and bills, and all the manuscripts too. I have to separate the material sent by clients from the hopefuls, you know...'

'The slush pile. The chaff. Yes, I saw it. I asked Patrick if there'd been anything delivered that was out of the ordinary.'

I heard another noise now, another muffled thump, though this resolved itself into a sob. When she came back on her voice was strangled with emotion. 'He took it off me as soon as he heard me... as soon as I opened it. He heard me. I suppose I must have sworn, or made some sort of noise. A cry of disgust.'

I rubbed my face. Polly sounded like the kind of highly strung individual who would make a noise of horror if someone opened a curtain too quickly, or overcooked a boiled egg.

'What was it?'

'There was blood,' she said. 'A manuscript. Horrible thing. Dirty. Fingerprints. Typed on the back of pre-used pages. Circulars. It was stained with coffee. Wine. Other stuff...'

'This can't be the first time you received anything... dodgy through the post,' I said. 'Don't you have some sort of company policy?'

'Usually we'd bin it straight away. And report it to the police. But Simm swept it all up and took it into his office.'

'Anything with an address on it?'

'I read some of it. The first page. I don't usually; it's not my job of course, but I needed to know... I needed to know what kind of mind could produce something like that.'

'An address, Polly.'

'It was terrible. Ugly. Inhuman. It wasn't fiction. It was fact dressed up as fiction. But Simm was adamant. He said we needed to keep it just in case it turned out to have something to do with the murders. He said we'd all be rolling in clover if he could represent a mad man.'

'Polly, who sent it?'

'I don't know – it talked about dismemberment. How difficult it is to take a body to pieces.'

'Where is it now? Can you get it?' I didn't want to shout in case she dropped the phone again and the link was lost; I doubted she'd pick up again. Despite that I wanted to reach through the wires and grab her around the throat and throttle an answer out of her. I wasn't sure she could even hear me any more.

But then: 'It will be in his safe. In the office. Unless he took it home with him.'

Every possibility, every chance to get nearer to this killer seemed to fork into multiple options. Not for the first time I wished for access to the police's resources.

'Do you have the combination to his safe?' I asked.

'Yes. But I don't want to have to touch it again. I washed and washed my hands…'

'Polly, I just need to see it. Maybe just take one page. We need something to work with. Patrick might be in danger.'

'And me too,' she said, in a voice leaden with awful epiphany.

'We're all at risk,' I said. 'Anyone caught up in this.'

She gave me Simm's home address and the office safe's access code and told me again, firmly, that she would help me no further. Her tone was relaxing though, softening. I was gearing up to try to work on her to go to the office for me when she gently put the phone down.

I nipped into a bar and ordered a beer. I stared at it and wondered what to do. I could march back to the Honey Badger's lair and force him to hand over the manuscript or I could go to his house and wait for him there; either choice, though attractive because it meant I'd get to manhandle the oily wanker, would only mean settling myself even deeper in to the trough of shit outside Mawker's door. Simm might be seriously hindering progress on this case but I would be involved in an assault charge if I wasn't careful.

And there was always the possibility that this grubby stack of pages might just have nothing to do with the deaths, a writer who hadn't observed the basic list of dos and don'ts involved when submitting work for consideration. But I couldn't entertain that possibility. I knew in my tripes that this was a bona fide lead. Simm knew it too, and wanted to get rich off the back of it. I swallowed half the pint, then the rest, trying to get the vile flavours of his intentions out of my mouth. Fuck the assault charge: I was going to pan the cunt.

I got back to his office and leaned on the buzzer. No response. I stepped back into the road and scanned his windows but there were no umbrella-eyed ghosts capering at the curtains. He'd gone out possibly to butter up some unscrupulous publisher with pound signs branded on his heart.

I buzzed the other offices but nobody was home, or they'd decided against letting in the shady character they could see on their entry cameras.

I went around the back. There was a fire escape but it looked rustier than Ian Mawker's pick-up lines. I'd have to chance it. There was a wall topped with razor wire so I tossed my jacket over and climbed up; I left the jacket where it was in case I needed to make a quick escape, then headed up the fire escape. As soon as I planted one boot upon it I knew it was fifty-fifty as to whether it would stay attached to the wall, or me to the stairs. It was corroded right through in places. It was like trying to climb a series of wafers.

Central London. Late. Me climbing the wall of a prominent building in an affluent area. Me, not looking affluent. Me, looking effluent. I was bound to be spotted. I reckoned I had ten minutes. Which probably meant five.

I took baby steps all the way. The fire escape groaned and swayed, and dry red rain landed in my hair and on my shoulders. I could see the screws and bolts dancing in their sockets. I reached an opaque window with a crack running diagonally through it. A toilet on Simm's floor. I placed my boot against the glass and tested it. The putty was old and crumbly. The crack spawned others. I pressed harder, trying to resist the temptation to kick the thing in as hard as possible. I didn't want to attract any unwarranted attention, nor sever my femoral artery. A large wedge of glass came free. I was able to waggle the rest loose after that.

I slipped into a narrow WC made narrower by cairns of toilet paper rolls ranged along one wall. There was a smell of apple Glade, bleach, and something older and more acrid. Simm's piss, most likely. Out into a gloomy corridor. There were the stairs I'd taken earlier. I went into Simm's office, fully expecting him to be sitting behind his desk perfecting his gecko look. But the room was empty. I checked his drawers in case he'd positioned the manuscript close to hand but he kept only the usual desk accoutrements here: business cards, comp slips, notebooks and pens.

I found his safe inside an attractive oak cupboard. Once I'd dialled in the combination, I opened it and looked inside. A tin of petty cash, some signed contracts. And a buff-coloured A4 envelope inside a clear plastic bag. I took it out, holding it gingerly by the edges. There were no stamps on it, no evidence of it having been fed through a franking machine. The address itself was restricted to SIMM. ALBEMARLE. No return details.

I teased the lips of the envelope open and slipped the manuscript out. No covering letter. No address. A musty, dusty exhalation. I was reminded of old school libraries, mushrooms, wet, autumnal woodlands. There was dried blood on the paper, smears and flecks and droplets. It was creased and torn and aged. But it was not all here. The manuscript started at page 244. Presumably Simm had hived off the first half of it, including whatever prefatory material the writer had included, to take home to read.

There was another envelope in the safe too. Smaller. Inside this were a series of short notes to Simm, ostensibly from the killer, detailing what he'd done, where, and to whom. These were details that only the police or the killer could know. Or me.

I stood there, stomach churning, trying to process this, how Simm must have been allowing the deaths to happen knowing that each one might add a zero to any eventual confession.

I borrowed one of Simm's envelopes and slid into it half a dozen pages from the middle of the manuscript. Then I took a selfie with the manuscript in front of his safe and emailed it to him, along with the message: *You think you're going to get rich off the back of this wanker but you're just as much in his sights as anybody. Maybe more so. I can help you. It's either that or prison for you, you grievous fuckhead.*

I left then, before the residents of W1S could nail me. Maybe they'd kept quiet, afraid of this leather-jacketed Spider-Man. Or more likely ashamed of the rusted fire escape.

19

I'd made it to Crawford Street, determined to give Mawker Simm's head on a platter, when a bronze Audi screeched to a halt in the middle of the road and Underdog leapt out of the passenger seat.

'Get in,' he said.

'Get fucked,' I said. 'I'm busy.'

He lifted the bottom of his hoodie and showed me the butt of a handgun sticking from his waistband – what looked like a Browning pistol; easy to get hold of, even for a tourist like this joker.

'Oh, the experience of buying a gun. I bet you called it a "piece", didn't you? I bet you handed over a "ton" for it, in used twenties.'

'Get in,' he said again. His face was pale and greasy. His eyes, usually so scornful and languid, now could not be more agitated. The 'little boy lost' shimmered just beneath the skin. I got in the back of the car and Underdog slid in beside me. The Browning, like most guns bought in the city on the black market, was probably just for show. A frightener. You had to pay extra for bullets (or 'food' as it was known) and once fired, your gun was unlikely ever to be sold again.

Odessa was behind the steering wheel. She looked similarly pale but it was countered by the inner steel she carried, a gutsiness that Underdog could only acquire by play-acting. But I still suspected him, nonetheless. I still looked at him askance. I imagined him puncturing and hacking. I could see him happily foisting pain and suffering in some twisted, retributive act.

Underdog slammed the door and we took off. I felt myself being pressed back into the leather.

'Nice car,' I said. 'What happened? Did you win first prize in a limerick competition?'

'You know, if I ever had to use this gun on you, I'd shoot it through your cocky fucking mouth first. I mean, don't you ever shut the fuck up?'

'Shutting the fuck up, sir,' I said.

He sighed and there were all kinds of defeat in it. 'You're a pain in the arse, Corkscrew,' he said. And then: 'Sorrell.'

'Ah,' I said. 'You've done some sleuthing. How did you find out?'

'It wasn't hard,' Underdog said. Triumph laced his voice. 'I thought there was copper in you so I went and asked the coppers down at Savile Row nick. "Anyone know this gobby scarface who's always sticking his nose in where it's not wanted?" Turns out you're not a copper. At least not any more. Turns out you're not as anonymous as you'd like to think. They were queuing up to tell me who you were and what a monumental pain in the arsehole you are. One of them even told me you lived on Homer Street. Ask a policeman, they say. Too right.'

'Well done,' I said, making a mental note to scour the

cunts at West End Central, find their snitch and perform the Riverdance on his face. 'So why don't we stop playing silly buggers and come clean on everybody's name. I'm fed up of all this *Mission Impossible* shit.'

'Fuck you,' Underdog said. 'I know you. You don't need to know m—'

'He's Sean. Sean Niker,' said Odessa. 'I'm Kim Pallant.'

'Did you have to do that?' Sean asked. He sounded like the kid at a party whose balloon has been popped.

'It's over, Sean,' Kim said. 'The Accelerants are finished.'

'Why are we doing this then?' I asked. 'Presumably you stole this car? We could have just met in the pub and chatted over nibbles.'

'It wasn't my idea,' Kim said. She was pasting it along the Euston Road, weaving in between the traffic, honking the horn as she approached pedestrian crossings, giving everyone at least a fighting chance to stay alive. At any other time I'd have been happy for her to ferry me around in a flashy machine like this, but fifty miles per hour in a thirty zone was giving me sphincter twitch. And the gun that Niker had pulled from his waistband didn't help.

'Where are we going?' I asked.

'We're going to shut the fuck up,' Niker said. 'I'm still in this. For the long haul, even if everyone else has wimped out.'

'For "wimped out" read "brutally murdered",' I reminded him. But he was in rant mode.

'My pursuit of experience, my euphoria, has not ended.'

A police car came howling out of Shepherdess Walk, skidding on to our tail so closely that I could see the light reflecting in the glasses of the driver.

The shock of it almost caused Kim to oversteer but she righted the car at the last moment, although I heard the kerb scrape against the expensive paintwork. Sirens wailed.

'How's your euphoria now?' I shouted.

We carried on along Bethnal Green Road before turning south through Stepney.

'You have to stop, Kim,' I shouted. 'You can't win this one!'

But she was deep in concentration, or she was choosing to ignore me. She turned sharp left on to Commercial Road. People backed off, or shot footage on their smartphones. Other cars were sounding their horns, maybe in support, more probably in condemnation. Sirens looped and twisted above the din: backup for the tenacious driver sticking with us as we belted east.

Kim nicked a thin roadside tree with the front nearside wing and I saw it split in two. The shock from the collision snapped my head back and wrenched the car to the left. Kim floored the accelerator and took us up a narrow alleyway. People screamed and swore. If she hit anyone, add x number of years to the rapidly accelerating count already on the wheel of incarceration.

Bags of rubbish erupted as she hit them and flung their slimy, rotting compost over the windscreen. The wipers succeeded only in smearing it more completely across the glass. She hit a hopper and it barrelled away in front of us, but something had happened to the car. A heavy, metallic clacking that sounded terminal. Our speed dropped off.

'Shit,' said Sean.

'You'd better lose that gun,' I said. 'Or you'll be looking at a ten stretch. At least.'

He turned in his seat and pointed the muzzle at me instead.

'Niker. Load that thing first. Then play "noisy penis compensation".'

'I think there's one in the chamber. To tell you the truth, in all this excitement I kind of lost track.'

'Christ,' I said. 'You really are a brain-dead twunt, aren't you?' I punched him in the eye and the gun went off about three inches north of my skull. The world went very quiet and I was momentarily blinded. Gunshot residue, I was guessing. It felt as though a thimbleful of hot sand had been thrown in my face. The only thing I *could* hear – though dully, as if coming to me through many layers of thick blanket (was I asleep? God yes, please make this a bad dream) – was the rise and fall of sirens. More than one, now, unless my insulted brain was fashioning elaborate echoes.

Somehow the car had stopped, the doors opened, and I was being led, blinking, eyes streaming, through dingy little veins of road and pathway, all of them furred with fly-tipped junk, all of them hazy with the feral mist of several species' worth of male piss. We climbed over fences and pushed our way through body-high walls of nettles. A police helicopter was blatting towards us; we had to find safe ground before it reached us or there'd be no escape. We scrambled across a no-man's land of back yards stippled with dog shit and puddles of electric-blue petrol. Big dogs on chains with jaws the size of firefighters' hydraulic cutting tools. Up stone steps carpeted with dead beetles and pebbles of reinforced glass. Along corridors lit by stuttering fluorescent tubes. Down scaffolds, feet slapping on duckboards. The shiver of brick netting. Yells of pursuit falling away. And then we were on level ground, down by the river somewhere. I had no idea where I was. This area might well be pink space on a map of uncharted territory. A sketch of a serpent and a warning: *Here be Dragons*. Christ I needed a beer and a lie down and Romy telling me how shit I was because my 'd' was too small.

I felt his punch before it landed; it seemed to push the air before it. It certainly pushed the air out of me. I fell to my knees and he punched me again, right on that painful little knot of nerves and glands at the top of the jaw. I couldn't see him to stop him; Kim's shouts at him to leave me alone were being ignored. A shadow fell across me; I pushed myself to one side and swept my leg around in a wide arc. I connected with leg. I hoped it wasn't Kim's. Niker's grunt as he landed confirmed I'd made the right choice. He swore and scrabbled after me, but now I knew what direction he was in I could keep all my dangerous edges pointed his way. I thrust a boot out when I sensed he was close enough and enjoyed the satisfying crunch as his nose became so much red putty in the centre of his face. That ended it. He was choking on blood, and reaching again for the gun. Kim screamed at him and slapped his hand down. She took him off to one side and tended to his blitzed schnozz with a handkerchief. By degrees she calmed him, though he didn't stop shooting me malicious looks every few seconds. It looked as if she had given him some instructions because he nodded twice and then sloped away, like a dog that has been reprimanded after shitting in the bath.

A jet took off, arse-shrivellingly close. City Airport? And when it faded, I could hear my hot, hard breathing, and that of another.

'Kim?' I asked. My eyes were still stinging, grit-filled. I felt as if I'd shifted a gallon of fluid from my tear ducts alone.

'You pair of testosterone pillocks,' she said. She tugged at my sleeve and cajoled when I stopped to hack my lungs up into my mouth.

'Am I shot?' I asked. I kept touching my head, where the heat of the round had burned my skin, and my hand kept coming away wet, but I could feel no wound.

'Don't be stupid,' she said. 'Sean put a hole in the roof. You were lucky.'

'So was he,' I said. 'Where is he?'

'Nearby.'

'Where are we going?'

She stilled me. 'Let's have a look at your face,' she said.

I couldn't keep my eyes open for longer than a second. Then blessed relief: she was splashing water on my face, irrigating my eyes, chasing away what felt like jags of hot glass.

'Can I have a swig of that?' I asked, and she put the bottle in my hand. 'What's going on?'

'Niker's convinced you have something to do with this. That you might actually be the killer.'

My sight was improving. We had entered a blasted land of derelict buildings: mills and warehouses and factories. We went inside one of them. I could see concourses of fractured concrete, sun-ravaged safety notices on walls topped with copings of shattered glass. There was a stormguard door in faded metallic blue with a sign painted on it in stark white capitals: IN CONSTANT USE. Barrels, a plastic chair, hubcaps, chicken wire. Arcane machinery frozen by time and oxidisation; valves and springs and pistons. Every pane smashed; every door sagging on buckled, rusted hinges. All of it could be fifty years old for all I knew. It seemed as if nobody had visited this district for decades. Dust was thicker than palace carpets.

Instead of gunsmoke and blood I could smell the river. And something Kim was wearing. Something subtle, something floral.

'It's strange knowing your real name,' I said. 'You look like an Odessa, weird as that might sound. You don't fit Kim quite as well, somehow.'

'This experience thing,' she said. 'Sometimes I think it's getting out of hand. Sometimes I think it's the best thing anybody could do. I've never felt so alive.'

'I'm happy for you,' I said. 'I'm happy to be experiencing your experiential joy right now.'

She ignored me. There was misery in her voice, despite the smile on her face. 'You know how this started for me? I've been thinking about it. I guess I must have been about seven or eight. We were learning stuff at school, science stuff. Temperatures. Expansions and contraction. I remember drinking super-cold iced drinks followed by cups of tea I'd scald my lip against. All so I could crack my teeth. I'm having enormous problems with the dentist now, but that's how I got the bug. Pushing myself to do crazy shit.'

'Crazy shit,' I said. 'I saw some crazy shit once. Not long after a dog ate a box of crayons.'

'What are you up to?' she asked. 'What is it you want from all of this?' There were a hundred stories I could spin. Anything to gain more time, to win back some trust. I guessed she liked me; I guessed she wanted to believe me, to be on my side, even though Niker felt the polar opposite. But I was tired of lying. It didn't matter any more. They knew me, I knew them. Nothing mattered except one thing.

'Solo,' I said. 'I know who she is. Her name is Sarah. I'm her father. I'm trying to find her. She was involved with Martin Gower.'

'I see,' she said. 'Well, you've got the lying skills for a career as a storyteller.'

'Have you seen her?'

'I told you, her attendance is erratic.'

'Do you know where she lives?'

'No. We all thought she lived with Martin. They seemed pretty close.'

'Martin lived with his parents.'

'So we gathered. You wouldn't think it, to listen to him. Mister Independent. Strong-minded. Used to take over our meetings. And then went home and got his mum to wash his socks.'

'What's she like?'

'I've never met Martin's mum.'

I gave her a look. 'You know who I'm talking about. I haven't seen her for five years. She was a kid when she ran away. She's an adult now. I'm not going to get those years back.'

Kim spread her hands. 'What do you want me to say? She was funny. Had some lip on her. Like you.'

'Is she a good person? I mean, would you say she was happy? Does she have… you know, people she can turn to if she needs them? Does she have a job?'

'I liked her, Corkscrew,' she said. 'She seemed streetwise. In control. I didn't see her too often. We didn't really talk. I read some of her stuff.'

'What did she write about?'

'Why don't you ask her that yourself, when you see her?'

I couldn't speak for a moment. I didn't know how to answer her. 'What will you do?' I said.

'Now? Lay low, I suppose. Write about it.'

'It's what the police would advise. It's clear this killer has a beef with you lot for some reason.'

'I don't believe it's an ex-member,' she said. 'The ones who left went abroad. Only President is still around, and he got out because he wants to write music.'

I wondered if that was the case. I was going to ask her if she really thought Niker was to be trusted, when he turned up on a motorbike, a knackered Suzuki Bandit. He didn't switch off the engine. He didn't take off his helmet. Through the visor I could see his eyes, like two pork pies with slits in them. Kim went to him and got on the back.

'It's an offence to ride without a helmet,' I said.

'It's an offence to steal a motorbike,' said Niker. 'So arrest us.'

'What about me?' I asked. 'You drag me halfway across London and then just maroon me? What about the experience of three on a bike?'

Kim waved. 'Check the drop from time to time,' she said. 'We left a warning for Solo. You never know.' Then they took off.

BLONDE ON A STiCK –
30 APRiL 1988 – ???

The manuscript was odds on favourite for the Big Black Bin, but that was before Roper came in with the coffee. Caffeine was his panacea for the Monday morning depressions he fell into when he shambled into the office. It was something that could have been cured by a simple furniture change, re-decoration, maybe even a couple of prints to brighten the walls but he was damned if it would come out of his pocket. No. Cofee was an immediate solution and it sufficed.

He was Don Philbert, editor of *Dark Candy*, a monthly magazine devoted to the macabre. It was a rag that had lasted ten years and he had been a co-founder along with Ralph McKean. Ralph had been claimed by throat cancer a year after the launch, lumbering Philbert with the unenvioable task of trying to make a success out of things. Which he did, partly through his own motivation, partly through a resurging interest in horror and fiction, and mostly due to a lucky break when James Herbert gave him a story back in 1982 which got *Dark Candy* noticed. That year also saw them rise from small press status into what Philbert called

'The Big Kids' Playground'. For him, the most important part of this promotion was the freedom to offer tempting payments for submissions. And he was inundated every day of the week – some of the manuscipts were top class – perhaps too good for *Dark Candy* (something Philbert would never admit to).

This particular morning was quite possibly the worst Monday since creation. A nuclear winter he decided would be mild compared to this. He climbed the steps to his office, noticing the crisp packet that was still pushed deep into the pointing of the brickwork. It had been there for at least five years. He couldn't care less.

The wind howled its annoyance when he closed the door behind him and sent a sudden barrage for rain to strafe the wiundows but Philbret was already at the stairs, shrugging off his mac and scarf and making yet another ascent. His mind flirted briefly with the idea that the steps, varnished wooden risers, should by now be displaying signs of age and excessive wear but no dips were apparent, only a few scuffs and scratches.

And it smelled here in this dark passage – some cat had magicked its way in and decorated with walls with a coating of urine or a rat had crawled under the stairs to die.

Philbret's office was L-shaped. From his seat he had a view of the entire room. Across from his was the large conference table he would use to interview any new masters of the genre (and wasn't that a laugh) for his Grave Words column. The last one had been a carpet-fitter from Hull called Nigel Willett who had a lisp and chronic halitosis.

Now Philbert opened one of the latest submission envelopes with his paper knife, its sheen considerably dulled from years of cutting, and pulled out the manuscript. What's this? He thought. The manuscript was an utter mess. It had been typed on the back of milk receipts, used envelopes, letters from the Gas Board, even on a section of cardboard from a box of Coco Pops. Coffee stains were on every 'page', the typing was atrocious and a basic knowledge of spelling was aparetnly lacking.

"What's THIS?!" He was getting angry. The gall of the man. And no SAE! The bastard. Right. He was going to... there was an accompanying letter with the story, slipped in between the fourth and fifth pages, almost as an afterthought.

Mr philbot.

itS TIME YOU HAD ONE OF MY STORYS. SEND THECHEQ THIS ~~WEEJ~~ WEEK.

ROMAN FORREST

It was getting comical. The name was obviously contrived – a fabrication that reeked with pretension. And for the man to virtually demand publication... What a colossal impertinence. Philbert laughed it off. He would perform an Elvis Presley and Return to Sender, but not before ripping this effort to shreds.

BLONDE on aSTIKC
By ROMAN FORREST

He loved knifes. Yeah. He loved there sharpness and beauty. He loved the way they could cut and slice flesh, the slick oily blood what coated the metal after...

What kind of ungrammatical crap was this? Philbert found his 'trigger' finger itching to shoot this Forrest into the ground and he pulled one of his rejkection slips close. But now his mood had lightened. Coffe,e, shelter from the storm, a comfortable leather chair. And he was a story that might give him a chuckle. He left the rejection slip alone and returned to the first page. He could play God to it later.

> …coated the cold metal after digging it in deep into unsuspecting victims and tugging through skin and grissle. Yeah, Jethro love playing with his knifes they was his toys…

At lunch time Philbret took the story down to the local pub – The EMPTY COW – and finished it off over a chicken pie and Guinness.

> …and then Jethro pulled thr knife out of his head and licked the blade clean. A nasty laugh rose into the night getting louder and louder. It only stopped when he begun to cry, kneeling over the girl with the knife in his hand.
>
> "I only wanted you to bleed on me,' he whispered, softly. "Is that such a crime?"
>
> A single teardrop splashed on the kniofe, making it glint in the moonlight.

THE END

Philbert paid for his lunch and walked back to the office, his trigger finger throbbing.

Dear Mr Forrest.

Have you ever been to school? If not, perhaps you ought to try it. It will help your spelling. I received (NB 'I' after 'e' except after 'c') your story but have to send it back for the following reasons:

A)   It was poorly presented.
B)   It was almost illegible.
C)   It was UTTER CRAP.

As you have not sent an SAE I will be forced to hold on to your story until you send return postage. Please do not send any more stories. If you have to submit them, sumbit them to a dustbin. Preferably one which is open.

Yours, DP.

Almost as soon as Philbert signed the letter he realised, with swooning dismay, that he did not have an address to send it to. It was pathetic. Even if he wanted to, he couldn't send the cheque this comedian wanted. With a cry of anger and frustration – Gaaaagh! – he threw the manuscript, complete with jam and coffee stains, into the bin.

The next day there was an envelope bearing Forrest's handwriting. There was a dead sparrow inside. And a letter.

Mr Philbot. I ET THIS BIRDS GUTS. I WUNDER HOW YORS TAYST. PUBLISH BLONDE ON A STIKC. PUT THE CHEQ IN THE POST. I HOPE YOU LIKD MY STORY. ROMAN FORREST.

Philbret scrunched the letter up and hurled it into the bin with enough force to create a dull clang. His fingers jittered for a moment. He'd had hate-mail before thanks to his style of criticism but the bird had shocked him. Usually it was along the lines of: You blind bastard. You wouldn't see a good story if it hit you. That's the last story you get from me.' But he was dealing with a nutter here. He

20

managed to find a taxi near the factory; a driver who had pulled off the main drag to eat a sandwich and read the *Daily Express*. I offered him a ton if he'd take me to Mayfair – I wanted a word with President, aka Craig Taft – and he asked if I wanted some of his sandwich. I was going to say no but then I realised I hadn't eaten for hours. I gratefully stomached it and it was not bad either: tuna and mayonnaise with tiny cubes of celery and cucumber and red pepper mixed up in it with lemon juice and lots of black pepper. It hurt like motherfuckers to eat, mind. Niker's blows bitched at me from under the skin. My entire head felt like a balloon inflated to breaking point.

We were slipping through Whitechapel (police helicopter still prowling around), night thick as nan's gravy, when my phone vibrated.

'Hi, Phil,' I said, through a jaw tender with raw pain. It would stiffen tonight. I'd be lucky if I managed to open it enough to be able to lick a stamp by tomorrow.

'How were your lamb chops?'

'Gnawed to the bone.'

'And the blow job? Gnawed to the bone too?'

'Nice... now hear this... it seems there was some calling card after all.'

'Beyond the book?'

'I heard about that. But yes, something else, something subtle, definitely left on the body.'

'Go on.'

'Both Martin Gower and Malachi Dawe were fond of tattoos. I found evidence of recent ink deposits in the lymph nodes of both victims, though on first appraisal, neither man wore tattoos you could describe as being other than a few years old.'

Kim had a tattoo, as did Sean Niker. I thought of the photographs of Sarah. The illegible tattoo beneath her left breast. I wondered if the killer was some kind of body mod fetishist, or a mental tattooist who wanted his ink back.

Clarke went on: 'It seems that something was added to the designs on their arms. Dawe had a full sleeve of mainly tribal art. Celtic designs and so forth. Gower had fewer tattoos, but they were more abstract stuff. More complex. A phoenix. Angels.'

'Get on with it, Clarkey.'

'Well, it seems text was added. Crudely. We're talking pins and biro ink here. But nestled in among the elaborate stuff. And small. I only caught it because the light favoured the new ink in a way that it didn't the rest.'

'What text?' My heart was shifting like Lemmy's thumb playing 'Ace of Spades'.

'On Malachi Dawe the words were "Maximum Creep". On Gower, "Maggot-Hearted You". Mean anything? Elaborate insults?'

'Maybe. Maybe something else. They sound like titles.'

'The titles to your autobiographies, maybe?'

'Cheers, Phil,' I said. 'Manhattans on me next time.'

I just about had the phone back in my pocket when it buzzed again. Simm, this time.

'Hello, honey,' I said.

'There are very strict laws in this country regarding the breaking and entering of private property.'

'Who said anything about B&E? I was just on my daily parkour jaunt and I fell through your dodgy khazi window. You're lucky I didn't cut myself or I'd sue your badger sac off.'

'I've already talked to lawyer friends, Sorrell. You don't have a leg to stand on. You even sent picture evidence of yourself in my office. Your arrogance is matched only by your stupidity.'

I could imagine his face and those blinkless eyes: Michael Caine meets Salman Rushdie via owls. Honey Badger my arse. I bet behind his back everyone, including his clients, called him Reptile Cuntlord.

'I'm ready to play *Who's the Naughtiest?*' I said. 'I'm willing to go to prison for trespassing on your property and noseying through your files. But you'll have some questions to answer too, regarding obstructing the police. Those nasty little love letters you've been collecting. Especially if this psycho gets his tools out for another one.'

'There's no evidence to suggest this is the same person,' Simm said, not unreasonably. I might have concurred had I not spoken to Phil Clarke. 'What if it's all a grand old game, in the spirit of the surrealists? A new kind of novel?'

'*Maggot-Hearted You*,' I said, thinking of the extra ink on Martin Gower. 'Does that ring any bells? Sounds like a novel, doesn't it? Something a horror writer might come up with. Something you received and chucked in the No Chance tray? Did you send him a form rejection? Or did you add some juicy little barbs? I bet you did. How about *Maximum Creep*? Title of a book? Or what I'll chisel on your headstone when Hackboy decides to pay you a visit?'

'Why should he pay *me* a visit?' Simm asked, but his voice was changing. It was defensive, edged with petulance. The kind of bitterness found in the voices of children who are being denied a treat for misbehaviour. 'I'll likely be able to sell this stuff now that he has a... profile.'

'A profile? Jesus Christ, Simm, the guy is a balls-out bedlamite. And it's too late. The damage is done. He's on the publishing shit list thanks to you, and that writers' group, and God knows how many publishers he approached directly. He knows that his magnum opus doesn't get published unless he's dead or in jail.'

There was silence for a while. The taxi turned into The Mall. I caught a glimpse of the mounted cavalry troopers at Horse Guards Parade.

'I'll split it with you,' he said. 'Fifty-fifty.'

'He'll split you fifty-fifty.'

'Think about it. Sleep on it.'

'I haven't got the time. Nor have you. You think he doesn't know where you live? You think you're safe?'

'I'm at a hotel.'

'See? You know the score. You're visible and you won't accept it. I'm talking to the police tomorrow. If they don't lock me away in a darkened room with a bunch of knuckles then I intend to propose we use that manuscript to tease this bastard out into the open.'

'Mr Sorrell, this could set me up for life.'

'Well that's lovely,' I said. 'But how much life do you reckon he'll allow you to have?'

I got him to agree to meet me in the morning, with the rest of the manuscript, and ended the call. The taxi driver was eyeing me through the rearview window as if I'd morphed into the worst passenger in the world. I asked him if he wanted his sandwich back. He shook his head and concentrated on the road. We were about to pull up at George Yard when I looked up at Taft's window. A light went out.

'Don't stop here,' I said. 'Pull up just around the corner.'

I got out and paid him and then stood on the corner thinking about what I'd just seen. So Craig Taft had just switched off his lights. So what? He was having an early night or he was just on his way out. Or maybe he liked to noodle on his six-string in the dark for added ambience. My heart was having none of it. Something was going on. I waited for him to show at the exit. I went around to the back of the building but nothing was going on around there. I tried calling him. No answer.

I went to his door and buzzed him. The door released. No 'Hello, who is this?' Just a silent *come on in*. The worst welcome there is.

I stood in the entrance hall and debated whether to call the police. I could hear radios and TVs playing. Muffled laughter. No shadows on the stairwell. Whatever was going to happen would be over by the time Mawker had tucked his shirt into his underpants and waddled over. I started climbing. The lights in the well opening went out. I was pretty sure they weren't on a timer. I edged back against the wall and moved up slowly to Taft's floor. His corridor was dark. At the end, the window cast frozen streetlight on to a corner of the carpet where a figure was sitting on the floor, hunched over, arms around its knees as if it was in pain, or crying. It was Taft, his silver ponytail gleaming in the soft light.

'Craig?' I said, and my voice was like a nail hammered into wood. 'Are you hurt?'

At least he was moving. Or was the dark deceiving me? The grains of night writhed all over it like insects. Surely he was moving. I approached, wishing I'd divested Niker of his shitty little point-and-shoot. I felt naked. But all the other guy ever seemed to use was a needle and a knife. A gun might mean he'd end up dead, and I couldn't have that. Not if he possessed knowledge of the whereabouts of my daughter. A tooth rocked in my gum where I'd taken a punch. I worried it with my tongue, and the pain focused me. I kept my eyes dead on him. I did not blink.

'Craig?' I said, but now it was all just breath. His door was cracked open a couple of inches. The black in that gap was deeper than any night I have known. It was a *congested* dark. Something you could grab hold of, if you were of a mind to. Someone was moving around in there, quite violently, it seemed. Maybe looking for something, now that Taft had been incapacitated. I could only hope that he hadn't been paralysed.

My breath quickened. This was it. I was going to nail the fucker tonight. I flicked the lights but they were out. He'd pulled the fuses. I flexed my fingers and pressed them against the door, tried to reimagine the layout from my previous visit. Inside I heard the intruder slamming against something. A door, maybe? But it didn't matter. I had to just charge in there and take him down as quickly and as brutally as possible. I had—

There were no torch beams.

Why would anybody be ransacking an apartment if they couldn't see what they were hunting for?

Something wasn't right here. Something was hideously wrong.

I spun around and bolted for the corridor. Taft was gone. THAT WASN'T FUCKING TAFT. *THAT WASN'T FUCKING TAFT.*

I could hear feet on the stone steps heading down, shifting fast and light. Stay or go? I darted after the runner, clattering down the stairs, tensed at every landing for a nest of shadows to unfold and fly towards me. I kept an arm in front of me in the hope that any sudden flurry of knife blows might be deflected. But he wasn't here. Of course he wasn't here. Outside the road was empty in each direction. He'd melted away. I had him in my sights. He'd been three feet away from me. And I'd let him go because I thought he was Craig Taft.

Taft. Christ.

I legged it back up the stairs, jabbing at the emergency button on my phone.

The ambulance took maybe five minutes, if that, but he was dead by then. He'd been scalped. The poor fucker had been scalped. But this was no trophy. This was a desperate act to create a disguise; that figure in the corridor had been wearing his ponytail. And I'd fallen for it. What if I'd gone to the figure first, in my mistaken belief that it was Taft? Gone to help him. I'd be dead.

I'd tried to staunch the wound – what turned out to be the fatal wound, that is – in his neck. The killer had ballsed this one up. The spinal puncture had not been accurate, but had still caused some damage. Not enough to incapacitate him though. Taft had fought back. Slashes in one hand showed where he had tried to defend himself; presumably his spinal injury had prevented him from using both. Had I disturbed this attack? My phone call, my ringing of the doorbell? Had the killer rushed? Made a mistake? I bagged the scalp with its trailing ponytail from the corridor and kept it for Mawker who might be able to lift a DNA trace from it. The noises I'd heard inside Taft's flat had been reflex actions: his shoe slamming against the side of a wardrobe as death tried to calm him.

I located the fuse box and got the lights back on. The police were on their way.

There were no signs of forced entry. So maybe Taft knew his attacker. Everything was pretty much as I remembered it, though there were signs of a struggle. I'd checked Taft's body but it was unlikely his attacker could have had the chance to tattoo him considering he couldn't even render him senseless. Taft did have one tattoo, but it wasn't as expansive as his erstwhile Accelerant colleagues: a grinning skull nestled within a scorched deck of playing cards, ace of spades most prominent. There had been nothing added to it. No crude DIY job. No emo horror title. Of course not. I'd spoilt that particular part of his game.

The guitars were still on the wall. The CDs were still stacked in their cases on the shelves. The music centre looking cool and functional with its dials and gauges and needles. Everything the same. Just striped with Taft's blood.

I got lengths of clingfilm from the kitchen and wrapped my hands with it. There was a plectrum stuck into the pick guard of one of his Gibsons. There was a bloody print on it. What was that about? I went to the wall and stared at it. None of his other guitars had any plectrums attached in such a manner. There was an old Altoids tin on his desk with a label that said *Take Your Pick*. That was where he kept his plectrums. So why was this one so inelegantly positioned? And the blood. Did he put it here after he'd been attacked? Was it a sign? A message?

I plucked it out. Nothing written on it. Not that you could fit much on it anyway. And he'd have been in no fit state to leave any messages. He was in extremis when this happened. Death was minutes away. I put the plectrum down and picked up the guitar. Nothing behind it. Nothing tucked under the strings. I put it back.

The guitar was positioned above a coffee table. Upon it was a photograph album. There was blood on that too. I turned pages. Taft performing at a gig. Taft showing off his guitars. Taft in Townshend mode, arm windmilling.

And then pictures I recognised. But these were clipped from a newspaper. Jeering figures at a stand-off between demonstrators and police in an Archway street. A photographer friend of mine, Neville Whitby, had taken them last year. I had prints of some of them on my wall: the ones containing Sarah. Why did Taft have them? And then the penny dropped. Sarah had been there of course. Taft had them as a gesture of solidarity. One of us gave it to Them.

I felt a bizarre kind of pride. *See, guys, that's how you do it. Yes, you could walk around the roof of a high rise or play chicken with the rush hour traffic. Or you could do what my girl did: take on the boys in blue.*

But then so, probably, had the others. This hadn't been any kind of political posturing. This was Accelerant experience gathering. I shuffled through the other clippings. Despite the scarves around noses and mouths, I thought I recognised Niker and Dawe and Pallant. And here was one picture that was different. A picture of a protester whose face was gleaming with reflected light from a Molotov cocktail, muscles bunched, coiled, right at the critical point when he was going to launch it at the line of police. Was that Craig Taft? I think, perhaps, it was. They'd all been at it.

There was someone else in the same shot that was new to me. None of the photographs I owned contained any pictures of this policeman. Most of the officers on duty that night were part of a blurred, black mass in the background. Batons raised, visors lowered, shields up. Those frames that did contain an identifiable face I had tracked down and talked to. Except this one on the Taft clipping.

I slipped the page into my pocket and continued looking around, but there was nothing else of note.

Mawker turned up and he flapped and swore and gesticulated and threatened and I sucked it all up and swallowed it all down and I waited until he had spent himself and then I leaned into him and told him that his mother confessed to me that his moods would improve if only he'd do her up the arse from time to time.

21

I called Romy. She was flat/cat-sitting for a friend in Islington and was about to settle down with a bottle of red and a box set.

'Why don't you come over?' she said. 'I'll cook us something.'

I made it to Angel within the hour and picked up a bottle of fizz from an off-licence on Upper Street. The flat was in a pretty square near a church off Liverpool Road. She answered wearing a bathrobe and a towel turban. Her face was a little flushed.

'I didn't think you were going to get here so quickly,' she said.

'At least you didn't fob me off with some excuse about washing your hair,' I said, and handed her the bottle.

'Your face,' she said.

'I punched myself shaving,' I said. 'Forget it. It's nothing.'

She led me through to the kitchen. A brindle cat was sitting on a stool next to the breakfast bar. It looked me up and down as if I was something often found on the sole of a cheap shoe.

'Something smells good,' I said. 'Dinner smells good too.'

'Hmm,' she said, and raised her eyebrow at me. 'Someone is in a cocky mood.'

'I'm just feeling better about everything,' I said. 'I see light at the end of the tunnel.'

'I see a knife at the end of your forearm,' she said, and handed me a large santoku blade. Light caught in the undulations of the steel and played in her eyes. 'You're on salad duty.'

'What's the cat's name?' I asked.

'Freckle.' She went off vigorously rubbing at her hair. I found a steel bucket and loaded it with ice from the freezer. I placed the bottle of fizz inside and got to work on the tomatoes and cucumbers and little gem lettuces. I heard the drone of a hairdryer. By the time she got back, little beads of condensation clung to the bucket and there was a bowl of beautifully sliced greens, though I do say so myself. *Freckle*, I thought. *Great name for a cat. Why couldn't I have come up with a name like that? Fucking Freckle.*

'I'm impressed,' she said. She was wearing a thin woollen cardigan over a strapless dress. Her wrists were obscured by thick metal bangles and a lump of polished steel hung on a leather thong around her neck. She was barefoot. I liked that she didn't wear nail polish on her toes.

'So am I,' I said. 'I managed to do that without adding one or two knuckles to the bowl. That's got to be the sharpest knife I have ever used.'

'My girlfriend, the one who owns this flat, she's training to be a chef. Her dad bought her a set of kitchen knives when she graduated. Serious money.'

She took me on a tour. The cat chaperoned us. It was a nice flat, but it had the air of someone trying too hard to display a level of taste that didn't quite come off. There were lots of clean surfaces broken by the occasional piece of glass or ceramic, or a subtle candle in a subtle holder. But then that would all be ruined because the sofa cushions didn't quite go with the colour scheme, or there was a framed 'Keep Calm' picture on a wall. Or there was just too much neutral going on, and you knew the names of the paint would make your teeth itch. Something like 'rolling fog' or 'latte' or 'damp mushroom'. We ended up in the living room. Flat-screen TV, but nothing too ostentatious. A mini stereo system. There were a few CDs on display – *Mezzanine*, *Maxinquaye*, *Trailer Park* – suggesting the owner was stuck in a trendy nineties trip-hop rut. Romy sat on the sofa and the cat curled up next to her. 'How do you say it in England? I could murder a drink?'

'I'll find you a suitable victim,' I said, and then wished I hadn't. The pages in my pocket burned as if invigorated by the joke.

I got to the kitchen and took the folder from my jacket pocket. Nowhere seemed like a suitable place to put them. The room seemed to darken with them here. Through the pale blue plastic I could see the blood stains. Some of the words were smudged where liquid – tears? Lymph? Piss? God knows – had spotted the paper. In the end I put it back in my pocket. I hunted down two champagne flutes and popped the cork.

'How's everything going?' she asked when I got back.

'All fine. I'll whip up some dressing if you li—'

'I meant with the killer,' she said. I sat down next to her. She stretched out a leg and rested it on my knee. *Europeans*, I thought. The cat widened its eyes as if to say, *The brass neck of some people.*

'We've got something to work with,' I said. 'The killer

made a mistake. He exposed himself. Vanity.'

'How do you mean?'

'He sent a manuscript to a London agent,' I said. 'Possibly... actually, probably before he started killing. The agent tried to row back on his earlier dismissal of it – the guy is shitting himself that his rejection means he's on the killer's grudge list – and now he reckons he can sell it for pots of cash. Blood money.'

'Ah, what a pleasant man.'

'Exactly. But I managed to squirrel away a bunch of pages. It's a pretty thick manuscript.'

'Tell me you brought it with you,' she said.

'Maybe we should eat first,' I said.

We returned to the kitchen where she lifted the lid off a pot of boiling water and expertly twisted a large handful of spaghetti into it. My stomach gurgled. The sauce she stirred was dark, reddish brown, glistening and unctuous, the kind of sauce that only comes about after very long cooking at a very low heat.

She poured more Prosecco, and spilled a little on her hand. She smiled at me and licked the fizz off her skin with a surprisingly long pink tongue. Something else gurgled and rumbled but it wasn't my stomach this time. Appetites were opening up all over me.

We ate and it was good and she put on a little music, some John Coltrane she had brought with her. We sat under a light and I took the folder out of my pocket and placed it on the table. The blood looked like old tea under the harsh kitchen bulbs.

'This your wallet? Or his?'

'I don't know if it's his,' I said. 'It might have been the agent's. Why?'

'I don't know,' she said. 'I'm nervous. I'm just filling silences.'

'You don't have to do this. I'm not sure how—'

'How helpful it might be? There is that, I suppose. Some see it as a parlour game. A silly trick. But there are consistencies. It has been proved. And it's only a small step, isn't it, to psychological profiling. It's all guesswork, in the end.'

'I believe you,' I said. We were sitting very close to each other. I could feel her shoulder against mine, and smell the ghost of soap on her skin.

'What does this get us?' she asked. Our voices had lowered almost to whispers. I felt like a kid on a first date. Heart tripping; cotton in the gaps of my head.

'It gets us under his skin, maybe,' I said. 'We've got enough ammunition to put holes in him on his writing alone, but I don't think that's enough. I don't think that matters to him any more. He's come this far; he's either developed a thick hide to the extent that he doesn't feel the slings and arrows, or he's toppled over into no-man's land. It's no longer about the writing, if it ever was.'

'So this is to attack his personality?'

'If we can.'

'Why not make it up? Why not just wade in with accusations that he's a paedophile, that he blows goats, that he likes to wear women's knickers and wank in public places?'

'For authenticity's sake,' I said.

'You wanted to see me,' she said.

'I wanted to see you.'

'You don't need an excuse.'

'No.'

'But you felt the need to offer one. Why is that?'

'Because I'm not sure I should be doing this.' I felt

responses being drawn out of me like hooks from a fish gullet. It was difficult – the words were halting, uncertain – but it felt good.

'Why not? You like me.'

'Yes, God, yes I like you. You're funny and intelligent and beautiful.'

'You are married?'

'I am. I was.'

'What happened?'

'She died.'

Romy lowered her foot and sat closer. She took my hand in hers. Her hands were tiny. Her fingers were slender and smooth. I felt her breath against my throat as she spoke.

'I'm sorry to hear that,' she said. 'Recent?'

'Six years ago.'

'It is still painful,' she said. 'It never stops. But maybe the pain becomes less sharp. Becomes more like an ache. With time.'

'Yes,' I said. 'I don't want the pain to go away.'

'And you feel what? Unfaithful, coming to me?'

'No, not really. We have not… we're not…'

'We are not lovers,' she said.

'No.'

'Not yet.'

'Romy.'

'Shhh. It's okay. But it's not just about that, is it?'

'You see so much in my handwriting.'

She laughed, but it did not reach her eyes. They remained intent, serious.

'No,' I admitted. 'It's not just about that. There another woman, last year. Someone I felt good about. She was kind. Innocent.'

'Innocent?'

'Yes.' I couldn't keep my voice from cracking.

Her fingers went to the blue folder and traced words through the plastic. 'Something happened to her?'

'Yes.'

'You feel you put her in danger?'

'I did. She became a target. She was a way for someone bad to get to me. And she never did anything to harm anyone. She was gentle. She was so caring.'

'And you worry that the same thing will happen again. That if I help you, it makes me visible?'

'Yes.'

'But this means your life is on hold,' she said. 'You cannot live fully while you think this way. It's not your choice. It's not your responsibility.'

'But I can control it,' I said. 'I can stand down, step away.'

'I have worked with the police before,' she said. 'Seconded for studies of manuscripts. This is not new to me.'

'It doesn't make it any easier,' I said. 'It doesn't make you safe.'

She sat up and removed her cardigan. A crackle of static electricity. I felt the hair on my arms rise. Her breasts moved beneath the sheer cotton of her dress. She placed a hand on my chest and one of her fingers slipped inside my shirt. I felt her nail dimpling my chest. My clothes, my skin, felt too tight for my body.

I was thinking of how I could explain how I felt, how I might put into words the exquisite dread she inspired in me. How things might be able to work if only I could find Sarah first and put away this psychopath. How—

She kissed me.

And the words were scattered and floating around my

mind like summer butterflies. I persuaded myself that everything would be fine, especially when she touched me there, like that. And bent to kiss me there, like that. And everything of hers that slid across my body, or curved into my hands, felt right and true. She tasted sweet and sour and I couldn't get enough of her on to my tongue. The textures and colours of our skin blended or contrasted, but eventually became seamless, united by a wrapping of sweat.

Later I heard her heart beating like that of a startled animal, and her breathing softened and she retreated into sleep and I watched her for an hour or so until the light in the room was so poor that she became indistinguishable from the grains of night.

22

I must have slept too, because the smell of coffee awoke me. Romy was sitting at the end of the bed. She was naked, dawn light tigering her body through the Venetian blinds. Her breasts were full and caramel-coloured; paler skin delineated the shape where a bikini had once been. I wondered which beach she had been lying upon, and with whom. But who cared? She was here, she was naked with me.

She was leafing through the manuscript pages, gingerly holding each piece of paper by the corner, possibly so she didn't corrupt the evidence with her fingerprints, but probably more so that she didn't have to touch too much of the disgusting thing. I felt bad then for bringing it at all. She was right. We should just make something up, but give it enough of a subtle spin to make it sound believable. What if she read this and concluded that it was a guy who bought chocolates for his grandmother at the weekends, fed stray dogs and gave regularly to children's charities?

'This stuff...' I said. 'It's typed. You said you were a graphologist.'

'That didn't bother you when you came over last night.'

'I came for you last night.'

'You gain some insight, staring at paper all day, handwritten, typed... scattered with ideograms or hieroglyphics. You develop... I don't know the word.'

'Empathy?'

'Empathy, yes. You see patterns and shapes. It doesn't matter, sometimes, how they were introduced to the page.'

'It's all just a kind of reading,' I said.

She nodded. And then: 'He's a loner,' she said.

'That makes sense,' I said. 'There can't be many serial killers who get away with this kind of thing with wives and children in tow.'

'He likes his work.'

Too much, I thought. *He doesn't even consider it work. Not any more.*

'He showed great promise as a youngster.'

'A youngster?'

'I'm guessing... look at the dates. 1988. Nearly thirty years ago.'

I took one of the pages from her. If she was right it meant that whoever had written them might be any age now between forty-five and sixty. '"Their teeth shone dully, mist filming their vision. Teeth long and wolfish, flashed in the light." It's got some rhythm to it, I'll give him that.'

'The sentences, though typed scruffily on a failing machine, are, if not grammatically correct, then trying their best. The spelling is not great. The punctuation is all over the place, but that might be because his typewriter doesn't work properly. Or it could be a stylistic choice. He feels as if he deserves some success, but it never came. The dog that never had its day. And like you point out, the sentences contain patterns, rhythms. Sometimes they're long and meandering;

sometimes staccato, very short. I'd be willing to bet they follow his moods. I imagine he is a moody person, prone to swift changes in his emotional state. And I think... I think he stands up to write.'

'Stands up? How do you work that out?'

'Look at how hard these keys have punched into the paper. You can feel them on the back, like Braille. And this is good-quality paper. I don't think you get that kind of leverage sitting down. Not consistently, anyway.'

'Anything else? Anything we might damage him with?'

'I don't know. There's some stuff... like this, at the beginning of "Bluebottle Jam": "I lie asleep in bed, but only sometimes. Mostly I'm awake, struggling with my fear of the dark, conscious of the sweat on my forehead. Conscious of the cruel silence. After ten years the dreams still bother me. Ten years."'

'You think, what? He goes walkies with the black dog?'

'Well, I wonder if he might play host to suicidal tendencies. These handwritten notes in the margin... you didn't add these, did you?'

'No,' I said.

'No, of course... but the way the line rises and falls here, where he's written "Shit... it's all shit". I don't know, it's difficult to say as there are no lines on the paper, but it's indicative. Perhaps it's nothing. But also... the stroke pressure is quite high. Like the type, you can feel the words through the page. This suggests a strong libido. Not quite the kind of thing we can bait him on. Although these smears, these blotches... you could point to a kind of sensual indecency, depravity even, a lack of control where indulgence is concerned. Appetites, you know.'

'That's better,' I said. 'I like it. Maybe we can build him up

with that, and then pull the rug out. This guy is a sex god…
oh no, hang on, I mean he's a pervert.'

'The way the words slant forwards, a heavy slant…' She
puffed out her cheeks. 'Wow. You could say the person is
hysterical, or is prone to hysteria. He overreacts. He loses
touch of himself, his inner feelings, his control, his self-
denial. And following on from that, he is influenced by
the emotional worth of a situation rather than any person
caught up within it. He is indifferent to feelings of others.'

'Jesus,' I said.

'And here, loops within loops… a tendency to secrecy.
Deliberate concealment. He omits. He deceives and misleads.
The omission of information in the hope it hides the truth. And
perhaps he does this even to conceal things from himself…'

'Is there anything here that chimes with what you saw
before, in that first batch of pages I gave you?'

'I don't think so,' she said. 'It's difficult to say. Writers…
writing changes from person to person, even within the
space of a few months. Circumstances can alter handwriting.
Moods. Illnesses.'

I glanced through some more of the sheets. Whatever
typewriter these pages had wound through was grimy and
knackered, or maybe just the misery in the words had turned
it that way. And some of the lines didn't hang quite right.
'*Sometimes I wonder what became of all the school friends.
It's natural.*' That impersonal '*the*' where you'd expect a
'*my*'. It said something about him. It gave me the creeps.

I rubbed my face. Days of stubble rasped back in
response. It was a loud sound in the room. I watched the
beat of Romy's heart transmit itself to the necklace hanging
against her sternum.

'How is *your* stroke pressure?' she asked. She placed

252

the papers on the floor and knelt on the bed. She lowered herself on to all fours. Her nipples grazed my thighs as she moved towards me.

'I've never had any complaints,' I said.

'When do you have to see the police?'

'Our meeting is at six a.m.'

'You have an hour.'

'What can we do in an hour?'

'Joel, Joel, Joel...' she whispered, a teacher admonishing a particularly thick pupil. Her nails scrawled mysterious ideograms across my chest. 'What *can't* we do?'

Mawker didn't agree with it; not at first. Hell, I wasn't even sure it was a good idea. I mean, the guy had obviously been on the wrong end of a lot of criticism. He'd already flipped his lid, retrieved it and tried to screw it on back to front. A bit more of a kicking was hardly going to make a difference. But it might. We had to try. Especially now that Niker and Pallant had gone dark and he was running out of targets. We dragged Simm in and read him the riot act. He kept pleading that he'd thought it was all just a big literary joke but the disgusted looks on our faces soon shut him up. He handed over the rest of the manuscript and the letters and Mawker told him he was lucky to be escaping a prison sentence. He sat there now, his face sadder than a diabetic's treat cupboard.

It was in all the papers that day. *The Hack*. I guessed Simm had been in touch with them. He was determined to get a payday of some kind it seemed. Fuck it. Get it out in the open. Maybe someone had seen something and would come forward. Maybe The Hack himself would suddenly find the pressure of nationwide coverage too great and either surrender to the police or top himself.

'This mad berk, this evil fucker,' Mawker said, 'is clearly trying to attain the notoriety he thought he'd get via publishing by knocking off people on his writerly shit list.'

'Have a promotion,' I said. He gave me a look but didn't react. We were in his office on the ninth floor at New Scotland Yard. No photographs on his desk. No Tupperware lunchbox, lovingly prepared for him. Instead there was a greasy cardboard box sticking out of the wastepaper bin, and the high reek of curry. Coke cans were strewn around like tokens on a coach's tactics board. He needed a haircut. His shoes were scuffed. What looked like a bead of apricot jam clung right at the tip of the V of his tie. It smelled in here, and not just of chicken jalfrezi. It was Mawker's sweat, a tart compost of anxiety and anger. No amount of Pledge or Windolene sprayed by the cleaners could shift it. On his desk was a computer. Someone had affixed a sticker to the back of it which read 'Ello, ello, ello, PC PC'. It was a laugh a minute in this place.

'And this moniker they've given him. The Hack. Because he has some ambitions as a writer. And also, it's a reference to his MO, although we haven't released any specific details on that.'

'Double promotion. Mawker, you are on fire, son.'

'Can it, Sorrell,' he said. 'I'm just summarising what we know.'

I handed him an index card from his desk. 'I reckon you could write everything *you* know on that card. With space left over to draw a giant cock. And balls.'

'We've had top brass talk to the BBC,' Mawker said. 'They'll let us run something during the ten o'clock news.

But there's no guarantee he'll be watching. If he's not writing or shedding blood, what? He sits up late at night with his Ovaltine to see how the latest McEwan has fared?'

'They don't do reviews on the ten o'clock news, Mawker. Do keep up.'

'Whatever the fuck it is.'

'Anyway, we have to try,' I said. 'Simm can do it. Or one of his publishing cronies. "This guy can't write for toffee. He couldn't write his way out of a wet paper bag. No future in this game." Really pile it on. Get the radio stations to pick it up for their bulletins. Get it on tomorrow's front pages.'

Simm licked his lips and flicked his attention from me to Mawker and back to me, as if we were playing invisible tennis. 'I'm not doing it,' he said, and widened his eyes for emphasis. They looked as if they might just bug out of his face and make a bid for freedom. 'And anyway, what would it achieve? You hit a wasps' nest with a stick, you won't do it again. I don't want him after me.'

'He's already after you,' I said. He blanched.

'We need to get him angry,' Mawker said. 'Lure him out. Get him to make a mistake.'

'And if he doesn't?' Simm was chipping away at my resolve. He was right. Of course he was right, but I had nothing else in the ideas tray. It was either this or wait for him to strike again. And we had no idea who his next victim was likely to be. What was crippling me was that it might be Sarah; he might know where she was, even if I didn't. At least this way we could set him up with some potential targets that we could keep close to until he made his move from the shadows.

'Like I said,' I said, 'we have to try. Anything come through from forensics, Ian?'

'You only call me "Ian" when you want something.'

'Well it is your name. Granted, it's not the one I choose to use half the time.'

'Nothing from forensics, not that it's any of your business. No prints. No DNA. He's not a knobber. No hairs or fibres, so either he's naked and bald as a coot when he attacks, or he's super lucky.'

'Or super cautious,' I said.

'In which case this might not work,' Simm said. It felt as if the words were leaping from his mouth, working on any little point of weakness so as to disarm, anything to take him further from where we wanted to go. His body followed up, repositioning itself, all eager, open. I decided he must be quite an act at the various negotiation tables of London's publishing industry. 'He'll smell a trap a mile off. And then he'll keep his head down for as long as it takes until things have cooled off. You'll scare him away. Maybe for good.'

'We take that risk,' Mawker said. 'At the very least the spree is over and we can go back over the evidence and approach this in a more thorough, by-the-numbers fashion. We'll catch him, but it'll take time. This way I think we get a crack at catching him more quickly.'

'I don't want anything to do with it,' Simm said. His body had closed up again, like a shellfish at low tide.

'It's too late for that,' I said, and then to Mawker: 'What's the setup?'

A BBC crew were coming around to New Scotland Yard the next morning. Ten a.m. sharp. Tula Barnes would be there, as well as an experienced and well-respected editor from Janner & Fyffe, one of the city's oldest publishers. The footage would then be able to be repeated as much as possible throughout the day, maximising the chance of The Hack seeing it.

'Let me see if I can bring something else to the party,' I said. 'If you think giving him a kicking over the quality of his metaphors isn't good enough, there might be some other way we can sting him.'

'Like what?' asked Mawker.

'Give me till tomorrow,' I said.

'We haven't got the time. We need to work on what we're going to say now.'

'Well do that then, but allow for some extra material.'

'Christ, Sorrell, this is going to be some ugly clusterfuck, I can feel it in my bladder.'

'Let's hope so,' I said.

It was five minutes quick march round the corner to check on the dead letter drop. As before I took my time, glancing up and down Birdcage Walk and across at the park, where the swans were being fatted for the Queen's table. It was late afternoon and the traffic was picking up, but there were few pedestrians down here. I watched a woman jog by with various high-end fitness gadgets appended to her torso and arms, then ducked next to the tree and found a piece of paper folded up into the knot of roots.

> 51°30'59.26"N 0°10'33.61"W
> 13.04. @ 0000 WTFIGO?!?
> Solo

Midnight tonight. I opened the map on my phone and fed in the co-ordinates: Paddington Station. I struggled for the literary link. Hadn't there been a Sherlock Holmes novel where they took a train from Paddington? *The Hound of the Baskervilles* maybe? Or was I thinking of the film? Fuck Sherlock Holmes and his hound. It didn't matter. I was hyperventilating.

Solo.

She was getting in touch. Presumably she'd caught wind of the shitstorm and was trying to make contact with allies. I ran my thumb over the dimpled surface of the typed note and my mouth went dry. She had written this. She had delivered this. WTFIGO? She used to say that when she was a kid: 'What the Figo?' I'd always assumed it had something to do with the Portuguese footballer, until Rebecca explained to me.

I snapped my head up, convinced she was here, that she was watching. I peered into every knot of bushes, every nest of shadows, and pareidolia tricked me into thinking there were faces there when there weren't. I pocketed the note and after a moment's pause, decided to leave one of my own.

I'll be there, I wrote. I couldn't sign it. I didn't want to risk scaring her off. I only hoped she didn't recognise my handwriting.

23

Praed Street, just shy of midnight. Little traffic, fewer pedestrians. Lights on everywhere. This city knows no darkness. Not any more. Not the literal kind, anyway. I hurried past St Mary's Hospital – the place gives me goosebumps for all manner of reasons (Sarah was born here; much later I met a monster within its walls).

The slip road down to the Paddington Station entrance is like a throat. You got a sense of how huge the floor space was way before you stepped upon it. The roof gave you a clue, as did the wide way in. Shadows stretched off, dense and palpable. The breath from that yawning mouth was every kind of hot: grease, diesel, resentment. Spent tickets shifted around the threshold in eddies of wind. I heard footsteps – brief, hurried – and they sounded like high heels. A woman rushing to make a last train. A lover hurrying into the arms of one who had waited for her arrival. There was a sense of the station winding down. You could hear its fatigue in the creak of the shutter doors and the tick of cooling engines. The smell of a thousand travel-weary bodies hung in the air, and I grew tired just getting the slightest hit of it; the pall clung to the shed roof, all the humours of a busy day in a London hub.

I stood just inside the entrance for a while, watching the shadows and light. Staff in dark blue uniforms clustered on a platform. I heard laughter. I saw sodium light glance off spectacle lenses. About a dozen people were staring at the departures board. I scanned the faces. I strained my eyes looking for the shape or the gait or the posture of a girl I no longer knew. I kept out of the pools of light and edged towards the escalators. The statue of Paddington Bear was just alongside. I stared at that little bronze creature for a while, remembering childhood afternoons watching the TV incarnation.

This wasn't right.

It was gone midnight, but that wasn't the problem. It just didn't feel right, in the way that Peter Pan had. Yes, things had changed. There was imminent threat now, blood on the ground, but the dead letter drop was designed to neutralise that. Only the Accelerants knew about its location.

Something had gone wrong. I wondered if there had been any kind of danger sign agreed, an abort code of sorts, should a meeting not look likely to be fulfilled. I stared down the platforms. I remembered when I first moved to London you could drive right in to the station from the north end. I'd dropped Rebecca off here once, when she had to catch a train to Bristol for some symposium or other. It had been noisier and smellier back then. Farting trains. Taxi fumes. Smoking on the platforms. Overly loud tannoy announcements by real people rather than today's pre-recorded digital robot voices.

Getting on for ten past. Just me and Padders. *Please look after this bear, thank you.*

She wasn't coming. Perhaps she had seen me and melted

into the night. I'd do the same thing if I'd been in receipt of a message written in a hand I didn't recognise. Do a recce, leg it if I wasn't happy. Maybe I was early and she was late. I moved, fast, and found a spot behind one of the ticket machines near the ticket office. A guy wearing headphones came through buffing the floor with an orbiter. A teenager with a large backpack was asleep on a bench.

She wasn't coming. Nobody was coming. Nobody I wanted to see, at least.

All the lights went out. The departures board stuttered and died.

I felt my back bristle. I moved out from behind the ticket machine and heard the consternation of staff on the platforms, and passengers cheated of their information. A fire alarm went off. People began moving towards the exit. I stayed put, shrinking into the deep shadow of an entrance corridor. I heard the clatter of roller shutters as they crashed down.

About a hundred metres away, a figure moved out of a thick darkness that was wadded up against the far wall. I kept losing it in the gloom. It wasn't Sarah, that was for sure. It was like a magnet shifting through iron filings. It coalesced and disintegrated. The absence of light, or of anything on the figure that might have reflected it – glasses, belt buckles, polished leather – meant that it sometimes shrank from view. I couldn't track it. And then it would be over there to the left, a little closer now. It was ranging from side to side. I had the horrible feeling that it was trying to sniff me out. I imagined something blind, something monstrous with unhinged jaws sucking in the flavour of my warm body, homing in. But now I did see something gleaming, and it was a broad blade. I thought it might be a machete, but that could have been fear enlarging it. I was torn between running for my life and sticking around in the hope that I might catch a clearer glimpse of my stalker and put a face to the threat, level this playing field. Maybe even disarm him, finish it tonight.

But fear was a series of tiny eggs hatching in my gut. The last time I'd fought a man with a blade, I'd almost ended up with a new mouth. I felt weak and tired, the comedown from a jag of adrenaline at the thought of being reunited with my daughter once again. And maybe this wasn't about me. Maybe this was a guy coming to rob Paddington Station. With a machete. Yeah, right. The shakes intensified when I thought of that weapon piercing Gower, Treacle and Taft, making steaks of them, life spraying in trajectories created by a millimetre-thick edge of steel.

I got moving myself, but not before I decided to match the figure's trickery. I slid my watch off my wrist and into my pocket. My wedding ring too. Buttoned my jacket and turned up the collar. I headed for the edge of Platform 1 and dropped on to the tracks as quietly as I was able. Hugging the wall under the lip, I made for open air, crouched low alongside the rails.

I passed under Bishop's Bridge Road, and waited for a while in its shelter. The space under the roof of the station was utterly black. How hard could it be to replace a fuse? And then a footfall on track ballast; the harsh music of crushed stone. The weapon was fully brandished now; it swept the air before it in broad, slow arcs. I backed away, ready to run if need be. The sight of the steel made the scar on my face ache.

I was relatively new to violence. That realisation bit deep, and I felt my confidence dissolve, as if the puddles of oil beneath this bridge were draining the vitality from me. I'd made up for it in the intervening years since that callow fifteen-year-old was kicked to a shrivelling pile of snot and tears outside a fish-and-chip shop in Childwall. I couldn't remember the name of the thug who'd attacked me, nor the reason for his assault. An askance look? A spilled drink? One of the two, or something else equally pointless. A girl, a car, a gesture.

I remember getting into the bath that night and my whole body felt raw, as if I'd been dragged along the road until my knees and elbows and knuckles had been skinned. I'd got out of bed like a guy who'd just had a hip operation. Bruises had opened up beneath the skin in science fiction colours. I was convinced that he'd loosened some of my teeth, but it was transitory. When you're a teenager, you heal fast and forget quicker. I got fit. I got fleet. I learned some moves. A bit of judo, a bit of boxing, a bit of karate. I picked up some krav maga later on. Just enough to know when something was coming, how to block it, create space, counterstrike and get away. Fists and feet and knees and heads I could cope with, despite the blunt force they provided. Sharp steel, though, and firearms – all of that was above my pay grade.

If I kept still, kept in these dark shoals, shrank, buried my head in my arms, slowed my breathing and listened to the sedate crunch of stones as he approached, he would walk right past me. I could grab a handful of aggregate, fling it in his face when he turned back, gain a split second, enough to unleash hell upon the soft parts of his body before he could reposition himself, bring the machete into play. Or I could just watch him go. Follow him to his lair. Either way I could end it. If I ran, he could sedately plot his route to my daughter's doorstep. But I'd been trying to do that for five years and she'd been a step ahead all the way. I had to believe that I was the professional PI here. He might know more about slice and dice, but I was the tracker. If I couldn't find my daughter in all that time – and my need was greater than his – then it wasn't a foregone conclusion that she was in any kind of immediate peril. She was not stupid. She had become even more of a ghost since Martin Gower died. She understood the danger and was concealing herself from it.

I was the stupid one, prepared to seize upon the first dodgy lead as having been authored by her. I'd fallen into a trap more crude than the one I was plotting with Mawker. I'd gone to it with open arms, never once suspecting that he knew more than we gave him credit for. He'd been ahead every step of the way. Slowly, sedulously, he was cutting down his targets, no matter the Accelerants' cute little codes and curfews. If I died here, she was alone. I had to make sure that when the confrontation did come, I had a definite, immediate reason to face it. I had to be between him and her. I couldn't risk a cold and lonely death, a pointless death, out here. Not tonight.

I pushed myself upright and began inching away. Once I was on the other side of the bridge I intended to find some way to shimmy up to roadside if at all possible. But I wasn't given the chance. I saw him stiffen and turn his face in my direction. It was in the cowl of a hood, pale and oval and stitched with shadows and intent. I had no idea of this guy's physique – it was locked up inside a heavily padded jacket – but if he was stocky, it didn't affect his speed or grace, because he came for me, hitting full pelt within seconds. I stared at him for a moment, shocked by his acceleration, and then took off myself, all thoughts of concealment gone.

I raced past closed security gates and doors and generator housings containing multiple warnings of death and trespass. Padlocks winked at me. I didn't look back. I didn't need to in order to know that he was gaining, despite that unwieldy machete.

A light up ahead. A train slowing for the buffers. If I could somehow get that train between me and my pursuer... but that wasn't going to work. Someone had obviously alerted the driver to the power failure because the train was coming to a stop way before the tracks split for the platforms. It would be stationary before I reached it. Maybe I could alert the driver? But at this rate, The Hack would be upon me way before I became visible to any staff in the cockpit.

I picked up my pace, but it was hard to run in the darkness on such unstable ground. I had to hope The Hack was suffering the same difficulties, although it didn't sound like it. The crunch of the stones was nearer, and had a confident rhythm about it. *Turn your fucking ankle*, I thought. *Trip and spear yourself on your own fucking weapon.*

A distant tannoy made an announcement nobody could hear. Westbourne Bridge was coming up. Across the tracks on the Westway side, I could see an area of flapping plastic net, where new constructions and refurbishments in the Basin abutted the railway. I angled right, hurdling the rails carefully. If I tripped I was dead.

I got to the fence and rammed through it, stumbling into a cordoned-off building site filled with Portakabins and orange plastic barriers. The structures were wrapped in scaffolds and brick nets. Harsh sodium lights blazed on brackets high up on concrete pillars. I tried a couple of the Portakabin doors but they were locked. I could hear him at the fence, the gritting of the blade against the wall as he hoisted himself up. I ran along a blind alley, casting covetous glances at a scooter parked by a service hatch. No keys in the ignition. Not enough time to hotwire. Didn't know how to do that anyway.

I came out into a polished quadrangle of high rises and a token postage stamp of green space to keep the office workers happy. There was a hairdressers and a deli, a noodle bar and a mini supermarket tucked into a rank of shops under a walkway. Behind me was a coffee shop and a pizza restaurant. I ran along a corridor studded with lights, flanked by plane trees in the direction of an office block with rounded corners and ice-blue lighting recessed in gills that ran up the side of the edifice. It was like being on a science fiction film set after shooting has stopped for the day.

I'd lost him. I was a couple of minutes away from Little Venice. I'd lost...

He came up out of the dark and the machete moved so quickly it left a trace of where it had been, like a swipe of motion in a comic book. In that moment, before I felt it connect with the side of my head, I saw another figure shifting in the near distance. It raised its hand and cried out. I tried to scream at it to go, to run, to get away, but my mouth was filling with blood. The black outlines of the trees, like spiders' legs frozen against the sky, began to twitch and move and grow. The thin black boughs swelled and blocked out all the interstices where there was light, until there no longer was any, and no longer any colours or smells or sounds. And I thought, *What a ridiculous way to die.*

'CANCER PLANET'

2 FEB – 10 FEB 1988

They were coming for her – the Shadow Walkers – eating up the ground, showering plumes of oily, dark soil/flesh behind them, stabbing the overcast spears forged from disease, catching the red rain on tongues reeling with foulness.

Thunder roiled and shuddered across the horizon, chasing them laughing and shrieking like hideous, mutated hyenas.

Their teeth shone dully, mist filming their vision. Teeth long and wolfish, flashed in the light.

They could see her.

And too late, she saw them, but the pain was already therre, already deep and spreading blackly through her as a malignant

cancer.

She wakes, threads of perspiration stinging her eyes. Dawn is rushing into the sky outside the hospital window, pouring honey-coloured light across the roads and houses. She sighs and the air rattles through her like wind soughing through october leaves. The nightmare clings on, leech like.

Shadow walkers.

Cancer.

The word injects fear into her bones and it buries deeper into her consciousness, wallowing in the damage it has already caused. It is as if she can feel herself steadily deteriorating: each doomed cell's useless fight with an ancient, well near unstoppable horror, the steady onslaught of the sickness taking over. She winces when she realises that, in a way, she is killing herself. Her body is gradually eating her from the inside out.

She reaches across to the bedside cabinet and gropes for the water jug. Her hand snags on something else and she tugs it towards her, appalled by her lack of strength. She holds the mirror up to her face and her reflection stares grimly back at her; a skull covered by a shrink rap of yellowing skin, punched with lifeless eyes. Her hair hangs in sparse clumps, the result of hours of chemotherapy.

She breathes in, wrestling with the fear of pain, and her lungs seem to shred and part in her chest like so much wet tissue paper and when the pain does come, like a gout of white flame, she is ready, and for the first time since the Shadow Walkers invaded her dreams, she is able to force the tears back.

The doctor arrives.

He prods and pokes at her emaciated body, his face neutral, as expressionless as cream cheese.

The doctor's breath is redolent of cigarette smoke and she suddenly hates him, despises the face that he is standing on the other side of the sheets, treating her, a non-smoker, for the very thing that he should be suffering.

He asks the questions, she answers, her voice distant and,

al=most comically, disembodied from her, as though she were the world's greatest ventriloquist.

She eats well today, forcing the food, but getting it places, to the corners of her body that crave sustenance. As she eats – the tines of her fork clattering nervously on cracked hospital plates, she watches the sky darkes, the clouds shifting broodily before the menace of night.

She contemplates reading a book, a collection of short stories by Ruth Rendell, but instead invites sleep and with it, the slow, seductive kiss of the nightmare. She acecpts that the kiss will be cold, but comforts herself with the knowledge that her fight has begun and the Shadow Walkers will not find her so easy to attack this time.

The clouds

filled her mind as well as the sky that night and echoes became a part of her dream. She could hear them, not necessarily close by but they were there all the same, perhaps sniffing the air for her, perhaps confused by this new aroma of determination.

Perhaps just biding their time. Stalking her.

She breathed the sweet, heavy air of her dream and found it refreshing and strengthening. She could feel the curl of a smile sweep across her lips. Then the clouds dispersed.

The Shadow Walkers stared at her from across the black, oozing wasteland; eyes baleful, bodies twisted and grotesque, heaving with anticipation.

Her smile widened.

And they came for her.

Or at least, that was the ida. Because, from behind her, hurtling out of her choking darkness, came a rush of diamond sharpo brightness, like the coruscating light flashing off storm torn water.

The Shadow Walkjers were consumed by it, turned into thraashing figures and then –

Then they were gone, their screams cut off with chilling finality.

And when she remembered to turn arouns, in case there were any more to devour her, there was nothing but a vast, lovely light.

Fourteen weeks later, a lithe, beautiful, slightly tired woman skips down the hospital steps, dark hair swirling in the

24

I came to a minute, an hour, a day later, I don't know. A dog was licking my face. I lifted my head and pain unravelled from it. Everything felt loose and unconnected. Nausea filled me up and I turned to one side to be sick. Stars leapt and crackled in the dark spaces inside my head. I batted the dog away before he could get excited about the warm snack I'd provided. The back of my neck felt hot and irritated, the skin wet and chewed. I guessed I must have collided with the pebble-dashed edge of a nearby bench on my way down. I pushed myself to my knees, paused for a while to allow everything to settle, then got to my feet. I closed my eyes to the sway until I reclaimed control. Now. Why hadn't he killed me?

Right. I remembered. The other figure. That was why.

The voice that had followed me down had belonged to an elderly man in a flat cap and a raincoat. Beneath it he wore an AC/DC T-shirt, although much of that was obscured by blood. Police sirens on the A104. Maybe they'd been there ever since I'd revived. Maybe they were on their way while I was still out. But they were for The Hack, or for me. Not for this guy. Everything was too late for him now. Blue strobes stitching into the black above *Blade Runner* town. I knelt down and thanked him and disappeared.

Two a.m. I was standing on the main road, staring down Homer Street, daring it to do something different, willing it to show me why I shouldn't go home. I was desperate to go home. I wanted a bath, a drink, a bandage and a bed. I wanted to see the look on my maniac cat's face when I tooled through the door looking like Joseph Merrick on a bad day. I wanted to talk to Mawker and find out the name of the guy who had inadvertently saved my life. I kept touching the area where the machete had hit me. Somehow, angles, fate, a shit aim: the blade had failed to lop the top off me like a boiled egg and had knocked me senseless instead. I had a lump the size of Berkshire growing out of the side of my head.

Homer Street was quiet. Cars parked along the left-hand side. Lights on in windows. *I get in and I'm safe. I stay out and I'm not. So move.* But I couldn't. There were sinkholes of darkness between me and the entrance. And as at Paddington, I was convinced I could see movement within them. I kept out of sight and moved away. At Baker Street Tube station I called Romy. She answered just as I was about to hang up. I shouldn't be leaning on her. I could just go and stay at Tokuzo's place after all. But I wanted to see a friendly face. I needed some positive physical proximity, to cancel out all the negatives of the last couple of hours.

'What is it?'

Her voice was thick and slow with sleep. I imagined her under the duvet. Soft, warm curves. Dips and swells. The smell of her.

'That pasta was good,' I said.

'There's some more in the fridge if you want it.'

'Can I come over?'

'What time is it?'

'It's late.'

'Are you okay?'

Traffic tore up and down the Euston Road, unimpressed by the hour. I thought of Sarah somewhere in the city, maybe sleeping, maybe not. I hoped she was safe and invisible. I sent her every good wish I could muster.

'I'm not that great,' I said.

'Of course you can come over. You don't need to ask.'

I waited some more before I descended into the Underground station. I kept an eye on the traffic and the few people meandering along the pavements. I had to be sure I wasn't followed before I went to her. I wouldn't put her at risk. And so, despite the burn to be with her, loops and false turns and switchbacks: Baker Street to Waterloo to Bank to Holborn to King's Cross and finally to Angel. People staring at the lump on my head. People trying not to stare. A splitting headache was building behind my left eye. Maybe my brain was swelling. Maybe they'd find me at five in the morning, cold and blue in my seat somewhere in south Wimbledon.

He'd known about the dead letter drop. How could that be? Either one of us had been clumsy and had been followed to the drop, or the killer was a member of the inner circle. I tried to marry the movements of my pursuer to the physical quirks and peccadilloes of Sean Niker. I couldn't be sure because of that padded jacket and the camouflage of darkness, but I couldn't see beyond him. Although it didn't make sense. I knew, deep down, that he had nothing to do with these deaths. I just wanted an excuse to mash his face against my knee for an afternoon.

She was at the window when I got to the flat, nearly two hours later. Her hair was tied back off her face. It was a good face, strong and kind. She was concerned about the state of my injuries and wanted to call an ambulance, but I showed her how well I could walk in a straight line. I counted backwards from twenty to one. I told her who the prime minister was, and the chancellor of the exchequer and the home and foreign secretaries. She drew me a hot bath while I raided the cupboards for painkillers. It seemed the trainee chef had suffered most of her life from cluster headaches and had a stock of weapons grade analgesics. I took two tablets that looked like rhinoceros suppositories and washed them down with a beaker of spiced rum.

I slipped into the bath and it was a tad too hot, but I needed it. I felt the water touch every raw red part of me and my skin screamed, but I relished it; a little masochism never did anyone any harm. Under the water my flesh was strange, like the membrane of a cuttlefish in flux between colours. I rested my head on the lip of the bath and wished I had some more rum.

Romy came in as if reading my mind and set a glass down. She was naked.

'Is there room for two?'

'At least,' I said. 'I was thinking of hosting a water polo tournament.'

She slid in opposite me. The water lifted her heavy breasts, and clung to her firm skin in beads. My pulse sent ripples through the water that broke against her.

'It's hot,' she said.

'Yep.'

She smiled. Her eyes went to my cock and appraised it. I swallowed and the sound was a sharp click in the steamy air.

'Nervous?' she asked.

'Booze and drugs…' I said. 'I'm just glad you're here in case I fall asleep.'

'We can't have you falling asleep,' she said.

'It's unlikely now. I mean, a beautiful woman gets into my bath with me. How could I possibly fall as— zzzzzzzz.'

'Very funny. Drink your rum.'

'I would, but my shoulder feels as if it's been dislocated and replaced with a bag of broken spanners.'

She sighed and rolled her eyes. She planted her hands on either side of the bath and raised herself to her knees. Muscles jumped in the smooth skin of her chest. She leaned forward to get the glass. A breast slid against the side of my cheek. I felt the weight of it against me and groaned. Her pussy was shaved but the hair was growing back; stubble grazed the head of my cock, snapping it awake.

'Oh, hello,' she said.

'Sorry,' I said. 'It's the only part of me that hasn't been destroyed.'

'I'm sure I can fix that,' she said. She began to rock her hips, sliding herself up and down the length of me.

'Romy,' I said. My voice was thick and ragged.

She took some rum into her mouth and leaned forward, dribbled it into mine. Her eyes were locked on me the whole time. 'Today I was piecing together fragments of a love letter from the seventeenth century,' she said. Spice danced on her breath. She didn't cease the slow back and forth of her hips. I felt the water move against me in beats, and the clinging wetness of her; it felt as if I was being massaged with hot oil. I reached up and pressed the spike of a nipple into the palm of my hand. She closed her eyes. 'Words of concern and ecstasy, older than the light from some of the stars up there. Written before Napoleon was born. Tattered and torn and lost to the world all through the events of the last three centuries. Those unknown... unknowable lovers who cared for each other once, a speck in history, gone forever. But something remaining of them. A shimmer of heat in all those cold layers of time.'

There was urgency in her movement now, and she was pressing against me harder with each stroke. I rose to meet it. I put my hand around her neck and drew her down to me and felt her tongue slide against mine. Pain was leaping around every corner of my body but the core of warmth and pleasure was keeping it at bay. She raised her hips higher and I slipped into her. Breath hissed. Water sloshed out of the bath. Control disappeared. I came hard and knocked the glass to the floor. I heard it smash as I felt the water slip over my head. I watched her through it, rising above me, her hands in her hair, and she was all sliced and blurred, her mouth a red O and all I could hear was the thud of my heart.

25

We were invited to use a studio at the BBC's Broadcasting House in Portland Place, but we decided it would be better, and safer for all concerned, if we recorded the piece at a neutral venue. In the end we borrowed a sequestered second-floor office in Poland Street. It was pretty packed in there. We had radio broadcasters, a TV crew, reporters and photographers from all the dailies. Mawker introduced me to Tula Barnes, who was huddled in a thick grey shawl, looking like an owl poking its head out of a nest. She was standing next to a guy in a cream jacket who surreptitiously wiped his hand after shaking mine. He was Jacob Briers, apparently, an editorial director at Janner & Fyffe. Neither had agreed to be filmed. They were there solely in a consulting capacity.

I agreed to assume the role of a literary critic, but it had to be a freelance position; none of the linens would agree to take me under their wing. They didn't want any attacks on their offices.

I said I'd start within five minutes and if people weren't ready then tough shit. There would be no second take. It wouldn't sound right if it came over too rehearsed.

I basically recited what Romy had fed me, adding a little spin of my own. I said that The Hack's serial rejection was incidental now, but it had been a pivotal moment early in his so-called career. I said that he was probably mentally ill, and prone to thoughts of sexual deviance. I suggested that he was unattractive, and possibly impotent. No doubt this was a violent person, but there was a likelihood that violence had been visited upon him all through his life, in many forms. Physical, emotional violence, of course, but also sexual abuse, likely from the key people in his life that he should have been able to trust. Was he an orphan? It wouldn't surprise me. Was he deformed? How could he not be? He was a bully, a thug, a brutal outcast. A freak. I ladled it on. And then I read out some choice pieces from the manuscript. All the howlers I could find. I chuckled. I derided. Contempt oozed from every syllable.

I watched the video cameras and the digital recorders blink. I watched the pencils form their curlicues of code in notebooks. Everything I said was a roundabout, fancified way of saying THIS IS A CUNT OF EPIC PROPORTIONS.

'Is he man enough to come in and debate this with me? I doubt it. He's a skulker, inhabits the shadows. He jumps you from behind. There is no nobility, no courage, no class to this person at all. He is a bottom feeder. He is a freak. He is a smear, the lowest form of life in the underclass. I pity and abhor him, and so should we all. He has nothing in his life. Some write as a form of therapy. Some write because they have great stories they wish to share. This vainglorious by-blow writes in the way the peacock spreads its feathers, but all his colours are grey and the plumage is collapsed and dusty. This man. This Hack. Is pathetic.'

The recorders clicked off. The biros clicked shut. Eddie Chesters, a shit-strainer from one of the tabloids, touched my arm as I was leaving. 'Don't hold back,' he said. 'Tell us what you *really* think about this guy.'

And then we got the hell out of there. I knew the owner of a basement cocktail bar nearby, and I steered Romy quickly into it before any of the journos could see us and follow suit. The guy who ran it, Mo Belper, an asthmatic with a grey face and a penchant for white leather jackets, locked the doors behind us and went to fix us drinks. Romy wanted a coffee, but I ordered myself a dirty martini and sank it quick. I felt dirty inside and out, as if breathing the same air as that pack of quote-hungry wolves had furred my lungs with filth, but also because it wasn't even eight a.m. yet, and I was ladling sauce down my throat.

'The breakfast of champions,' Romy said.

'That was not the most pleasant thing I've ever done,' I said. I was shaking.

'You could have had an Americano, like me.'

'I'm not talking about the martini.'

'It's done now. Maybe it will work, maybe it won't, but now you can forget about it. You did a good job. If it was me you were talking about in there I'd come out all guns blazing.'

'Is that a good thing, though, really?' I asked. I was no longer so sure. 'What if it just causes him to withdraw into himself, make him harder to find? He's not stupid. He'll realise how hot a property he is, how much fear he's instilling in people, how much we want to nail him. He could go off the radar completely.'

'I don't think so.'

'Why not?'

'Because this is his time, Joel. Why couldn't he have

done this years ago? Why now? Because of the way the chips fall. Because the voices tell him it's now. Because of planet alignment. Maybe he doesn't care if he's caught. He's determined to finish whatever is on that to-do list.'

Belper punctuated that with a hit on his inhaler. It broke the spell. The world filtered through. I heard the traffic outside, and a radio talk show playing in a back room of the bar. I smelled burned toast. The martini had given my appetite a tickle; I wanted something to eat.

'I'll leave you to it,' she said. 'I have a fragmented love letter to return to, remember?'

'What if it was fragmented not because it's ancient, but because the person who received it tore it to pieces? What if it was unrequited?'

She reached out and cradled my chin with her hand. 'Look at you,' she said. She was smiling but there was sadness in her voice. 'Bruises and cuts. Don't let your heart go the same way.'

She kissed me and left.

Mo Belper, who had been sweeping the floor nearby, kicked my shin.

'What was that for?'

'You,' he said. His voice was deep and fractured, the result of a lifetime of firing salbutamol and tar at his lungs. 'Always seeing red lights. You sit with a beautiful woman and you send her away on a downer. We all get the face we deserve, Joel.'

'Your face is going to deserve that broom if you don't piss off and fix me a bacon sandwich,' I said.

Refuelled, I stood at the doorway looking up and down the street. Clear.

I caught a cab for the flat, in need of fresh clothes. Streets blurred past the window, and it seemed like a speeded-up version of the past few days, slogging along roads searching, running to, running away from. My hips, knees and ankles twinged with the effort of all the miles I'd clocked up. I wondered about holidays. Difficult to do when you have a stay-at-home cat, but now I daydreamed a little about putting the little fucker in a cattery, or paying for a sitter, or sticking him in a gulag with armed guards. Jet off for a week to a beach. South of France. Portugal. Drag Romy with me. Sarah too. Because I was going to find her. She was close enough I could touch her; I could smell the strawberry lip balm she always used.

Mengele was there to greet me. I say 'greet' but 'assault' might be more accurate. His tail lashed at me and he stared at it, mildly alarmed, perhaps thinking what he might achieve if he attached razor blades to it. I bent to scratch his ear and he bit me, actually breaking the little web of skin between my thumb and forefinger.

26

I dreamed we were in the claustrophobic office on Poland Street. Standing room only. All attention on me at the front of the room. A light blazed in my face alongside the unblinking shark's eye of the TV camera. Nerves rioting in my gut like a nest of snakes sprayed with petrol. Pencils poised. I speak and I can't hear the words. They fold and jumble in my head like shapes I once knew but no longer recognise. Journalists transcribe anyway. I see the jag of graphite on paper, the weird hieroglyphics of Pitman and Teeline. And a shadow growing.

Romy Toussaint with a collapsing smile on her mouth, nodding in encouragement, but perhaps taken aback by the savagery of what I'm saying. Ian Mawker looking tired and worn, stretched thin like his underpant elastic. I stare into that lens and see the soul of The Hack welling like black oil from the cracked engine block of a car too dangerous to drive any more. The words go straight into him like hooks. All distance is concertinaed; I'm pulling him into the midst of us. The shadow grows. He's here. Everyone touched by that elongating black figure shrinks in pain, cradling charred limbs. A photographer with an arm like a mackerel-striped log left in the embers of a bonfire trips backward, his camera melting, fusing to his skin. A woman falls to her knees, her face blasted red, the flesh hanging off her like shreds left on a barbecue rack, eyes poached in their sockets, milk-white, puckered dry.

The shadow has his arm curled around his notepad; a kid at school protecting his work from the copycats. Steam and smoke rises from his grinning mouth, and the black hoods where his own eyes should be. The pencil crackles and crumbles on paper turned to sheaves of grey wafer in the heat.

Notes and queries, he said, but his voice was all breath, like some mystic wind in a far-flung desert. *Skeletons on the page*.

I was backing away. I could feel the heat coming off him. I felt my eyebrows crisp. Moisture fled from my skin. I reached out to Romy but she burst into flames before I could touch her.

I came out of sleep roaring.

Mengele was on the other side of the room, watching me warily. I must have been crying out in my sleep. Sweat speckled my brow; I felt it trickle down the small of my back. I took a hot shower and checked myself in the mirror. I looked like a filleted chicken skin with the bones put in ass backwards. I wrapped a towel around my waist and retrieved the bottle of Grey Goose from the freezer. I got a shot glass, thought better of it, and picked out a chunky tumbler. I poured in an inch, thought better of it, and half-filled the glass.

I went out on to the balcony. It was okay, but you could feel the plucking fingers of winter just past trying to cling on. I stared out at the rooftops and the cranes and felt a tremor of fear at the thought of going out there again. I never seemed to do what normal people did any more. And it was getting harder to remember what that was, exactly. Not much of the last five years could be entered into the 'mundane' column of life's ledger. The last time I went to the cinema, Rebecca and Sarah had been with me. I didn't have long lunches any more. I didn't go out to the pub with mates. I didn't see any mates. I didn't have any mates. Not close ones, the kind you can call any time to bend their ear. The kind you can drop in on, unannounced. Tokuzo, maybe, but she'd argue the toss.

The drink was going down all too easily. I wanted another. But I knew another was going to skew everything. But that was all right. I needed some down time, some me time. A couple of drinks at home, a delivered pizza. Unexpected cat attacks and news programmes on the radio, or some music. I was dead on my feet, I suggested to myself. I deserved a night off, I persuaded.

I put on my bathrobe as a way to underline that thought, and poured myself another drink. I ordered a pizza online with more toppings than gravity could deal with and put on some music. I hadn't listened to Zbigniew Preisner since Rebecca had died – she loved his music – so I listened to that, expecting the floods to come, but it was okay. I had a drink to celebrate that Rubicon moment. The pizza turned up and I ate the lot, heroically fending off Mengele with one hand while I scarfed down anchovies, olives, hot green peppers and mushrooms. I drank some more. I didn't notice the CD finish. I didn't tune in to the news. I sat in the dark and listened to the rasp of Mengele's tongue on the pizza box and drank until the glass was empty and then I refilled the glass and did it all again.

Drinking released the fear I'd locked away in me. Drinking was the only way to deal with it too. An hour later and the fear was too big for me to contain it in my small living room and the vodka wasn't putting too much of a dent in it. I went out on to the balcony again and breathed hard and deep. I rested the hand holding the glass on the railing but I misjudged and instead knocked the glass out of my fingers. I almost went over the railing after it, trying to catch it; it was the last of the glasses from our wedding list, a set of beautiful Polish tumblers. Really chunky numbers – very heavy: a third of it was a solid glass base – and they'd all been broken over the years but I'd been extra special careful with this one, until now. I heard it shatter in the communal back alley, the place where everyone in this block kept their bins. Ignominious ending. The sound seemed to go on for minutes.

Another little link to Rebecca erased; soon all that remained of our marriage, the only tangible proofs, would be a certificate in a tin in a box in the attic. And Sarah.

And the attic might catch fire one day. And one day Sarah would die. She might die tonight. She might be dying right now, while pizza congealed in my gut and I kept milking a bottle of vodka.

I reeled to the bedroom and threw on some clothes. I had no idea where I was heading but wherever it was I was in no fit state to be there. I fell over twice before I'd even got my jeans on, and even then they were back to front. Mengele looked bug-eyed frightened: a first. This was in no job description he'd been privy to. Idiot opens cans – check. Idiot supplies arms/legs for general scarring – check. Idiot thrashes around failing to get dressed properly – WTF?

I jack-knifed over the corner of the bed and cracked my head on the edge of the skirting board. Mengele turned his back on me and left the room. I opened the bedroom window and screamed Sarah's name. I kept screaming until the guy next door – the guy who must have a cock made of splintered steel if his girlfriend's coital shrieks were anything to go by – started hammering on the wall for me to be quiet. By that time I'd pulled something in my throat, or stripped it raw, and I couldn't produce any more sound anyway. I shambled back to the kitchen and poured another drink, just a small one, to alleviate the pain.

And then I was in a bar I didn't recognise and a woman who was at least as pissed as me was jouncing around on her stool laughing at some joke I'd told or she'd told. Or maybe there was no joke and she was just insane. Loud music was playing and someone was dancing on a table. A couple in a corner sat next to each other, drinks neatly aligned in front of them. They said nothing. His hand palpated her right breast as if he was searching for his keys; death couldn't have made her features less thrilled.

'Where's Sarah?' I asked the barman.

'Where's Sarah?' I asked the doorman.

'Where's Sarah?' I asked the woman in the bus queue.

Outside a bar in Meard Street I asked a guy tapping the screen of an iPhone.

'Sarah?' he said. 'I know where Sarah is.'

'Is she safe?'

'She's safe. You want to see her?'

'I need to see her.'

'It'll cost you.'

Red descent. It wasn't so much the content as the delivery; he wouldn't look up from his fucking screen. I slapped the phone from his hands and grabbed him around the throat.

'Where is she?'

He seemed utterly unfazed, although his voice now sounded like Donald Duck speaking through a eunuch flute. 'It'll cost you.'

I got his hand and folded it and sent it up his back. He yelled out. I folded it a little more. He begged me to stop. I told him to take me to Sarah.

Somehow we got to D'Arblay Street and he led me into a mews filled with shadows and blocks of tired red light. He was saying something over and over – *you'll pay for this* – but I was past listening to him.

'Just get the fucking door open,' I said.

Inside three women unfolded from a sofa in front of a small TV. They were wearing fishnet stockings and push-up bras. They looked at us with a mixture of defeat and amusement.

'Who's this?' asked one, in an accent I couldn't place. She looked European at least. There was a smell of peppermint tea and scorched hair.

'Where's Sarah?' I yelled.

'Whichever one you want,' said the guy. 'You let go of me you'd better be ready to pay double or I'll paint the fucking walls with you.'

I broke his arm and left him pale-faced, cradling himself in the corner of the room while the girls huddled together. One of them pulled a Taser out of her bag and aimed it at me.

'Get out,' she said.

I left.

I ordered vodka and a Kronenbourg chaser in a bar where the walls were decorated with what looked like cow hides. It was the last drink I managed that night. The woman sitting next to me was vaping on something that looked like a steampunk sonic screwdriver. She frowned whenever I spoke to her.

'Warsaw?' she said. 'Warsaw? What the fuck are you on, mister?'

I blacked out.

When I revived I was outside. I'd pissed myself and I was wearing a bib of vomit. The smell of undigested alcohol hung in a pall around me. The sky looked like a funky bandage removed from an infected wound: all ochre and deep purple; there was even a soft band of green in there.

I struggled upright and recognised where I was. Welbeck Street. At least I'd been heading home in vaguely the right direction before my gas ran out. The area below my left eye was stiff; I reckon someone had punched me at some point. Just the one person? Bonus. All things considered I'd got off lightly, although the evening wouldn't return to me in glorious Technicolor. I got little snippets and excerpts granted me by the fear editor in my head. *Look at what you did, you arsehole. Remember this? You did this too, look. You complete twat-meister.*

Another fifteen minutes and I was turning into Homer Street. All my gauges were at zero. Needles shivering in red zones. I was going to have a bath and sleep it all away.

'Hey.'

Another stranger. I'd had enough of strangers. It was folded into itself, crouched in my doorway, hooded. I saw the faintest spots of light where its eyes must have been. I hung back. I don't like strangers who know where I live, strangers waiting for me.

The figure stood up. It was Niker. His posture spoke of defeat. He looked finished.

'What do you want?' I asked. Despite my fatigue I felt

myself instantly back on guard. I was on my toes. I was fight or flight.

'Jesus,' he said. 'You look like a mop in the gastroenteritis ward.'

'Save it for your fiction,' I said. 'What are you doing here?'

'I'm scared,' he said. 'I think I'm being followed.'

'So you came here?' I said. 'You fucking legend.'

'I had nowhere else to go.'

I was sizing up the cars parked on my street, deciding if I recognised them or not, deciding if they were empty, or containing shadows of intent. 'Where's Kim?' I asked. I shook the door keys from my pocket. A taxi pulled up at the end of the street and two men got out. They stood together, talking in hushed voices, while the taxi driver pulled away.

'I don't know,' he said. 'I think... I think shuh-shuh-she's... I think...' His voice was cracking and crumbling all over the place. I thought, *Clever cover, good talent.*

'Get inside,' I said, and stepped past him, got the door open. The figures at the end of the street were still huddled together, but they were watching me now. I felt the familiar scuttle of adrenaline as it charged up and down my spine. I was drunk and exhausted, but the needles were rising out of the red zone for a while.

We went up to my flat. Niker's skin was pale enough to light the way. His eyes wouldn't focus. I thought maybe he'd taken something, or drunk too much, but it was just the thousand-yard stare. I see that a lot. I've worn it a couple of times. It was shock, and seeing too much of what was bad for you. It was a combination of terrible memories and a future that wouldn't resolve itself no matter what decisions or choices you made. The stare was an incremental shutting down.

Mengele had fallen asleep on the sofa, but not before

dragging a stack of papers to the floor. I eyed the vodka bottle on the floor and thought a return to oblivion would be great, but I didn't have the energy to lift it. Niker sat by the cat and pressed a hand against its flank. Mengele jerked awake.

'You might want to retreat a little if you want to leave this place in one piece,' I said. 'He has a trophy room filled with the limbs of those he's bested in the past.'

But already Mengele was purring like a two-stroke engine at full throttle. He turned over and showed Niker his belly.

'Well, I've never seen that before,' I said. 'You have The Touch, I'll give you that.'

But Niker wasn't paying attention. He was staring at the wall, and shivering from time to time, the way I sometimes do when I've remembered something cringe-inducing from a night of too much sauce.

I left them to their mutual masturbation session and checked the street from my bedroom. The guys were still on the corner. One of them was on the phone. A couple of minutes later and a van pulled up. They got in. It left. Just guys waiting for a lift. Not everyone wanted to fill me full of holes.

Relieved, I went back to the living room. Mengele was sitting up now, a possessive paw resting on Niker's knee. He shot me a look with those green, coin-slot eyes as if to say, *Can we keep him, Master?*

I went to the bathroom and peeled off my crust of sick. I showered and shampooed. I put on some jogging pants and a T-shirt. In the kitchen I made a pot of nuclear-strength coffee. 'You hungry?' I asked.

'I can't eat,' he said.

I dumped sausages in a pan anyway, and served them to him in a sandwich with plenty of ketchup and English mustard.

'Best hangover cure I know,' I said, wolfing mine. 'This or

pho made with tons of hot chillies.'

'I don't have a hangover,' he said.

'Maybe you need one,' I said.

'You drink too much,' he said.

'Define "too much". Personally, I think I don't drink enough.'

'You found Solo yet?'

'Her name's Sarah.'

'Getting warm?'

'I'm working on it,' I said. I waited for him to get to what it was he wanted from me. 'Have you heard from her?'

He shook his head. 'No. I don't think she liked me very much. I heard her telling Odessa once that she thought I was a gobby cuntbuster.'

I winced. 'Well she didn't get that language from me,' I said. I finished my sandwich and fetched the coffee. He was more enthusiastic about that than the food. After a few hefty swigs he closed his eyes and leaned back on the sofa. 'My God, that's better,' he said.

'Who's Ronnie?'

'Who?'

'That's what I said. Who is he?'

'I don't know any Ronnie,' he said.

'Name cropping up in this freak's manuscripts. Along with your initials.'

'Really?'

'Really.'

'Mine and probably ten million other people.'

'It could be a coincidence. Or it could be you.'

'It isn't me.'

I believed him. The angriest thing about him at that moment was the crease in his trousers.

'I always knew there was something screwy about you,' he said. 'Right from the off.'

'How so?'

'You weirded me out. That first night. The way you threw yourself at that tower. I knew we weren't dealing with some wannabe short story writer. That there was something more to you than that. And I was right.'

'Just a dad trying to find his little girl.'

'Maybe.'

'And who are you? Behind the cocky look. Full of cum and attitude. What's behind all that?'

He bowed his lip. 'I want to be a writer. It's all I've ever wanted. All the other stuff. It was nearly compensation. I pushed myself. I did things. I experienced. The others thought I was reckless. Thought I was pushing the self-destruction button. But that's me. All or nothing.'

'You submitted work?'

'Yes,' he said. He looked sheepish, hunted.

'I mean to agencies. Publishers.'

'Yes.'

'And?'

'What do you think? Everything bombed. I wrote, redrafted dozens of times, I honed, I polished, I read all the "How to" manuals. I read fiction like oxygen for the lungs. A novel – sometimes two novels – a week for years. I sent it in and it came straight back. Form rejection.

'Do you have any idea what it's like to knock on the door in your Sunday best every day of your life only to find nobody ever opens it? Nobody ever *sees* you?'

'I can think of parallels,' I said.

'Not many,' he insisted. 'Not nearly as crushing. And what's worse…' He sat up, sat forward. The thing that was pissing him off the most was also making him the most animated. '...is that I wouldn't be happy even if I did get a taste of it. If I sold a story I'd be buried in the contents. I wouldn't open the fucking book. I wouldn't close the fucking book. I'd be lost amid the *names*. I think it would be worse to be one of the "many others".'

'The goalposts are always moving,' I said.

'Yeah, well, I'm finished. I thought I was good at it. I thought I was a stand out. I used to love writing, just love it for the fun of it, for what it was. I loved it before I knew you could be published or paid. But once you get on that conveyor belt... it gets so you can't think of anything else. You forget why you were doing it in the first place. All you ever seem to do is hear of younger writers landing big deals and film adaptations and "Hey, everybody, just finished another one..." and it all looks so easy and effortless and you sit alone in your room grinding out some piece of shit that took months and months and it's bad, it's derivative and clunky and... just... bad.'

'Where's Kim?' I asked him.

He looked at me and there was terror in his eyes.

'She's dead,' he said.

'What happened?'

'I think she's dead.'

'Sean,' I said. 'Back up. Relax. Tell me.'

'We were together. Last night. This morning. Late. We had decided to stick together until this was over. This morning we were going to catch a train to stay with my mother in Leeds. We caught the Tube at Leicester Square. She went through the barriers but my ticket didn't work properly. She was on the escalator. She turned to me and I saw her sink out of sight. By the time one of the staff let me through the escalator was empty. I couldn't find her at the bottom. She wasn't on the platform. A train had just departed. I guessed she'd caught it – I mean, what else could she have done? – but when I got to Tufnell Park she wasn't there either. I tried calling her but she wasn't answering her phone. A little later I received a text from her number.'

'What text?' I asked. 'What did it say?'

He slipped his phone from his pocket and fiddled with the screen, passed it over.

New experience

'She's playing with you,' I said. 'She's teasing you.'

'She wouldn't tease me about this. She was scared rigid. Me too. We talked about it for hours after President died. We knew we were being targeted. I'm the only one left now. Well, me and Solo, if she's even—'

'Don't you fucking dare,' I said, and counted to ten. 'You don't know for sure. Kim could turn up. You'll feel such a prick when she does.'

'Come on,' Niker said. 'You know who sent that text. You know what "new experience" he was referring to.'

I sighed. 'The kind you can never write about.'

'You said it. And I'll be next. Me or—'

'I told you to leave it.'

'So what now?'

'Go to Leeds,' I said. 'Right now. Get out of Dodge. But be careful. Don't get a taxi. Walk. Take the Tube. But don't go direct. Mix it up. Make sure at every step that there's nobody at your back. Stay among crowds. Keep moving. Go to Leeds. Stay there until it's over. Write a classic.'

'You make it sound easy.'

'Stay then,' I said. 'Die. Like I give a shit.'

I stared at him until he stood up. He pulled his jacket closer around him. I saw the child beneath the stubble, in the wide-eyed shock of people who become what they never thought they'd be.

'I thought he was you, for a while,' I said. 'The initials. And when you showed up here I thought you were reacting to the come on we put out on the TV and radio.'

He seemed a little confused, then he seemed a little angry, but he couldn't sustain it. He sighed and pinched the bridge of his nose. 'Tough guy.'

'Wannabe tough guy. One step away from needing a hug from Mummy.'

'Whatever, Sorrell,' he said. He pressed his lips together, looked around my flat. 'I saw the broadcast. I thought it was... desperate.'

'We *are* desperate.'

'He'll know that.'

'I want him to know that. I want him to react. If he reacts because he's narked, great. If he reacts because he thinks he's untouchable, superior, that's great too. We need him to make his move.'

'He's made plenty. We're all dead.'

'Not all,' I said, but it was a whisper he didn't hear, or chose to ignore.

27

After he'd gone I dunked my head into a sink full of iced water and kept it there until it felt as if my skull was beginning to compress my brain. Pain ricocheted all around, but it felt great. It felt as if it was zapping all the bad stuff in there; slapping the drunk molecules awake and telling them to get a grip. I surfaced and let out a blast of air mingled with a strange trumpeting that felt like triumph and despair mixed.

'Hi,' I said to my reflection. 'My name is Joel Sorrell and I have a drink problem. The problem is this: I can't drink as much as I need to get rid of the frighteners in my mind. Please send help. Or if not help, more booze.'

I blew a kiss and towelled myself dry.

The living room was a tip. Mengele sat imperious at the centre of it all. If he knew the gesture he'd have been giving me the Vs. 'That's right, clean it all up, bitch,' I imagined he was saying, probably in a James Mason voice, as I began scooping up magazines and books and stacked plates that his paws had disturbed.

My fingers found the envelope that the manuscript to

Patrick Simm had arrived in. The lack of stamps or franking materials was frustrating, and I had to admire the nerve of the guy, stepping up and delivering the thing by hand in broad daylight. He might have been spotted.

But that didn't make sense. He'd been careful every step. No fingerprints. No sightings. I raised the envelope to my face and inhaled. Utterly neutral. No embossings. No labels. No return addresses. I shook the envelope. I rubbed it like Aladdin, thinking a Royal Mail genie might pop out and offer me three wishes but only if they were correctly addressed and weighed no more than one hundred grams. I spread the flaps and stared inside. Something. A sticker with a barcode on it, and a name: Mustard Bikes.

The Hack hadn't delivered the parcel in person after all. He'd paid a cycle courier to do it for him.

Mustard Bikes was based in one of the arches near Stamford Brook station in Chiswick. It took a while to find it. I got there early to find a controller sitting at a desk just inside the red concertina doors. He was eating noodles from a cup and speaking into a radio. Something about a bag of video cassettes to be taken to Lewisham from Wardour Street. Behind him was a bicycle in bits on a large piece of tarpaulin, and a set of tools.

'Help you?' he said. He lifted the noodles on a fork and sucked them through a pursed mouth that looked like something prolapsed from a jungle ape's backside. He wiped his mouth against his arm: his sleeve was streaked with stock.

'Breakfast of champions,' I said, thinking of Romy.

'Fuck all else in. Except for a packet of Malted Milk biscuits, and they taste like sick don't they?'

'Are you Jay Taylor? Is this Mustard Bikes?'

'Yes and yes.'

'Recently,' I said, 'a package – an envelope filled with papers – was delivered by one of your couriers to an address in Mayfair. Albemarle Street. I need to know who booked that job.'

'"One of my couriers",' he said. His voice was full of mockery. 'I've only got one.'

'Right. Mustard *Bike*, then. I could do with speaking to him. Or you, if you've got an originating address.'

'I have to be honest,' he said, as he put the cup of noodles down and drew a large ledger towards him, 'I almost never make a note of what job is going where, never mind where it came from.'

'An organised outfit,' I said.

'We do okay,' he said, smiling.

'I'm surprised,' I said. 'You must be shelling out at least ten grand on this place in rent each year. Plus business rates. And you've got just the one cyclist? What's he pulling in per job. Three quid? Four?'

'Around that, yeah. The tiddlers, yeah. But there are still some people out there who prefer the personal touch, rather than faxes and emails. And some pay well, for, you know, special jobs.'

'I can believe it,' I said. 'What was the Albemarle job? Was that special?'

'I can't see it in here,' the controller was saying, pointedly studying the reams of blank pages.

'Come on,' I said. 'Ditch the comedy. This is important.'

'Unpack what you mean by "important" using, oh, I don't know, monetary terms.'

'How about I unpack it in pints of blood shed from your worthless sack of shit body?'

He pushed himself back from his desk and stood up. He was half a foot taller than me, but clearly he sat at a desk all day sucking noodles through his arsehole mouth. His belly hung over the waistband of his pants. I punched him straight away, right in the neck. He went down, coughing and spluttering, surprised more than anything. I picked up the cup of noodles and emptied them over his head. Then I grabbed hold of his hair and dragged him over the open ledger. I pressed his face into the blank page.

'Look really close,' I said. 'Study it hard and tell me what you see. I'd be fascinated to hear.'

'Cuh-unt,' he said, in a strangled voice. I made it even more strangled by grabbing his wattle and really digging my nails in. He made a weird animal shriek. I smelled garlic and soy sauce on his breath.

'People are dead,' I said. 'I want to stop it. This is the only lead I have at the moment. I would like to follow it. You are preventing that. Now spill your fucking guts or I will spill your fucking guts.'

'All right, all right,' he said, as if he'd only been having a bit of fun with me and I'd gone over the top with my reaction. I let him go and he sat up. His throat looked as though someone had bitten him. Noodles clung to his hair and skin like a kid's pasta collage gone wrong. 'I don't enter details on hush jobs.'

'Hush jobs,' I said. 'You mean bent jobs.'

He ignored me. 'I don't know where it originated from,' he said. 'You'd have to talk to my brother. His address is on the job list.' He flicked a piece of paper in my direction.

'Your brother, the courier?'

'Yeah, we're a family business.'

'So where is he now?'

'I don't know. Sucking down porridge. On his fucking bike somewhere, delivering shit.'

'Call him.'

'Fuck you.'

'But you'll call him when I've gone.'

'Fucking dead right.'

I picked up his rig and hurled it at the wall.

'That's the best part of a grand you owe me.'

I grabbed his hair and twisted. When he raised his hands to try to loosen my grip, I slipped my free hand into his pocket and relieved him of his phone. I smashed that against the wall too.

'Keys,' I said.

'Just fucking leave,' he said.

'Keys, or I'll throw *you* against the wall.'

He handed over his keys. Outside I shut the concertina doors and locked them. Then I dropped his keys through the grate of a drain and hurried back to my own car. I was shaking with the buzz that comes from acts of violence, more so that they seemed these days to be emanating from me. The closer to getting what I needed, the nastier I was becoming. I wasn't sure I was too happy with that, although, I thought, as I perused the list Jay Taylor had given up, at least it meant quicker results.

Ryan Taylor lived in a flat in an estate in Dalston. I got there by nine a.m., pessimistic about my chances of catching him before he went off on his jobs for the day. There was a guy sitting in a Ford Kuga smoking a cigarette and reading the newspaper. I asked him if he knew Ryan Taylor and he nodded.

'Out though,' he said. 'Early bird. Back late and all.'

I thanked him and checked the list of jobs again. I'd arranged them into order travelling south to north from this Dalston beauty spot. There was no guarantee that Ryan would have done the same, but it made sense to do it this way, especially if speed was of the essence.

I really didn't want to do this, but I couldn't think of a way around it. It might eat up a big chunk of the day; there was every chance I'd only catch up with him when he arrived back at his flat. At least, if that happened, he'd be dead on his feet and unlikely to give me any trouble.

In the end I found him almost immediately. But I was lucky. He'd stopped off at a café on Kingsland Road for his breakfast and he'd locked his bike – a stripped-back single-speed Dawes Mono in bright yellow, a real mustard bike – at head height on a railing opposite, presumably so he could keep his eye on it while he waited for his bacon bap.

I stood by his bike and let the air out of his tyres. He came out with a white paper bag, the cleats on his soles skittering on the pavement. He was hunched over to balance himself against any sudden slips and he wore one of those ridiculous speed helmets that resembles an elongated teardrop.

'You look like a shit velociraptor,' I said.

'You're the cunt gave my brother grief,' he said.

'So he managed to call you after all? Anyway, he gave himself grief. Everyone has the option to make the right decision and avoid grief. The alternative is time-wasting and bruises. I wonder which way you'll go.'

'You made my decision for me when you let the air out of my Halos. You fuckhead.'

'I just want to know who booked the delivery of a

manuscript to a literary agent – Patrick Simm – on Albemarle Street in the recent past.'

'Who gives a fuck?'

'I do. And so do the police. We've got reason to believe the person who sent it is a murderer. We want to stop him before it happens again. You could help.'

'I'll consider it after I've used my pump on your arse.'

'Leave your filthy little fetishes for your Dalston hellhole,' I said.

He came for me and I sidestepped easily. His cleats slipped on the pavement and he fell awkwardly, his left leg shooting out to the side.

'Ooh,' I said, wincing. 'Unintentional yoga.'

He got up, haltingly, and leaned back against the railing. 'You've fucked my groin,' he said.

'Words I hope never to hear ever again,' I said.

'That's me buggered today,' he said. 'That's my wedge gone.'

'I'll compensate you. The full whack. In return for some information.'

He slid down to the ground and pressed a gloved hand against the top of his thigh. 'What makes you think I should remember a job that might have happened weeks ago?'

'I don't know. Maybe because it was unusual in some way. Maybe you saw something you didn't want to see. Not a usual client. A client who paid over the odds to do something that the post office could have done for much less.'

It was starting to rain, but it was little more than a fine mist. It beaded on Ryan's woollen cycling jersey. The radio fastened to the bandolier around his chest chuckled and chirped. He wore Lycra cycling shorts; his calves were taut, nut brown, cabled with veins. He stared at me.

'Come on,' I said. 'I need to get a wiggle on. Rack what passes for your brains.'

'Woman,' he said. 'Older woman. But toned, you know. A MILF. Hell, maybe even a GILF. I've got no qualms about ancient pussy, as long as it's bookended by top tatas and a bubble arse.'

'I'm sure she'd be thrilled to know that,' I said. 'Name?'

'No name.'

'Address then?'

'I don't remember. Somewhere out in Waltham Cross.'

'If you could narrow that down a bit.'

'I don't remember.'

Yeah, you do, I thought. *A guy like you who might be fit, but has bad teeth and eyes that are too close together. A guy whose hair always looks greasy and lank no matter how much you wash it. You haven't had a girlfriend for some time because they don't like your shithole address or your shithole brother or your shithole mouth. Or maybe it's your total lack of respect for anyone, let alone the women you lust after. The smirk on your lips – unnecessary, unsuccessful, unearned – that makes you look contemptuous, not beguiling or sexy or mysterious, as you'd have it. Your eyes constantly looking at the tatas or the bubble and never any deeper than that. Evenings in the pub with your no-mark mates, leaning back against the bar. Do that. Had her. Till it bled. And then back home to a microwaved pot and Pornhub and a spit-slicked fist.*

I came to and his face was a bubbling, fizzing mask of blood and snot. He was moaning at me, maybe he was begging me to stop. My right hand was mashed into a fist, hair matted against it. I'd hit him so hard that one of my knuckles had been dislocated and driven back into my hand. Sirens wailed. So did he.

I let go of him and dropped to my knees. 'Where in Waltham Cross?'

And then I heard that he wasn't begging me to stop. He was reciting an address, over and over. I leaned in close to his mouth.

Station Approach.

PART THREE

ENDPAPERS

28

I was heading back to the car when a plain-clothes crime-fighting duo in an unmarked black BMW 3 Series pulled up, blocking my way. Their radio hissed and spat with dead code as they pushed me into the back seat.

'We don't need to do this,' I said. 'Not now at least.'

'We do, actually,' said the driver. He was bald and there were spidery white scars all over the skin. 'We had a complaint from a guy about you. This guy was wearing his breakfast. Noodles, apparently. Someone saw him stuck in a window of an archway warehouse in W6 and called the police. He wasn't trying to break in, he was trying to break out. It was his shop. Someone had locked him in. You, specifically.'

'Hello, Ian,' I said.

Ian Mawker was sitting in the back seat reading the *Daily Mail*. He was sucking food out of his teeth and he pointedly did not look up when I joined him.

'You're under arrest,' he said.

'Oh, fuck off, Ian. I've got an address.'

'An address for who?'

'It's "whom". And it's him. The Hack. We can be there in

half an hour if you stick your ice cream jingle on.'

'Where you'll be in half an hour is a cell in Stoke Newington nick. What's the address?'

'You don't play this game very well, do you? You think I'm going to tell you unless you loosen your girdle and relax? We go together or not at all.'

'If you don't tell us, nobody goes, and time ticks on. Sarah could still be okay now. In half an hour, who knows? Or is that "whom" as well?'

'Hey, Humpty,' I said to the driver. His eyes drilled into mine via the rearview mirror. 'Did you know that an anagram of "Ian Mawker" is "I am a cunt"?'

'Wanker, surely,' said passenger seat, a virulent-looking streak of dung with his hair styled in what we used to call a fanny fringe back in junior school.

'Shut it, Pascoe,' said Mawker.

'Ian,' I said. 'Let me in on this.'

'No. Fucking. Chance.' He folded his *Daily Mail* and slipped it into his inner pocket. 'But I'll cut you a deal. You give us this address, we collar the bastard, you walk. No arrest. No charges. You're free to go back to missing the urinals at your favourite watering holes. You can go home to your psycho cat and frot yourself off against him some more.'

I stared at him. He was serious. He wore that goading expression of his, a look that said: *Go on, test me, see what happens.* He wanted me to push my luck. He wanted me in a cell.

I decided to push anyway, one last little go. 'This is my daughter, you fuckhead. If she dies because you go in there with a hard-on—'

'We'll play it by the book, I promise.'

'I don't trust you to piss through the right hole,' I said.

'You know, you never say anything nice to me,' he said. 'I'm not sure you ever have, even when we were cadets. And I'm not too bothered about that. That ship has sailed the fuck off. If you said something nice to me now it wouldn't sound right. It doesn't sit nicely with you, saying nice things. I imagine it tastes bad on your tongue. It wouldn't surprise me if you called your mother Old Vinegar Tits. And the so-called women you spend your nights with, I bet they don't hang around too long because of it.'

My hands were white fists on my thighs. If I punched him now then that would be it, no matter if I gave him the address and offered him a massage and breakfast in bed.

'If I walk away and you find Sarah, you bring me back. You let me see her straight away, no matter what state she's in.'

'You have my word.'

I gave him the address in Waltham Cross and stepped out of the car.

There was a coffee shop. There was a bar. I wanted coffee. So I chose the bar, because (I kidded myself) I could always order my coffee there. Booze was a backup, if I really needed it. I'd never be able to order a cocktail from a bean-dedicated barista. Not that I was going to sink a hard one at this time of the day. Haha. No way.

I resisted the urge to hop in a cab and welly it up the road to Waltham Cross. I'd only muddy the waters and distract Mawker from fucking everything up in his own special way. Better to wait and listen for the fallout.

I took my cucumber martini to a dark corner; fatigue followed me. I sat and traced the frosted sides of the glass with a finger and felt the strain of the week hunker down

311

on my eyelids. The pale green drink reminded me of the colour of the eyes of a cat that once used to visit us in the garden of our house in Lime Grove. It was a pretty cat, ash grey, with beautiful eyes. It walked with a pronounced limp. One of its rear legs was stiff from an accident or some congenital condition, and it hobbled around, but without any apparent discomfort.

In that room of hot, hard camera lights.

Sarah made friends with the cat. If I got close it would give me the slow blink and the question mark tail but any attempt to pat it would be met with claws and teeth. But not for her. It would roll on its belly and allow her to tickle its chest and throat.

The click of mechanical pencils and digital recorders. Pages flipped in reporters' notebooks.

Alien colours roamed around the back of my eyelids. I wasn't going to sleep. What was it my nana used to say when she sat back in her armchair? When I was a kid, visiting with Mum and Adam. 'I'm not having a nap, I'm resting my eyes.'

I thought of Martin Gower in a seedy little room of urban heat and fashionable decay. The soft, buttery light from a flash. Sarah parading in front of an arctic-white photographic background. Fan on. Catch lights in her eyes. A light coating of Vaseline on the slender muscles of her calves.

Journalists in here too, somehow, scribbling descriptions into their pads, leaning in close to ask questions. *How long do you think you've got, Miss Sorrell?*

It's Peart. And it's Ms.

P-E-R-T...

P-E-A-R-T, you perve. Don't they teach you how to spell in journalism school?

Journalism school. The Teeline shorthand book in Gower's room.

I flew out of sleep and knocked the martini to the floor. The glass smashed, and faces at the bar whipped my way. I was thinking of skltns.

SLX Sesh.

SLX had nothing to do with camera models or photographic studios. It was a street name that Gower had written down, but minus the vowels, which is what journalists do with words before they turn them into shorthand squiggles.

I asked the guy at the bar if he had a *London A–Z* map, and he handed one over after he'd underlined the seriousness of my crime by noisily emptying the dustpan of broken glass into the bin.

I flipped to the index and ran my finger down the S columns. Nothing under 'Sa' or 'Se'. But here: *Silex Street, SE1.*

I checked my watch. Twenty minutes since I'd been planted on the street by Mawker. They probably wouldn't even be in Waltham Cross yet. Southwark wasn't a million miles away. It was something to do. I might at least find some evidence of where Sarah was staying, if it wasn't Silex Street itself. She might even be there now.

I called Jimmy Two and told him where the car was and asked him to pick it up for me at a time suitable to his schedule within the next half hour thanks very much. Then I caught the London Overground from Haggerston down to Canada Water where I nipped on to the Jubilee Line. I was in Southwark within forty minutes. No calls or texts from Mawker. They must be there now. I closed my eyes against the suggestion that there must be a stand-off between police and villain. The Hack firing pot shots at them from a bedroom window, or worse, holding Sarah hostage while

Mawker utterly fucked up the negotiations.

I checked my phone again. No headlines. Nothing happening. Not yet.

Silex Street was around a five-minute walk south of the Tube. It was a nondescript street of mainly purpose-built flats. None of the windows suggested the airy room in which Sarah had been photographed by Martin Gower, but at the north end there was a substantial building largely boarded up, with some of the higher windows smashed. At some point in its history it had been known as Newspaper House, but that sign over the main door was now little more than a series of ghosted letters, chipped off by vandals or weather and time.

I tried the door but it was locked. I had to climb over a concrete wall at the end to access the rear of the building. Locked containers rusted on a wasteland of aggregate and plastic. A chain-link leash was attached to a metal post driven into the ground, but whatever dog had been tied to it was no longer around.

There was a metal door at the back with a corner eaten through by rust. There was enough space to crawl in. Someone else was doing so on a regular basis: you could tell from the tracks in the dirt. I got on my belly and wriggled under. I could smell dead candles and hot grease in Styrofoam containers – somebody was inhabiting this space. I was in some kind of antechamber; not quite warehouse, not quite loading bay. A place where minions stacked and unstacked. A forklift zone. A huge roll of paper turned to pulp, bruised with mould, stood like a monument to the age of hot metal. There was a stack of trade magazines shrink-wrapped in plastic and lengths of nylon binding. Rats had chewed this protective coating away and shredded the innards for nests.

I listened to the air circulating through the chambers and channels of the building for a few moments. I tried to detect some current warmth within it; the flavours of chewing gum and coffee. The surfacing of lipstick and leather. But it was all just stale and sour and old.

I pushed on, trying to avoid the feeling that I was being consumed.

29

The way was partially blocked by a water-bloated door that sagged on its hinges. Someone had laid a mat inside, the kind you use to wipe off your wellies before setting foot in a house. The words GO AWAY were branded into the centre.

I went through the doorway and into an area where once had existed some kind of machinery; printing presses perhaps, although all of it was gone now. There were only a series of grooves in the cement floor, and a variety of bolts and brackets and sockets. A folder, swollen with moisture, containing old copies of the *Southwark Advertiser* had been left in a corner. A calendar girl from 1989 wore a cherry-coloured bikini and hair so back-combed it was porcupinian. Someone had scrawled fresh marker pen over her breasts and pudenda, given her a moustache and googly eyes. I had to stifle a breath because I thought I knew who had done it.

SLX sesh. Silex session.

This was some squat, some roughly photogenic make-do urban studio blessed with the kind of scarred brickwork and large arched windows that a cameraman likes to use to create a mood. It was a cliché mood, but it never seemed to go out of fashion. Grunge was popular, whether off the back of a musical legacy twenty years old, or linked to policies of austerity. It spoke of us against them. It gave those lacking privilege and entitlement something of an edge.

Now under the scorched smell of wax and stale reefer I could detect other notes, notes closer to home. White Musk, a scent Sarah always liked; cheap but distinct. Perhaps a little too cloying, but a kid's scent; a young woman's scent. The hot, vinegary smell of takeaway Chinese. *Dad, can I have sweet and sour pork?* A bottle of Strongbow cider.

Jesus Christ, Mawker, get on the blower and tell me you've nailed the swine. How much time do you need?

But he wouldn't, would he? He wouldn't be able to bring himself to contact you. If. You know, if.

Stone steps. One became two became many as the acoustics created greedy echoes, as if the building was revelling in a noise it had not known for many years. It gave the impression of pursuit, and it took me a while to relax and understand that I was alone. But that wasn't true. Somebody was living here. A person was making a small corner of this old newspaper factory into their home. I came upon a den of sorts, off a corridor on the third floor. Patterned throws bulldog-clipped to cracked windows. A sleeping bag. A nest of make-up. Newspapers stacked haphazardly: *The Independent. The Guardian.* A headstrong daughter. A dad who failed.

Books lined a wall, their pages bloated with damp. Caitlin Moran. Joan Didion. Siri Hustvedt. Clothes strewn around the lip of a gaping suitcase. I checked them. T-shirts and leggings and jeans in the main. Size ten. Doc Martens. Converse. Size five. Nothing else in the case beyond a few hotel soaps in their wrappers. A few free Barclays biros. Some forced experience this was. I hoped there might be a diary. Something to make concrete this suspicion that I was in the midst of my daughter's life.

In a zip-up pocket of the suitcase there was an envelope of photographs. Sarah with Mum. I felt the breath punched from me. I hadn't seen these pictures in years. Clowning for the camera. Dancing. Funny faces – *you'll stick like that if the wind changes* – and exaggerated hugs. There were no pictures of me, which pierced me a little, but it didn't matter. It was okay. I was the one holding the camera ninety-nine per cent of the time anyway. It was either that or lopped heads, inaccurate focus, fingers in front of the lens; Rebecca never tried to hide the fact she was a dreadful photographer. That was my reasoning, anyway. I clung to it.

I sat down on the sleeping bag and closed my eyes. The fan of photographs in one hand. Swatches of the bag in the other. As if I was trying to commune with the dead by holding physical links to her. *Stop that. Stop that.*

I hunted for warmth in the sleeping bag but I was so psyched up by my discovery that I couldn't tell if the heat beneath my fingers was evidence of recent occupancy or the mischief of my tommy gun heart.

Be here soon. Be anywhere other than that monster's lair in Waltham Cross.

I pulled out my phone, but before I could hit some numbers it leapt in my hand. It was Mawker. His call almost triggered an anatomical first for the human race: a man shitting out his own skeleton.

'Ian,' I said. My voice was flat and cold against the lonely stone. 'Tell me you've got him.'

'We've got him,' he said. But his voice was all wrong. There was none of the tart triumph I recognised in him whenever he had some high-level intelligence he wanted to use to lord it over me. All the moisture fled from my mouth. I had to work to unstick the strip of jerky tongue from the roof.

'Sarah,' I managed, little more than a puff of air.

'No. Joel. No, it's okay. I'm sorry. Sarah… she's not here.'

'Then what's up with you? You sound as if you've stumbled upon the grim truth behind your species' relatives.'

'This guy we've got. I know him.'

'You know him? What? He's someone on a wanted list? Ex-con?'

'No. He's ex-service. Name's Nyx. Scott Nyx. When I say I know him, I mean he was one of us. But he was only in the force six months. He left just last year. Post-traumatic stress disorder.'

'Because?' I was getting narked. Mawker was withholding something, worming around the truth. He wouldn't talk to me. And I was cheesed off that he was the one feeling this bastard's collar when it was me that had found him.

'That Archway fracas. You know. The one Sarah was involved in. According to the PSU roster he was on duty that night.'

He said it as if she was responsible for the whole thing. And for this guy Nyx's PTSD too.

'What, he couldn't cope with a bunch of shouty kids?'

'It was more than that. Bricks and bottles. Nyx was hit. But I don't… I don't get it.'

'What don't you get?'

There was some commotion going on in the background and I heard Mawker cover the phone while he yelled instructions. I felt an old twinge of excitement. The police raid. The battering ram. Entries and exits. Chasing down those chancers who make a break for it out of a rear window. I craved that for a moment. I itched to be back in the saddle with the others.

'Christ, Mawker, what don't you get?'

Behind me there was the merest scrape of metal on concrete, so faint you could be forgiven for thinking it was little more than the peculiar song of a tired old building, or the wind testing its areas of weakness, or some weird collision of neurons in the brain; the inexplicable mischief of a tired body, wound-up too tightly like a spring. I turned but there was just the big, empty space of a room filled with dust and fusty air and ghosts.

I was straining for another instance of it, to confirm or deny, to trigger some form of action as yet undecided, but then Mawker was back and he was saying something but his hand must have still partially been covering the phone because I didn't hear him properly. Or if I did, then it made no sense, and maybe that was right, maybe this was what Mawker didn't get.

'Say again, Ian,' I said. 'It sounded as if you said—'

'Yeah, you heard right. He's a quadriplegic. We found him sitting in his wheelchair.'

'So... he's *not* our guy? We got the address wrong?'

'No. We're in the right place. Sound-proofed cellar. We're waiting for forensics to check that out but it's looking very red from up here. We've found a bunch of manuscripts. Same mish-mash of papers. Same typewriter. Old stuff going back to the eighties. Short stories and partially written novels with shocker titles. *Maggot-Hearted You*, for fuck's sake. *Blonde on a Stick. Cancer Planet.* Christ. I'm no reader but some of this shit you wouldn't believe. Purpler than something you'd find hanging out the back of a baboon.'

'Thanks for that, F.R. Leavis,' I said. '*Maggot-Hearted You* was one of the tattoos Phil Clarke found on Martin Gower. Maybe this guy, this Nyx, he's a victim? Next on the list? We got to him before The Hack could settle in for another night's arts and crafts?'

'I don't think so, Joel. There's no neck puncture. And he's clean. No evidence of injury. He looks as if… well, he's been well looked after.'

'What does he say?'

'He's not said anything yet – I'm not even sure he can – but I'm getting creeped out. This guy's eyes are following me around the room like a fucking oil painting. He's got some fucking scar on him. His head looks like a bucket that's been given a real kicking.'

'You wouldn't get that from someone chucking half a brick.'

'Looks like a gunshot wound.'

'Anything on Sarah?'

'Nothing we've found. I'll let you know. We've got to decide what we're going to do. Stake this place out. Take this guy in. I don't know yet. I think the person we're looking for is Nyx's partner.'

'Male? Female? Anything on record? He married? The courier said it was a woman gave him the package.'

'We're looking. There's nothing here but pages and Wheelchair Guy.'

'You're sure he's immobile? You're sure he's not kidding?'

'His legs are like pipe cleaners.'

'Pinch him,' I said. 'Stab him in the thigh.'

'I'm not about to do anything like that. He's a raspberry. Believe me, you can tell. He isn't faking.'

Another pause. Another muffled order. An expletive. A shuffle of papers.

'Hang on,' he said.

'What is it?'

'We've got something here. It's a page with a bunch of postcodes on it. Typewritten. Crossed through. Well, most of them.'

'Go on.'

'Um... W12, crossed through. That's Ellerslie Road. Malachi Dawe.'

'What about the others?'

'NW5, crossed through. W10, untouched—'

'NW5 is Kim Pallant. W10 I don't know. Maybe Niker. He's gone. Left London. He had a feeling Pallant was dead. What about Taft?'

'Yep, W1 is crossed through. Gower's – N21 – that as well.'

'Is mine on there?'

'W1H? No. The only other one listed is SE1. Untouched.'

'Southwark. That's where I am now.'

'You what?'

'I had a breakthrough – Gower was using shorthand. A makeshift studio where he took those shots of Sarah. It's on Silex Street.'

'I'm sending a squad car over now. We can't take any chances.' I heard the phone moving in his hand, heard a barked question, presumably aimed at Nyx, and the line was cold before he'd finished it.

Another scrape of metal. I felt my scalp tighten. This wasn't a breeze pressing its shoulders against the door. I made to call Sarah's name, but I couldn't do it. It felt suddenly too foreign in my mouth. But that wasn't it. *That's not it, is it, Joel?*

It wasn't her.

It wasn't the sound of a person coming back to a habitat

they know well. It was an exploratory testing of barriers. It was too cautious. And then my confusion increased, because now I heard footsteps, light and quick. *Above me.*

I felt a weird tingling of the flesh, as if everything was trying to draw in, conceal itself. The hedgehog frightened into a ball. But there was also an expansion as if part of me wanted to explode into action. Run for my fucking life. Fight for my fucking life. My leg started to shake and I was adding my own sound – a violent tattoo against worm-bitten floorboards – to those sounds snaking around on the levels above and below me.

I stood up to try to control the trembling. It served only to shift it to my hands. Memories of pain, of near-death incidents in my recent past. Here was more of it. I couldn't deal with it any more. Fuck forced experience. Fuck the thrill of the chase. I wanted to be away. Why had I even come here? Sarah was grown up. I should just accept that. She had managed to fend for herself as a kid and now she was fending for herself as an adult. The fantasy – that she would run crying into the arms of Daddy, the brave knight come to protect her once more – was dead. All I was doing was putting myself in a corner and inviting the shadows to smother me. I didn't need to do this any more. She'd released me years ago. The problem was that *I* hadn't released me yet.

Sounds were rising and falling like amplified breath, as if the building was coming to life. I couldn't pinpoint their origins. One moment I thought I was backing away from noise when it suddenly transpired I was shifting towards it. I heard the footsteps halt on the wood and then make a shushing sound as direction was altered, then they began again. Slow but light. They were descending.

I placed the photographs back in the envelope and

returned to the corridor, moving as quietly as I could. Air trapped in old pipes scarred with flaking paint made a borborygmic din that drowned out the footsteps. I felt the area around my pelvis and bowels turn to iced liquid.

I stood in the corridor and waited for a while. Part of the ceiling had rotted through revealing batons of wood like misshapen ribs. A rat lay stiff and mummified in a corner, its insides having been hollowed out by insects long ago. There was a wooden chair with a vinyl seat that had perished to reveal nicotine-coloured foam beneath. A copy of a discarded newspaper had been bleached nude. I saw it but I took none of it in. It was just bland background. It was wallpaper. The space became granular with night. It grew difficult to discern detail. There had been no torch by the sleeping bag; it was fanciful in the extreme to think that any electricity still coursed through the bones of this place.

I could no longer hear anything on the ground floor and there was nothing but the swarm of darkness; nothing substantial within it. I could still hear the subtle tap of feet on the stone steps coming down to this level. Up ahead, the stairs rose into a blade of deep shadow. I kept my eye on its cut-off point, ready for some forced experience the moment a foot should drop into view.

I thought I heard a siren outside, far off, maybe coming closer, and I felt a warmth towards Mawker that I'd never experienced before, and then shook it away. Any warm feelings I was likely to have would be down to pissing my pants with fear. But I was glad he was sending backup.

I wondered if Sarah was here, if it had been her making those kid steps on the floor above before coming down to see who was in her den. I remembered she used to do ballet, and she used to perform yoga moves with Rebecca on a Sunday night.

I wondered if The Hack might have arrived for some fun too.

That got me moving.

I was at the steps, about to ascend, ready to call Sarah's name and beggar the quiet and the consequences, implore her to run, just as I felt a presence rise in the space behind me. I smelled the wake of air it pressed before it, and I was reminded of my mother's home. I was trying to understand why (perfume?) when I felt it – explosive, invasive – and immediately understood what was happening. Somehow, within the mushroom cloud of pain that fired up through the base of my head, I forced myself to act, to collapse as I would have been expected to do.

It was dark, I said to myself. *His aim was not true. He missed and he suspects that might be the case. He will lean over you to make sure. He will get it right this time.* I managed to think this through the smothering mists of pain. I heard the sirens and they helped but I thought, *They won't get here in time.* I could feel blood, a lot of it, drizzling across my shoulders and taking a slide down my spine to pool in the small of my back. An artery might have been nicked. So death was in the vicinity, or had at least hailed a cab to get here *tout de suite*.

Pain and panic was filling all the gaps and crevices in my mind. I wanted to writhe around and try to scream. I wanted to beg for help. But I had to lie still and take the one chance I would be afforded. I might be on my way out, but I had to take the fucker with me, otherwise Sarah was dead too.

'Once upon a time,' she said, in a sing-song voice. 'In a

dark, dark wood. The big, bad wolf. Who's been sleeping in my bed? One feather is of no use to me, I must have the whole bird. Mirror, mirror, on the wall. What great teeth you have. Trip-trap, trip-trap. Nibble, nibble, gnaw.' Her voice was cracked. I thought of the wicked witch of the west. *This woman cries a lot. This woman screams a lot. She does not sleep. She. Is. Insane.*

I grasped on to that as she dipped in towards me out of the dark, like a pale owl zeroing in on its prey. I didn't know this darkness, but neither did she. We were both strangers here.

I saw the flash of a blade.

'Off with his head,' she said, and I felt her hand in my hair, gathering it into her fist. I felt her breath on my cheek and I smelled bad coffee and raw alcohol and the sour stench of desperation.

I knew it would hurt beyond all knowledge, enough to make me black out even, so I had to get it right. I wrenched myself to the side and felt about a square foot of my hair tear free of my scalp under her nails. That hurt a lot, but it was a manageable hurt, and I relished it, almost, because it shone through the fog of that other pain, which meant that the initial insult was not as serious as I had thought.

I kicked out and connected with something soft. She let out a grunt and I heard her weapon clatter across the floor. I pushed myself to my feet and the wound opened in the back of my neck. It felt as if someone was pouring molten metal into it.

'I'm not a part of your vendetta,' I said, but the words came out as a garbled shriek of air.

She came at me again and I lifted the chair and hurled it at her. She dodged it and a window shattered. Now the light flooded in and I saw her. Her hair was short; I saw the clean angles of her jaw. Her eyes were hidden within deep shelves of shadow. She bared her teeth.

'I know what happened to Scott,' I said, and my voice sounded better this time. 'Your husband? Your son? We can find out who did it. They can be made to pay.'

But there was no getting through to her. They were already being made to pay. Her justice. I kept myself between her and the stairs, the way out. I listened to the sirens, and waited for the slew of braking tyres and the floodlights.

The mistake I made was thinking that because her machete was on the floor, far out of reach, she didn't have another. She came at me with her hands frozen into claws and as I raised my arms to bat her away, she magicked a knife from somewhere in her jacket. I was off-balance, and so was she. She fell into me and I tried to knock her arm down, away from my chest. I felt the knife slide deep into the junction between thigh and abdomen.

Her mistake was that she did not let go.

We went down together. I managed to twist and land on her. I felt her teeth sink into my forearm. I screamed and the sound cut through the anaesthesia of all those endorphins flooding my bloodstream. The body's way of allaying the panic, the pointless struggle, swaddling you as death took over.

There was enough fight left in me to grab a scimitar of window glass and drive it into her eye until it ground against bone, until she stiffened into an arch, flinging me free of her. I heard her feet shiver and kick in the throes, but I was too busy with my own end to care much about hers. Blood was jetting from my thigh; I knew she had severed the femoral artery. I only hoped it was a clean cut. I stared at my fingers wondering if I could find somewhere to wash them, and choked on bitter laughter. *Get in there, dickhead*, I hissed to myself.

Lying in the dark, trying to locate a tube the diameter of a drinking straw in a cleaved piece of warm meat is not the easiest task I've ever been presented with. It also hurts like fury. I tried to not think of those chunks of striated muscle as my own, and that instead I was cleaning a slab of steak, hunting for the integument and the veins and the gristle... all the stuff that gets caught in your teeth.

Blood flashed across the back of my knuckles. I found the end of the artery and tried to plug it with my little finger, but I lost it instantly because of the blaze of agony and the fact it was so slippery. It would have been easier to hold a thrashing fish in hands drenched with baby oil. I almost fainted from the pain, but I had to keep it together or it was death for sure. Just five minutes and the place would be crawling with boys in blue.

I felt the hot squirt of the opened vessel and sank my finger into the aperture. Again the surge of pain, but I bit down against it. I made a fist with my other hand and pressed it hard as if I was trying to pin my belly against my spin. Hopefully that might compress the main artery to all points south. I held on. I held on.

I was going to die here. With this crazed bitch lying next to me. I'd been so close to finding her. I'd had her blankets in my hands. Sweet dreams.

I didn't want Mawker to find me with any fear or pain on my face. So I thought of Sarah, and I felt myself relax though I knew I had maybe thirty seconds before I lost consciousness. I thought of her before the death of my wife, when we would play chess together, or sit on the sofa watching Disney films. She had bottle green eyes and freckles. She had caramel hair and a ready smile. She used to have a ready smile.

The sirens might or might not still be wailing into the skies above Bankside. I was beyond hearing. I was beyond smelling anything but the iron of my own blood. I could taste it too, rising in the back of my throat. I concentrated on Sarah's face, willing it to remain though my sight was fading fast.

Her face coalesced in my thoughts, dipping towards me, out of the dark, and she wasn't smiling, but there was concern in her face. At least there was that. I could cling on to the dream of that. Not a bad final illusion. Your daughter. Your life. I'd imagined some maturity into the bone structure. Gone was the puppy fat. This was, after all, a woman. No longer a little girl (my baby, always my baby). Bad knowledge put shadows in her eyes, but there was concern too. Here was love.

'Happy ever after,' I said, and blacked out.

eepingblistersonhandspushingandpullingsolongtheturno-
facircleandthehaironthebackofyourneckmapscatsandfire-
hydrantsangelcakeroadsofbonesandcoalscuttlesdrycough-
honeydropyousavedmefrommyselfandgavemehopeallthe-
yearsispentinsidebeopenlakereallyoldteachandfindmyway-
therouteisdeadilivedinwalesapostapocalypseshedrevealand-
someonesoldthereisnoneedtocryorfoldaposterofasuperfilm-
nopracticalusetomeisgoingtotheheadillaneedgetdarknes-
sallwitslessengonethepathofknowingmychildrenoutoftimey-
oureadmyworkandloveditvoureadmylifeandlovedmeitisun-
likelybudgeoutofwoodlandthecrustroadsomewheretheheat-
badgerswalkinsunsetnobodybeststhebadgerroadnotoad-
sweaselsmonkeysandratsjustbadgersandtheroadhaslast-
edforcenturiesnobodyknowswhereitisbecauseitismulesall-
thewayforsomeoneyoucannotfindajunctionyouhelped-
meandihelpedyouintheendbutmyhelpwasnotgoodenoughi-
couldnotdowhatyouwantedicouldnotgothroughwithitev-
enthoughyoubeggedmeallicoulddowasholdyoutightwhiley-
oupulledthetriggerandthencleanupafterwardsandgetyou-
fixedwhenitwentwrongandtrytogiveyousomekindoflifean-

dtrytofindyousomeformofclosureeventhoughtheclosurey-
oureallywantedhadfailedsoicommittedmyselftoyouasyou-
hadtomeandisworeiwouldfindthemisworeiwoulddotothem-
whathadbeendonetoyoueyetoothheartlifeeveninglaybysore-
petrolstationsorcarssocksforbiddentowalkalongwhenalarm-
clockwhiteoutforwardmarchaprononesadbirthdaythatwill-
notarrivecoatandcandlethatcannotbeleftthebeatofthescalpe-
landanarmfullofbastedfingersroolsstalestalkerfromaviary-
toparklandatthecentreofatownworryopenheartsurgeryouto-
nbusesdrivenbyoffdutyarrestteamslloingforbusinessandthe-
anceintartofbathingfacesatshadowedshardsonslifftopsand-
fallingtotheskytheyneedtogettoseethecitysexwhiterolled-
outcookerybenchovenfrenchrewardandhadslowatomando-
penallhoursandstiffcrycuntsmackmoneyimissyourbodyon-
topofoldropeandgormlessoutofdateanachronisticletteropen-
erfrightwigshedoesprogrammesonpoorantsmuscularla-
dyremnantstotheedgeofthecityandadogfurstoleoutofcon-
trolterrainapefoughtiwillnotgobackinsideiwillcherishyou-
nomatterwhatshapeyoufindyourselfadoptingiwillcherishy-
ouindeathandiwillensureyoudonotgotothegraveunavenged-
strictstripclubbentdonkeywhelpcavesharptheendoftheend-
ofweallgohomeandiwatchyouandyoumoveifistareforlong-
enoughwhoamikiddingwhoarewe

30

Jim Thompson was a writer. I've read some of his books. They're pretty good. Pretty dark. Plenty dark, actually. He's long dead, but when he was active, back in the 1950s, he produced harrowing crime novels that weren't as surface as the stuff Chandler, say, was writing. He got his hands dirty. He delved into the grim interiors of his characters and came up with red fistfuls of truth. His characters were dark and snide and ugly. They were unreliable. They were real people, in other words. Anyway, he said something once about writing and it has always chimed with me, because it's pertinent to life too.

There is only one plot – things are not what they seem.

Of course, what would be helpful for a guy like me, is to work this out at the time. Hindsight? I'm the greatest unlocker of puzzles on the planet. And I had a lot of time for hindsight. I was in hospital for twenty days and spent seventeen hours of those in the operating theatre. I suffered what's known as the triad of death. Apparently, when a body haemorrhages (I lost twenty pints of blood during what they call a 'massive transfusion') it causes a depletion in oxygen delivery to the organs and can lead to hypothermia. Oxygen is needed when blood coagulates, so clotting goes out of the window too. And because of that lack of O_2, the body starts burning glucose for energy, which releases acids into the bloodstream and organs aren't big fans of acids. They start to malfunction. Nutshell: like a porn star in a gang-bang, I was fucked in all kinds of directions. A doctor told me this (the stuff about the triad of death that is, not the gang-bang).

It was touch and go for a while as to whether I'd have to have my leg amputated. But here I am. Still whole. Adding to my scar collection nicely.

Suck on that for experience, Accelerants.

Mawker sent me a card. *Did you know that Joel Sorrell is an anagram of 'Dumb Bastard'?* He also wrote: *Me and the boys hope you get better soon, and find your way out of that hospital bed, if only so we can put you straight back in it, you twat.* Credit to him, he also sent me details about the woman who had almost put me in the grave. I felt cheated by the fact that I had killed her. I wanted to talk to her, to find out what had driven her to such extreme behaviour.

Her name was Veronica Lake. But she hated it, hated the fact that someone famous had lived with the name before her, so she always went by the name Ronnie.

It seemed she had been taken under Nyx's wing after her arrest, aged seventeen, back in 2002, for a series of violent robberies she committed with her boyfriend, a career criminal called Naylor, a decade her senior, who committed suicide in prison one year into a twenty-five-year stretch.

Lake was sent to Holloway for ten years but was let out

after four for good behaviour. It was widely believed that she had been diverted off the path of righteousness by her boyfriend, but there were plenty who thought it was the other way around. Nyx had kept up correspondence with her and was there to provide comfort and support when she got out. Lake had no family. Nyx was suddenly everything to her.

Nyx should never have been anywhere near the police force. He concealed a drug habit and had a lifelong sexual preference for minors. He was a hothead. He played rugby for a team in Regent's Park and regularly put opposing players in the hospital or the dentist's chair. He got into countless fights on the pitch. He took that aggressive attitude with him out on the beat too. There were a number of reprimands for his 'heavy-handedness', which sometimes spilled over into violence, but nothing could ever be proven.

Lake thought she was going to be a great writer some day. She thought her notoriety would light a fire under things. She was stewing in the juices of sour grapes for years. Crime and violence and porridge and a guy she thought loved her committing suicide as soon as the bars closed on him. It all provided bitter bloody grist for her mill. God knows what the relevance of the anthology was. Maybe she had thought of submitting. Maybe she was angry at the way the planet was going to the toilet. Methane and apathy. Deforestation and political short-termism. Maybe she submitted one of her non-stories after all and it was rejected out of hand. *Dear Whoever you are. No thanks. Don't bother again. Fuck the fuck off.*

But there was Nyx. He worshipped Lake. She looked up to him, adored him. There were rumours that they embarked upon a depraved sexual relationship, but that might have just been the red tops retro-salivating. Whatever the situation, she was into him enough to become the weapon his hands could never hold.

Because then he was taken away from her too. After he left the police, cowed by a night of violence he was no match for (and that in itself must have been a sobering experience for a guy used to meting out plenty of rough stuff), he tried to kill himself with a pistol he'd squirrelled away from some arms amnesty or other. He got it wrong and served only to paralyse himself from the neck down. It was enough to send her over the edge, or further over than she already was. They had been tinder for each other: the final spark to blow each other's fuel stacks sky high.

I don't know how she tracked down the Accelerants. Maybe she did it like me, using photographs and feelings... I'm sure Nyx, with his contacts, was able to open channels that might otherwise have been unavailable. In any case, she infiltrated them, for a short while. She'd made it to the audition, at least. I remembered the name 'Veronica Lake' on Odessa's list of potential members, with a red cross against it. A red cross... Christ. It should have been given a black cross too. It should have been cut out. Smeared with tar and feathers. It should have been burned to ash. Even with them she didn't fit in but wow, did she ever live some experience.

Here was her novel, her great work, something she felt she could finish, unlike all those incomplete manuscripts. Nyx was her magnum opus and these kids who pissed about, playing at being writers, playing at living their lives, became the pages she carved into truth with blood-red italicised capitals.

* * *

336

I had a number of visitors, all of them while I was unconscious. Mum, Adam, Lorraine Tokuzo (who brought me a small box of expensive truffles and took bites out of them all).

There had been another visitor too, apparently, but she didn't stay for long and she didn't leave her name. She placed a single flower from a dianthus bush by my bed. I agonised over that for days. What did it mean? It used to mean she was sorry. Did it now mean *I forgive you*? Did it mean hello? Goodbye? She had saved my life. She had saved my life.

Romy came to visit me, a couple of days before I was released. The weather was getting cooler. It seemed every time I lifted my head to look outside there were rain spots on the windows.

She was beautiful and I told her so. She held my hand and passed on her father's regards. She tucked a piece of paper under my pillow and kissed me. I ran my fingers through the dense, heavy wonder of her hair. She told me to rest. She told me she would see me soon.

When she'd gone I retrieved the paper. It was a photocopy of a letter she had been working on. It had originated in a tomb in Gyeongju, South Korea, and it was dated June 1587. It was from a daughter to her father, who had died in battle.

I want to go to wherever you are. Please bring me to you. My love for you I cannot and will not change in this world and my grief knows no limit. Where do I place my heart now? And how can I live like this, my father, knowing that I will miss you for the rest of my life?

JOEL SORRELL WiLL RETURN iN

HELL iS EMPTY

JULY 2017

ACKNOWLEDGMENTS

Thanks to Rhonda for keeping me sane. Thanks to Ethan, Ripley and Zac for keeping me insane. Thanks to Ali Karim, Stav Sherez, Sarah Pinborough, Guy Adams, James Sallis, Steve Mosby, Mike Parker, Paul Finch and Fergus McNeill for kind words. Thanks to my agent, James Wills, for encouragement and football talk. Thanks to Miranda Jewess for her patience. Thanks to Mum and Dad. Thanks to my cat, Reddie, for sitting by me through thick and thin in that sweary study of mine...

ABOUT THE AUTHOR

Conrad Williams is the author of eight novels, four novellas and a collection of short stories. *One* was the winner of the August Derleth Award for Best Novel (British Fantasy Awards 2010), while *The Unblemished* won the International Horror Guild Award for Best Novel in 2007 (he beat the shortlisted Stephen King on both occasions). He won the British Fantasy Award for Best Newcomer in 1993, and another British Fantasy Award for Best Novella (*The Scalding Rooms*) in 2008. His first crime novel, and the first Joel Sorrell thriller, *Dust and Desire*, was published in 2015. He lives in Manchester.

DUST AND DESIRE
A JOEL SORRELL NOVEL

CONRAD WILLIAMS

Joel Sorrell, a bruised, bad-mouthed PI, is a sucker for missing person cases. And not just because he's searching for his daughter, who vanished five years after his wife was murdered. Joel feels a kinship with the desperate and the damned. He feels, somehow, responsible. So when the mysterious Kara Geenan begs him to find her missing brother, Joel agrees. Then an attempt is made on his life, and Kara vanishes... A vicious serial killer is on the hunt, and as those close to Joel are sucked into his nightmare, he suspects that answers may lie in his own hellish past.

"An exciting new voice in crime fiction"
Mark Billingham, No. 1 bestselling author of *Rush of Blood*

"Top quality crime writing from one of the best"
Paul Finch, No. 1 bestselling author of *Stalkers*

"A beautifully written, pitch-black slice of London noir"
Steve Mosby, author of *The Nightmare Place*

HELL IS EMPTY
A JOEL SORRELL NOVEL

CONRAD WILLIAMS

Joel Sorrell is drinking hard while his personal life collapses around him. An SOS from a childhood sweetheart springs him into action, but nothing about her or her problem seems to make any sense. Everything points towards an old enemy of Joel's, who has risen to prominence while incarcerated. On the run and in fear for his life, Joel finds himself tangled in a web affecting both the present and the past, and most certainly the people closest to him.

AVAILABLE NOVEMBER 2016

THE BLOOD STRAND
A FAROES NOVEL

CHRIS OULD

Having left the Faroes as a child, Jan Reyna is now a British police detective, and the islands are foreign to him. But he is drawn back when his estranged father is found unconscious with a shotgun by his side and someone else's blood at the scene. Then a man's body is washed up on an isolated beach. Is Reyna's father responsible? Looking for answers, Reyna falls in with local detective Hjalti Hentze. But as the stakes get higher and Reyna learns more about his family and the truth behind his mother's flight from the Faroes, he must decide whether to stay, or to forsake the strange, windswept islands for good.

"This one is a winner… For fans of Henning Mankell and Elizabeth George"
Booklist (starred review)

"An absorbing new mystery"
Library Journal

"The plot takes many unexpected twists en route to the satisfying ending"
Publishers Weekly

HACK
AN F.X. SHEPHERD NOVEL

KIERAN CROWLEY

It's a dog-eat-dog world at the infamous tabloid the *New York Mail*, where brand new pet columnist F.X. Shepherd accidentally finds himself on the trail of The Hacker, a serial killer targeting unpleasant celebrities in inventive—and often decorative—ways. And it's only his second day on the job. Luckily Shepherd has hidden talents, not to mention a hidden agenda. But as bodies and suspects accumulate, he finds himself running afoul of cutthroat office politics, the NYPD, and Ginny Mac, an attractive but ruthless reporter for a competing newspaper. And when Shepherd himself is contacted by The Hacker, he realizes he may be next on the killer's list…

"A rollicking, sharp-witted crime novel"
Kirkus Reviews

"Laugh out loud funny and suspenseful—it's like Jack Reacher meets Jack Black" Rebecca Cantrell, *New York Times* bestselling author of *The Blood Gospel*

"A joy to read and captures the imagination"
Long Island Press

THE AGE OF TREACHERY
A DUNCAN FORRESTER NOVEL

GAVIN SCOTT

It is the winter of 1946, and after years of war, ex-Special Operations Executive agent Duncan Forrester is back at his Oxford college as a junior Ancient History Fellow. But his peace is shattered when a hated colleague is found dead, and his closest friend is arrested for the murder. Convinced that the police have the wrong man, and hearing rumours that the victim was in possession of a mysterious Viking saga, Forrester follows the trail of the manuscript from the ruins of Berlin to the forests of Norway, hoping that it is the key to the man's death. But he is not alone in his search, and he soon discovers that old adversaries are still at war…

"A wonderful historical setting, brilliantly captured"
Maureen Jennings, bestselling author of
The Murdoch Mysteries

"A suspenseful murder mystery that holds the reader's interest to the last page" Michael Kurland, award-winning author of *The Infernal Device*

"Fans of Morse will love it. Intelligently plotted and elegantly written" Mark Oldfield, bestselling author of *The Sentinel*

THE BURSAR'S WIFE
A GEORGE KOCHARYAN NOVEL

E.G. RODFORD

Meet George Kocharyan, Cambridge Confidential Services' one and only private investigator. Amidst the usual jobs following unfaithful spouses, he is approached by the glamorous Sylvia Booker, who fears that her daughter Lucy has fallen in with the wrong crowd. Aided by his assistant Sandra and her teenage son, George soon discovers that Sylvia has good reason to be concerned. Then an unfaithful wife he had been following is found dead. As his investigation continues—enlivened by a mild stabbing and the unwanted attention of Detective Inspector Vicky Stubbing—George begins to wonder if all the threads are connected…

"An absolute delight. A gumshoe thriller that reminded me of Raymond Chandler."
Steven Dunne, author of *A Killing Moon*

"A quirky and persuasive new entry into the ranks of British crime fiction."
Barry Forshaw, *Crime Time*

"A controlled, artful crime story starring an arch PI and a host of acutely observed characters. A treat."
Conrad Williams, author of *Dust and Desire*

For more fantastic fiction, author events, exclusive excerpts,
competitions, limited editions and more

VISIT OUR WEBSITE
titanbooks.com

LIKE US ON FACEBOOK
facebook.com/titanbooks

FOLLOW US ON TWITTER
@TitanBooks

EMAIL US
readerfeedback@titanemail.com